P9-DOH-905

TUMBLING BLOCKS

Earlene Fowler

BERKLEY PRIME CRIME, NEW YORK

THE BERKLEY PUBLISHING GROUP
Published by the Penguin Group
Penguin Group (USA) Inc.
375 Hudson Street, New York, New York 10014, USA
Penguin Group (Canada), 90 Eglinton Avenue East, Suite 700, Toronto, Ontario M4P 2Y3, Canada
(a division of Pearson Penguin Canada Inc.)
Penguin Books Ltd., 80 Strand, London WC2R 0RL, England
Penguin Group Ireland, 25 St. Stephen's Green, Dublin 2, Ireland (a division of Penguin Books Ltd.)
Penguin Group (Australia), 250 Camberwell Road, Camberwell, Victoria 3124, Australia
(a division of Pearson Australia Group Pty. Ltd.)
Penguin Books India Pvt. Ltd., 11 Community Centre, Panchsheel Park, New Delhi—110 017, India
Penguin Group (NZ), 67 Apollo Drive, Rosedale, North Shore 0632, New Zealand
(a division of Pearson New Zealand Ltd.)
Penguin Books (South Africa) (Pty.) Ltd., 24 Sturdee Avenue, Rosebank, Johannesburg 2196,
South Africa

Penguin Books Ltd., Registered Offices: 80 Strand, London WC2R 0RL, England

This is a work of fiction. Names, characters, places, and incidents either are the product of the author's imagination or are used fictitiously, and any resemblance to actual persons, living or dead, business establishments, events, or locales is entirely coincidental. The publisher does not have any control over and does not assume any responsibility for author or third-party websites or their content.

TUMBLING BLOCKS

A Berkley Prime Crime Book / published by arrangement with the author

PRINTING HISTORY
Berkley Prime Crime hardcover edition / May 2007
Berkley Prime Crime mass-market edition / May 2008

Copyright © 2007 by Earlene Fowler.
Cover art by One by Two, Martucci / Greisbach.
Cover design by George Long.

ISBN: 978-0-425-22123-5

BERKLEY® PRIME CRIME
Berkley Prime Crime Books are published by The Berkley Publishing Group,
a division of Penguin Group (USA) Inc.,
375 Hudson Street, New York, New York 10014.
The name BERKLEY PRIME CRIME and the BERKLEY PRIME CRIME design
are trademarks belonging to Penguin Group (USA) Inc.

PRINTED IN THE UNITED STATES OF AMERICA

10 9 8 7 6 5 4 3 2 1

For
Ruth "Babs" Gibson
and
Barbara Peters
with my love and gratitude

Acknowledgments

Even to your old age and gray hairs I am He, I am He who will sustain you. I have made you and I will carry you; I will sustain you and I will rescue you.

Isaiah 46:4

My gratitude to: God the Father, God the Son and God the Holy Spirit.

Also my thanks to:

Ellen Geiger, my agent, a most gracious and truly fine human being.

Christine Zika, a gem among editors.

George Long, the wonderful art director who designs and coordinates my incredible covers. You are the best.

Cheryl Griesbach and Stanley Martucci, the artists who have painted all my covers. Your work is always beautiful.

Tina and Tom Davis, my good friends and Webmasters, I will always be indebted to you.

ACKNOWLEDGMENTS

Margrit and David Hall for their help in how to "execute" the perfect murder.

You gotta have friends, and I am blessed with good and faithful ones: Beebs and Millee, Jo Ellen Heil, Nini Hill, Jo-Ann Mapson, Karen Olson, Lela Satterfield, Kathy Vieira, Laura Ross Wingfield.

Always with love to my husband, Allen. It's been a long and winding road. I'm blessed to be traveling it with you.

A Note from the Author

When I started the Benni Harper series in 1992, the first book, *Fool's Puzzle*, was written in "real time." It was 1992 in Benni's life as well as mine. Time in a long-running series is tricky. Since it often takes a book almost two years from the time the author starts writing it to the point when it is actually in the reader's hands, time sequences can become confusing. Each author deals with this dilemma in a different way. I decided from the beginning that I would age my characters more slowly than I and my readers were aging. With Dove being seventy-five in the first book, I wanted to keep her active and vital, and I also wanted to explore the early stages of Benni and Gabe's complex relationship. Keep in mind while reading *Tumbling Blocks* that it takes place in December 1996, one month after *Delectable Mountains*.

Tumbling Blocks

Tumbling Blocks is one of the optical illusion quilt patterns that can be traced back as early as the 1850s. It was during this time that domestic textile production was on the rise, and fabric was easier and cheaper for women to buy. Because of this, block-work quilts became popular for many American quilters. The fool-the-eye, three-dimensional effect of the Tumbling Blocks pattern is achieved using light, medium and dark fabrics. Though diamonds are actually utilized to make the design, the image of blocks tumbling in an endless falling motion is the desired outcome. It is a deceptive pattern that changes depending on how you view it. It must be carefully pieced, the corners coming together perfectly, to produce the mesmerizing effect. Blocks were a popular toy for children in the early nineteenth century, so Tumbling Blocks was often used in baby quilts. One of the earliest examples of a silk Tumbling Blocks quilt was made in 1852 by an Alabama slave. Other names for this pattern are Stairsteps, Cubework, Shifting Cubes, Heavenly Stairs, Pandora's Box and Baby Blocks.

Quilt Histories

People often ask me where they can find histories of quilt patterns. There is no single book that tells all the histories of every quilt pattern. Like making a patchwork quilt, I piece together the history of each quilt pattern using a variety of sources such as books, magazines, newspapers and the Internet. I have found the following books particularly helpful in my search.

Encyclopedia of Pieced Quilt Patterns, compiled by Barbara Brackman

Quilts: Identification and Price Guide, Liz Greenbacker and Kathleen Barach

Old Patchwork Quilts and the Women Who Made Them, Ruth E. Finley

Quilts: Their Story and How to Make Them, Marie D. Webster

QUILT HISTORIES

The Romance of the Patchwork Quilt in America, Carrie A. Hall and Rose G. Kretsinger

101 Patchwork Patterns, Ruby McKim

The New Quilting & Patchwork Dictionary, Rhoda Ochser Goldberg

849 Traditional Patchwork Patterns, Susan Winter Mills

PROLOGUE

December 1996

$\mathcal{D}$EAR ALICE,

It's hard to believe, but it's that time of year again and, as I promised thirty-two years ago, I'm writing to let you know how Benni is doing.

It's been quite a year. In January, our girl helped a nice young couple get their dude ranch up and running. There was some excitement involving a love triangle and a fire, but, thankfully, Benni wasn't hurt. The Broken Dishes ranch is doing a real brisk business now, not a little bit because of her. She's a good and loyal friend who I wouldn't mind having on my team any day. Then again, could be I'm a tiny bit partial.

Things went along pretty smoothly through the spring and summer. We don't see each other as much as we used to, what with her responsibilities as museum curator and being a police chief's wife. We did have some real fun times putting up strawberry and plum jam. The strawberries were plentiful this year. She is always right there to help me whenever I ask.

She's done much better being a police chief's wife than I expected, not that I should ever underestimate her. As you well know, she's a good worker and always tries her best, something I know she inherited partly from you. I remember those last days when you struggled so hard to fight that cancer. I guess it just wasn't in God's plan. Like I told you that last day you had on earth, when you were so scared your sweet girl would face her whole life without you there to help her, that I would take care of her for you and let you know every year at Christmas how she's doing. Someday, when I head up there myself, Benni will find these letters and know that all along you and I have been partners, watching over her.

Oh, dear Alice, we almost lost her last month if that hostage situation had turned out differently. Those were some hard, hard hours. There were moments when I thought Gabe was going to just fold up and die. I do believe he would if something happened to Benni. That man is so in love with her. When Jack came up there to be with y'all, I truly thought Benni would end up like me, alone for most of her life (though Isaac has been such a joy and well worth waiting for). But I couldn't have in all my imagination thought up a man more suited to her than Gabe. He'd do anything for her, stand in front of a bullet to protect her, if need be. He's a good man.

Despite what she went through, she seems happier than I've seen her for a long time.

You know, I've learned a lot watching Benni with Gabe's son, Sam, her cousin, Emory, Elvia and her family and the people where she works. She throws herself into helping whoever crosses her path. That has taught me something about who we should consider family. I don't think I would have been able to open myself up to marrying a second time if I hadn't seen how willing she was to love again. As you well know, I'm real good with giving advice, not so good at taking it. There I was telling her to take a chance on love again, when I'd been so scared to do that very same thing for most of my life. She has taught me courage.

I'm so proud of her, as I know you are too. She went through a lot last month, and though she hasn't said it, I know she thinks that she failed with Gabe's cousin Luis. She and I have talked a little about what happened. I've told her that what she did was right, but I can tell she still relives it in her head, wondering if she could have done something different. Truth is, though we want to believe we have the ability to change others, every one of us has free will to choose. She'll understand that better as she gets older. Though my heart hurts a lot more for people now, I don't blame myself as much when I can't help them. Ultimately, each of us just has to flat out decide on our own what we're going to do with this gift of life that God has given us.

Right now, I can see that she's worried about Gabe. His mother is here, and there is some big sadness between those two that I'm praying will be resolved. I'm worried about Benni worrying about him. And Isaac's worried about me worrying about Benni. I guess that's what family is, a basket weave of people loving and worrying on each other.

You know, I picture heaven being a place where every person we worry about is right there for us to see—all safe and happy and healthy. A place where we never have to worry again. Am I right about that, Alice? I know you can't answer, but it seems right to me. I guess I'll find out eventually.

Well, I'd better get moving. The chickens are getting restless. I bought myself a bunch of Holland Whites. I'm not sure how they are going to do, they seem rather flighty, but they are fun to watch. Though I'd never admit this to anyone but you, I name my ladies. I'm here to tell you, it makes it hard to make a stew out of them. Just between us, I give my favorites away simply because I can't bear the thought of them in a bowl of dumplings. That's my true confession for this year. Some ranchwoman I am, ha-ha!

The alfalfa's looking good, and our Ben's just as stubborn and sweet as ever. I always felt bad that after you passed on my son never found someone else to love. As you can imagine, there have been plenty of willing ladies throughout the years. But he swore he could never love anyone but you. Who am I to doubt him? I knew you were special the moment he brought you home. He has a new colt and a new puppy, so that's keeping him busy.

I look forward to seeing you again, sweetie. Until then, know that I'm watching over our girl, not that she needs it so much anymore. We miss you every day and long for the time when we will all be together again in that place where there is no darkness, no pain and no sorrow. Say hello to the Lord for me. Tell Him I'll see Him soon (But not too soon! I still have plenty to do down here).

I remain always, your loving mother-in-law,
Dove

CHAPTER 1

"$\mathcal{M}$Y SYSTEM IS RUINED!" ELVIA GLARED AT OUR IM-
ages in the oak and brass full-length mirror while I
attempted to zip up her gray fitted Anne Klein dress. The
zipper wasn't cooperating. Screaming in protest might
have been a more accurate description. My friend's two-
month pregnancy was already creating havoc with her
precisely tailored wardrobe.

"Your system?" I tugged gently at the zipper. There
was no way I could sneak it past her definitely thickening
waist.

"My clothing system," she said. Her tone was snappish
as a water turtle.

Attempting to restrain the laugh gurgling in my throat,
I answered, "You have a clothing system?"

6

She arched one dark eyebrow. "Within a six-month period, I never wear the same combination of clothing. My schedule is computerized and makes suggestions for alternate choices due to weather fluctuations. Today is the pewter Anne Klein silk dress with my black Dolce & Gabbana wool jacket. It's on the list."

"You have a computerized list?" I watched my mirrored mouth gape in surprise. "It takes the weather forecast into consideration?"

Her tone grew haughty. "Don't act so superior. Everyone has a system. Mine is just a little more organized than most people's. Admit it, you have a system."

I couldn't hold back. Laughter burst from my mouth. Arrows shot out of her glossy black eyes, causing me to hold up my hands in apology. "Sure, whatever is clean and closest to what is appropriate for what I'm doing that day is what I wear. That's my system." *And*, I added mentally, *the system of most normal people*.

She growled at me, sounding like an angry little terrier. "I refuse to let this pregnancy ruin my system." She stomped one foot for punctuation. The burnished oak floor of the airy upstairs bedroom reverberated. We were in one of the guest bedrooms in the flawlessly restored Victorian house that she shared with her husband, my cousin, Emory Littleton. This particular room held three armoires, which housed only a small part of her extensive wardrobe. Emory had wisely hightailed it out of here about ten seconds after I arrived, though he was kind enough to give me a vague heads-up.

"Just a warnin', sweetcakes," he'd said in his loamy but sexy Arkansas drawl. "My darlin' wife is huntin' bear this morning." He gave me a quick peck on the cheek, then shrugged into his navy suit coat. "Best put on your flak jacket and try to dodge all incoming flaming arrows."

"That is such a weird image I'm going to pretend I didn't hear it," I said, laughing. "For the record, I don't feel a bit sorry for you. It's your fault she's in this emotional tizzy." I straightened a slightly skewed velvet and crystal cupid ornament on their ten-foot blue spruce Christmas tree.

He had grinned, not even trying to hide his pride at his upcoming fatherhood. "She might've been a willing participant at some point in the festivities."

"We could safety pin the back of your dress," I suggested to a still-glowering Elvia. "Just don't take off your jacket. No one will know." I admit, I was trying to wrap this dilemma up quickly so we could focus on my many problems, one of whom was arriving by train from Wichita this very day.

She whirled around, her glossy red mouth grimacing in horror. "Safety pin it? Are you crazy?"

"Yes, I am," I said, in my most soothing keep-the-temperamental-artist-or-rich-patron-calm voice. It was a voice I'd cultivated to perfection in my job as curator at the Josiah Sinclair Folk Art Museum and Artists' Co-op. "I am completely insane. What was I thinking? Please, forgive me. I have an idea. Let's simplify your system. I could run down to Target and pick you up a couple of Hawaiian muumuus to see you through the next seven months. Wash one, wear one." I grinned at her, proud of my joke. Actually, Target didn't carry muumuus, something Elvia wouldn't know, because I was certain she'd never bought any clothes there.

She was speechless for a moment. Her bottom lip began to tremble, and tears moistened her dark-lashed eyes. "Don't make fun of my system," she whispered. "It's my . . ." Her voice faltered. ". . . my system."

Seeing my normally levelheaded friend about to melt down because of a stuck zipper and an out-of-order dress stirred a flood of pity inside me.

"Oh, Ellie Mae," I said, using the childhood nickname I only used when she was really sad or upset because its silliness and absolute incongruity always made her smile. I reached over and took her cold hand. "Did you really think you could have a baby without putting on any weight?"

A single tear ran down Elvia's smooth, brown cheek. She must have been wearing waterproof mascara, because it was as clear and lovely as the diamonds on her wedding band. "I'm being silly," she said, swallowing hard.

"You're allowed," I said, putting my arm around her shoulders. "My advice is, take advantage of the next seven months and make my cousin and all six of your brothers wait on you hand and foot."

She gave a wet, unladylike sniff, causing both of us to laugh. "My brothers have been avoiding me like a poor relative. Emory, on the other hand, would carry me around in his pocket if he could. He's driving me loco."

"Welcome to the club. He's always driven me crazy."

Downstairs we could hear her housekeeper, Janey, singing an old Broadway musical song my gramma Dove used to sing to us as children while she was rubbing shampoo into our hair: "I'm Gonna Wash That Man Right Outa My Hair." It always made us giggle.

"Remember when you asked Dove why a man was in her hair?" I said, trying to make her smile.

Elvia inhaled a shuddering breath. "I took things so literally."

I started flipping through the dresses in the open armoire. "Everything's literal when you're in the second grade. Now, until we can track you down some outrageously cool and hip maternity clothes, let's be wild, throw your system to the wind, and find you something to wear this fine December day."

"Okay," she said, suddenly docile. "I have a bunch of catalogs. You have to help me pick out some clothes."

Now I knew that my friend had gone completely round the bend, asking me, the queen of manure-caked boots and Wrangler jeans, to help her pick out a new wardrobe. I had a sneaking suspicion that she'd be fine by this afternoon and that soon Emory would fly her down to Orange County to hit all the fancy maternity shops at South Coast Plaza and Newport Fashion Island. She'd develop a new system in no time with weight gain and swollen ankles factored in.

"Sure," I said. "And no muumuus. At least, not with this first child."

"Not *ever*," she replied, giving a slight shudder. My fashionista friend had returned.

"How about this?" I pulled out a black-and-white dress that appeared a little more boxy in the waist.

She nodded. "It's an early January, but it'll have to do." She slipped out of the gray silk and took the black-

and-white dress from me. This time, the zipper slid up without a hitch.

"This was always big on me," she said. "That's why I usually wear it in January. In case I ate too many of Mama's tamales over the holidays."

"Good, now let's concentrate on my problems."

"Talk to me while I fix my hair."

I followed her into the master bedroom decorated in a classy burgundy and deep navy Victorian style that matched the house. I sat on the edge of their king-size bed and moaned out loud. "Amtrak is delivering Kathryn today, and I'm nowhere near ready for her."

Kathryn Smith Ortiz, my husband, Gabe's, long-widowed mother, was a retired fifth grade schoolteacher. We'd met a few years ago when Gabe and I were first married and we'd flown back to Wichita so I could be officially presented to his mother, his twin sisters and a large array of friends and family. It was a second marriage for both Gabe and me. Because it happened so quickly and without her knowledge of my existence, Kathryn had, with great reluctance, accepted me as her new daughter-in-law. This year, when his two sisters ended up having other plans for Christmas, Gabe, in an uncharacteristically impulsive moment, invited Kathryn to our house here in San Celina on the Central Coast of California.

"Come spend the holidays with Benni and me. It'll be great," he'd said on the phone to her last week while I stared at him in unbelieving horror. He completely ignored my frantic finger-across-the-throat gesture.

"You'll love San Celina at Christmas," he continued. "There's no snow, but the town really goes all out for the

11

holidays. If you arrive on Friday, you'll be able to see the Christmas parade Saturday morning. Benni and her dad are riding their horses in it." When he hung up, his handsome brown face was animated with boyish excitement. "My mom's coming here for Christmas!"

"Did it ever occur to you to ask *me* before you asked her?" My tone and expression were somewhere between snappish and whining. It was not, I know, an attractive combination.

He cocked his head, his blue-gray eyes confused and slightly hurt. "You don't want my mom to come to our home for Christmas?"

I sighed, shook my head and lied my socks off. "Of course I do. It's just that it was so . . . unplanned." I'm certain my smile was less than convincing. *She's my mother-in-law,* I wanted to scream. *Do you have any idea what kind of preparation is necessary to get ready for her visit?* It occurred to me at that moment that she was arriving on Friday the thirteenth. How appropriate. The Wicked Witch of the West music from *The Wizard of Oz* echoed through my brain.

"You're always saying I need to be more spontaneous," he said, his tone accusing.

I smiled at him again, trying to tune out the ominous music in my head. To be honest, it was good to see my normally stressed-out, police chief husband excited about something. He'd been sad and quiet since the death of his cousin Luis last month. We'd both come through a tough time because of the tragic circumstances surrounding it and were just now tentatively talking about what happened. I'd been looking forward to a peaceful holiday at my dad's ranch with my gramma Dove in charge of the whole shebang, something she still loved to do. Now, it looked like I'd have to switch to warp speed to prepare our house for my mother-in-law's arrival.

"It'll be fun," I lied again, wrapping my arms around his waist. What was that saying, fake it until you make it? Maybe I could fake it until I felt it.

"Kathryn arrives at the Amtrak station at six p.m.," I said to Elvia, lying back on her bed and throwing my forearm over my eyes. "Can I just stay here until New Year's?"

"Is she bringing her dog?" Elvia faced me, her hair fashioned into a classy French twist.

"Bite your tongue!" I said, horrified at the thought. "If God has any compassion for me at all, that animal will not leave the state of Kansas. You know I love dogs, but I make an exception for Daphne. To be honest, I don't think she's really a dog. She's a gargoyle come to life."

My mother-in-law's Boston terrier, Daphne, had taken an instant dislike to me the minute I stepped over the threshold of Gabe's childhood home in Derby, Kansas. Nothing I tried could win that dog over, which had made Kathryn even more suspicious of the woman her only son had married.

"It's very odd," Elvia said. "Aren't Boston terriers called America's gentlemen?"

"Yes, they are known for being easygoing and loving. I think Daphne needs some queen-size Prozac pills."

"Or you will, if Kathryn brings her," Elvia said, laughing.

I was happy to see my small-fry troubles had made my friend temporarily forget her hormonally induced emotions. "My family doctor is on speed dial. How're things looking at the bookstore?" Elvia owned Blind Harry's Bookstore, the last independent bookstore between Santa Barbara and San Francisco.

She picked up a square black leather briefcase. "It looks like it's going to be a good holiday season. Sales are up from this time last year."

"Did my shipment of outsider art books come in yet?" I asked.

Elvia had ordered some books for the museum's two gift shops. One was located in the museum's small lobby and the other, our new shop, called Local Hands, was downtown on Lopez Street, not far from Blind Harry's. A special exhibit of California outsider art was opening this Wednesday at the museum. I always liked stocking a few books on whatever folk art we were highlighting at the museum.

"Yes, you can pick them up today. Did the Finch painting finally arrive?"

The star of our California Outsider Art exhibit was an original painting donated by a popular, fairly new member of San Celina society, Nola Maxwell Finch. She was the great-niece of the famous and reclusive Nevada outsider artist, Abe Adam Finch, whose arresting and original paintings captivated the art scene ten years ago. Some of his original paintings now sold for close to thirty thousand dollars.

"I signed for it this morning," I said, sitting down on a silk-covered dressing stool and retying the laces of my

New Balance tennis shoes. No flat-heeled Justin boots for me today. I had a dozen places to go in less than eight hours, and my arches would need some major support. "It's incredible. The details are amazing."

The painting, called *Abraham's Tree of Life Equal and Everlasting Amen*, was an eleven-by-fourteen depiction of a fantasy tree, part oak, part pine. It had the thick, swirly trunk of an oak and dark green leaves that appeared to have pine needles poking out from them. A riotous combination of unlikely fruits, birds and animals lived in the tree—zebras, dogs, cats, rabbits, moles, bears, blue jays, magpies—animals and birds from all over the world and some, it appeared, not even of this planet. The colors were both bold and muted, the background a soft golden glow, like the sun setting or rising. It was an odd combination of naive and sophisticated, which made the viewer wonder about the artist. Was he a visionary, a true genius, or was this the art of the insane? So little was known about Abe Adam Finch that it was speculated that he was a painting savant, locked away somewhere painting his colorful, haunting paintings that were promoted tirelessly by his great-niece, Nola Finch. He was not represented by any art gallery, something Nola said he insisted on, which only added to the speculation of who he was. His signature was small, almost childlike, printed as if with great care. All the letters were of the same small case size.

"Right now," I told Elvia, "it's locked in my bedroom closet being watched over by the best four-legged security system in San Celina. But Gabe's probably picked it up by now. We'll keep it in his office until

D-Daddy checks the museum's security system one more time."

"Is Scout feeling better?" she asked, snapping her purse closed.

I followed her out the bedroom door and down the long staircase. My chocolate-colored, half-Lab, half–German shepherd dog had jumped a little too enthusiastically for a Frisbee last week at the dog park. "The vet said it was just a strain. No rough play for a couple of weeks and some anti-inflammatory drugs. I bought him an orthopedic bed that cost a fortune, but it'll be worth it if he sleeps better."

"I can sympathize," Elvia said. "I can't seem to find a comfortable position to sleep in myself. I feel so off-kilter. Emory offered to buy us a new mattress set, but I'm not sure that'll do any good."

We parted ways at the sidewalk. I headed for my purple Ford Ranger truck parked two blocks away in front of my and Gabe's California Craftsman bungalow that I'd been frantically cleaning since that fateful phone call a week ago. I'd also baked pies, biscuits, muffins and casseroles, frozen now and ready to cook each night. I couldn't make too much fun of my friend's obsession with her clothes, because I'd planned for this visit from Gabe's mother like it was Sherman's march into Atlanta. Gabe had wisely moved out of my way and did whatever I commanded without one syllable of back talk.

"You know," he'd said, when he walked in on me earlier this week in the kitchen marking pages in my Cattlewomen's Association and San Celina First Baptist Church Women's Missionary Union cookbooks, "we could just eat out like we usually do."

"Not on your life, mister," I'd replied, pulling out another favorite source of recipes, Dove's stained and ancient Sugartree, Arkansas, Cemetery Association cookbook. There was a hashed brown potato casserole I'd remembered was really good. "Going out to eat every night would really give your mama a month of stories to tell her friends back in Derby."

"What could she say?"

"That you'd married a woman who couldn't—or worse, wouldn't—cook for her husband."

"What do you care what a bunch of old biddies back in Derby think about you?" he foolishly asked.

I looked up and stared at him, not blinking.

"Go rake the leaves in the backyard," I finally replied. There was no way a man could ever understand why it was crucial for a woman to make at least a modicum of a good impression on his mother, the first, some say the most important, woman in a man's life. "And clean up the dog poop. Your turn."

"Yes, ma'am," he said, saluting me and grinning with an easiness I hadn't seen in a few months. "Anything you say, ma'am. I live to serve."

I couldn't help smiling at his teasing. His toothpaste-commercial white teeth against his beautiful copper skin were among the first things that attracted me to him. He hadn't been smiling much since his cousin died, so if me going emotionally bananas over impressing his mother made him laugh, it seemed a small price to pay. "Get lost, Joe Friday. I've got important things to do."

He left whistling, always loving it when I called him by the nickname I'd bestowed upon him the first time we met.

I thought about his smile this morning as I drove from Elvia's house toward the folk art museum. It made me feel hopeful on this perfect Central Coast winter day. The sun was bright, but we'd had some early November rain, which turned the hills surrounding San Celina into a mixed salad of shaded greens that brought joy to every rancher's heart. The more rain, the less hay we'd have to buy. Not to mention that it decorated the town with a natural Christmas cheer that had to gladden even the most cynical holiday Scrooge.

On Lopez Street, San Celina's main drag, the downtown merchants had gone all out this year with the old-fashioned streetlamps twisted with artificial pine boughs and twinkling white lights. More than one pickup truck passed me sporting a wreath on its grill; a couple had menorahs in the wreaths' centers. Today, Elvia had told me, was the judging of the holiday window displays. The folk art museum's new downtown store, Local Hands, was giving Blind Harry's a run for the ribbon this year.

I turned into the parking lot of the folk art museum, pleased by its neat-as-a-fried-pie appearance. Not a red tile was out of place on the old hacienda's Spanish-style roof, and the whitewashed adobe walls were spotless. My underpaid assistant, D-Daddy Boudreaux, was out front watering the whiskey barrel planters overflowing with native winter wildflowers. I would have to talk to Constance about giving him a raise. Since he'd become not only my assistant but virtually the museum and co-op's facilities manager, the grounds looked perfect. He deserved a raise, even if I had to have it taken from my own paycheck.

"Hey, D-Daddy," I called, climbing down from my truck.

"How's your old hound?" he asked, turning his trickling hose to another barrel filled with wild mustard and sky-blue columbine.

"He's doing okay. The vet gave him pills to relieve most of the pain, but he's more than happy to lie in his new bed. I've put it on the front porch so he can watch the neighborhood between naps."

"He be a good dog, him," D-Daddy said, reaching around to turn off the spigot. "Miz Constance, she called. On her way down she say to talk 'bout some important bizness."

I sighed. With Constance, I never knew if what she wanted to talk about was actually important or just a burr under her very expensive, custom-made saddle. But she was our biggest, most dependable patron, so catering to her burrs was part of my job. "Did she give a hint about what was bothering her?"

He shook his head no, his head of pure white hair glinting in the bright morning sun. "She be huntin' bear sound like."

"You know, that's the second time I've heard that comment this morning. I think bears are getting a bad rap."

He glanced over my shoulder and gave a cheerful wave. "Your buddy's here, *ange*."

I turned to look at the bright red Dodge Ram pickup parking next to my Ranger. The driver was something to me, though I'm not sure the term *buddy* covered it. Detective Ford "Hud" Hudson and I had a sort of friendship. Our relationship had its share of tension and sometimes outright animosity, but something in it had shifted when we'd gone through some heavy stress together last month when his daughter, Maisie, and I were involved in a hostage situation. The incident had moved our relationship past its teasing, semiflirtatious mode into something I'd not yet been able to classify.

"Hey, ranch girl," he said, climbing down from the truck.

"Ohhhh." I gave a long sigh when I saw what he held in his arms. "Please, let me hold it."

He grinned at D-Daddy. "You know, if I wasn't such a gentleman, I could take that comment completely the wrong way." He held the drowsy puppy out to me.

"Shut up," I said, taking the chubby, tricolored male puppy from him. "He's adorable." The puppy let out a large yawn and settled, without fear, into my arms. I put my face down into his downy fur, inhaling his sweet, clean puppy scent. His tiny sandpaper tongue licked my hand, causing me to coo again.

"What's his name?" I asked, rubbing my cheek against the puppy's head.

"Boudin," he said.

"Boo-what?" I said.

"Boo-dan," D-Daddy said slowly and deliberately. Then he chuckled. "It's Cajun sausage."

"And as D-Daddy can tell you," Hud added, "it's actually pronounced Boo-da, but it's easier just to tell people Boo-dan. I'm calling him Boo for short."

"I get it!" I said, suddenly recognizing his breed. "He's a corgi!" He had one upright satellite ear and one floppy ear that hadn't come up yet. "Did one of Sally's dogs have another litter?" Sally Schuler was San Celina's sheriff and Hud's boss. She raised Pembroke Welsh corgis as a hobby.

"Yep," Hud said, smiling. "She said Boo is a half brother to your daddy's dog, so I think that makes us kinfolk."

"In your dreams," I said. "Did you get him for Maisie?"

"Yeah, but Laura Lee says he has to live with me. We're doing a joint custody thing now, so Maisie has a room at both our houses. I bought a house over by Laguna Lake two blocks from them."

Hud had come to San Celina a few years ago after his ex-wife moved here to be near her only sister. A part-Cajun native of Texas, he'd finally forged a place for himself in our community.

"Excusez-moi," D-Daddy said, rolling up the hose. "I've got to go work on the second potting wheel. Motor's running rough. Don't want the potters getting all heated up."

"D-Daddy," I said. "What would we do without you?"

He grinned, shrugged and patted me on the back before he went inside the museum.

I turned back and looked at Hud's suntanned, boy-next-door face. Even though he was close to my own thirty-eight years, he looked as youthful as a college senior. Considering his job at the sheriff's department, cold case investigations, I wondered how he stayed so carefree. "So, what brings you to the folk art museum?"

He reached over and scratched under Boo's chin. The

white-chested puppy slitted his eyes in contentment. "I have a favor to ask you."

"What's that?"

In the past, I would have been suspicious, certain it was something not entirely seemly. He'd had a bit of a crush on me since we met, powered, I've always suspected, more than anything by the fact that I was absolutely unavailable.

"It's huge," he said, taking off his pale white Stetson. "And you're the only one I can ask." His face held a beseeching expression.

Now I was starting to get nervous. "I have my mother-in-law arriving for the Christmas holidays today, and I've got about a million things to do before Christmas day, so it can't be something that takes up too much time."

He kicked the dirt with his dark green lizard cowboy boot. It was one of two dozen pairs he owned. "There's no one else in the world I trust more than you. In a nutshell, I promised Maisie and Laurie I'd go back to Texas with them for the holidays. It's Laurie's grandma's ninety-fifth birthday, and Grandmama Lilly always liked me and, Laurie asked me . . ." He flashed his most winning smile.

Then it dawned on me. I held the fat little puppy out to him like it had just peed on my shirt. "Not a chance in the world! I'm not babysitting your pup. Hud, I can't. He's cute, but he's a . . . puppy!"

He took two steps backward. I followed him, holding out Boo, who starting yapping, thinking we were playing a game. "Take him back right now. I mean it." The puppy wiggled in my hands, and I pulled him back to my chest.

"Please, please," he said, holding his hands in prayer

and bowing. "I'll do anything, pay anything. I have no place to leave him . . ."

"What about Iry?" Hud's grandfather had moved to San Celina not long ago and lived in senior apartments near the folk art museum.

"He's going with us."

The puppy let out a little squeak, settling himself against my chest. He let out a big sigh and licked my forearm. I felt my resolve start to melt.

"Look, he already thinks of you as his aunt Benni," Hud said. "I swear, I'll pay you whatever you ask. I've put a thousand-dollar retainer at All Paws on Board, the doggie day care place next door. You can leave him there whenever you can't watch him. He's just past four months, has all his shots. But they don't do overnight care, and he's so little and helpless and at the vet he'd be stuck in a cage . . ."

The soft bundle of fur against my chest snuggled deeper, rested his head on my forearm and let out a little chirrup. That was the sound that did me in.

"Oh, Hud," I said, weakening.

"Thank you, thank you," he said, rushing over to his truck. "You are an angel, my hero, I'll love you forever. I have all his bedding, toys, food and other stuff here in my truck. We'll be home the day after Christmas. You're a lifesaver. Maisie will be so happy that you are taking care of Boo. It was killing her having to leave him so soon after we got him. She was afraid he'd be lonely."

I watched in dismay as he started unloading enough dog paraphernalia to open his own pet store. "Hud, how much have you spent on this dog?"

His face colored slightly as he put a green and white L.L.Bean bag full of plush toys in the back of my truck. The bag was personalized with Boo's name and a picture of a corgi. "I know it seems a bit much, but this little guy's been a godsend to Maisie . . . and I admit, to me and Laurie too. After what happened to Maisie, we needed something to take our minds off the trauma." He lifted a dark green dog crate into my truck bed. "We're going to counseling, and the child psychologist said she thought the puppy was a good idea, gave us all something in common to think about, concentrate on. Something that was positive and life affirming."

I ran my finger up the white stripe on Boo's nose. His eyes were covered with a furry black mask, and his two maple-brown eyebrows twitched. "I understand. I was told by the police psychologist at Gabe's office that something like what we went through will possibly show itself in unpredictable emotional ways and that we should be aware of that. A kind of post-traumatic stress syndrome, he said."

"Are you okay?" he asked, his expression concerned.

I nodded. "Gabe and I are doing all right. I have some trouble with insomnia, but . . ." I shrugged. "It's livable. Gabe was a little down, but his mother coming for Christmas seems to have cheered him up."

"And what's this visit doing to you?" He crossed his arms over his chest.

I shrugged again. "You know how it goes. It's my mother-in-law. Gabe's her only son and her first child. I'm not sure I'm exactly who she would have chosen for him."

"Her bad judgment then. Gabe's a lucky man."

I laughed at his words. "Cut the bull pucky. I've already agreed to puppy sit your little sausage dog. Tell Maisie that Boo is in good hands."

He lifted a twenty-pound bag of puppy food into the back of my truck.

"Whoa," I said. "Just how long did you say you were going to be gone?"

He grinned and leaned against the side of my truck. "Two weeks, tops. I just didn't want you to run out of food. I don't want this to cost you a penny." He pulled out his wallet.

"Put that away, Clouseau." I'd given him the nickname of the bumbling French detective because Hud was anything but bumbling when it came to his work. "We're friends. I won't accept money for doing this."

"What if he needs to go to the vet?" Hud asked.

"Who's his vet?"

"Dr. Catalina Vieira."

"She's Scout's vet too. No problem. She'll just bill you."

"Okay, great," he said, putting his wallet away. He took a card from the inside of his jacket. "Here's the numbers where we'll be if you need to contact me. My cell phone's on there too, but the ranch is pretty far out. I'm not sure how good the service is."

"If I need you, I'll find you." I took the card and smiled at him. "Don't worry, Boo is in good hands."

"That I know for sure, ranch girl," he said, reaching over to stroke Boo's head.

"Have a safe trip. Say hey to Laura Lee for me."

He slipped his Stetson back on his head. "I'll do that. Merry Christmas, ranch girl. And I meant it, you know."

"Meant what?"

"Gabe's a lucky man."

"Merry Christmas, Clouseau."

As Boo and I watched his red truck leave the parking lot, the sound of his horn blaring "The Yellow Rose of Texas" echoing through the stand of eucalyptus trees, another car barreled past him into the parking lot. A black Mercedes-Benz without a speck of dirt on it. The Wicked Witch of the West music reverberated through my head for the second time in a week. The car stopped a few feet from me, and Constance Sinclair, the folk museum's personal patroness of the arts, stepped out.

"Boo, I don't think we're in Kansas anymore," I whispered, rubbing my lips across the silky top of his warm puppy head.

She slammed the car door and marched toward us, her two-toned pumps making crackling sounds as they ate up the gravel parking lot. Her thin, Italian greyhound face was flushed pink with agitation. My mind frantically searched for something I could have possibly said or done to bring on this hissy fit. Nothing sprang immediately to mind. I clutched Boo closer to my chest.

"Benni Harper," she bellowed when she reached me. "You simply have to help me. Pinky has been murdered."

CHAPTER 2

"*E*XCUSE ME?" I SAID. *PINKY? MURDER?*

"What is that?" She stared with open disgust at Boo.

"A puppy," I replied, still dumbfounded by her declaration and a bit afraid to ask who Pinky was.

"I know *that*. What are *you* doing with it here? I hope it won't interfere with your job."

"Watching him for a friend." I just realized at that moment that Hud had not told me anything about Boo's personality, tastes, habits and most important, how far along in the toilet training process the little guy was. Typical man. I shifted the dog in my arms. "And, no, he won't interfere with my job. Don't forget, our new neighbors are a doggie day care facility."

"Most ridiculous thing I've ever heard. Day care for dogs."

I might have agreed with her at one time, but holding this puppy in my arms and trying to figure out how I'll get all the things done I need to get done in the next two weeks, doggie day care seemed a lifesaver.

Changing the subject seemed prudent at this moment. "Who is Pinky?"

"You know her as Arva Edmondson." Constance's bright blue eyes filmed over, displaying an emotion I'd never seen in her: sadness. "Her friends called her Pinky. She was my dearest friend. She died five days ago." She dipped her head, leaving me to inspect the top of her teased, champagne-colored hair. "She was only sixty years old."

"I'm so sorry, Constance," I said, truly feeling bad for her, despite our often fractious relationship. I couldn't imagine my life without Elvia. "Is there anything I can do?"

I'd met Arva "Pinky" Edmondson at a few museum functions and vaguely remembered a slender, dark-haired woman with a laugh that was a tad more brassy than most society ladies, not that anyone faulted her on it. She seemed to be one of the leaders of Constance's very elite group. It was not a surprise that I didn't know her nickname. Like most of Constance's friends, she hadn't had any reason to do more than ask me to fetch her another glass of champagne. She was younger than most of Constance's friends, who tended to be closer to her own age, somewhere in the mid to late seventies.

Her head popped up, the determined and self-confident

Constance back. "Yes, there is. You can find her murderer."

I must admit, her statement gave me pause. I was thinking more along the lines of baking a pie or helping her pick out music for Pinky's memorial service.

"Well," I said, drawing the word out, trying to buy myself time. "That's not exactly my job here at the folk art museum. Have you talked to the police?" Boo started to wiggle in my arms, his short nap over. I set him down on the ground, and he immediately squatted and relieved himself.

"Oh, for heaven's sakes," Constance said. "I hope you'll clean that up before the museum opens."

"Of course I will," I said evenly. "Now, what happened to Pinky?"

"I told you," she said, enunciating each word. "She. Was. Murdered."

"How?"

She waved her hand. "That doesn't matter."

I waited a second before answering, a bit shocked by her statement. "Of course it matters, Constance. How did she die?"

"Your husband," she said, spitting the words out like they were a bite of sour orange.

I inhaled deeply, mentally counting to ten. "What about him?"

"He refuses to investigate."

This was awkward. But, I had to admit, she'd aroused my curiosity. "What do you mean?"

"He *refuses to investigate* my friend's murder," she snapped. "What part of that sentence don't you understand?"

Boo scampered behind one of the whiskey barrel planters, and I darted after him. He was as fast as a toddler. "Back where I can see you, Mister Boo," I said, scooping him up with one hand and placing him at my feet. He pounced on the tassel dangling from Constance's right dress pump.

"Get away, you beast," she said, jerking her foot. He chased after it, excited by the new game.

"Come back here, you," I said, pulling the scrunchie from my hair and dangling it at him. Luckily, the attention span of a puppy is nanoseconds. He grabbed the scrunchie and shook it like it was captured prey. "Let's go into my office, Constance, and talk about this in a more comfortable setting." I scooped up Boo.

"He's coming with us?" Her pale eyes bugged slightly.

"I can't leave him out here. He's just a puppy, and people will start driving in soon."

"All right," she said reluctantly. "But we just had your office carpeted. He'd better control himself."

We followed Constance through the museum toward the co-op studio in back, which was once the hacienda's stables. These buildings, I wanted to inform Constance, had seen their share of animal droppings. Instead, I whispered into Boo's upright ear, "If you must piddle, please stay away from her expensive shoes."

Once inside my small office, I found a basket, emptied it of its magazines, arranged my sweatshirt for some padding, and settled Boo in his makeshift bed. He immediately stuck his shiny nose inside one of the sleeves and went to sleep. From experience, I knew his nap would probably last for about twenty or thirty minutes, then he'd be ready to play again. Hopefully, by then, Constance would be gone.

"Tell me everything," I said, sitting down across from her in one of the two padded visitor's chairs. "From the beginning."

"First, I want to say how disappointed I am in your husband. You know, I've half a mind to report him to the mayor."

I contemplated reminding her that the mayor wasn't Gabe's boss, the city manager was. On a quick second thought, I decided to keep that to myself. "What did Gabe do?"

"It's what he's *not* doing." Beads of sweat darkened the whitish down on her upper lip.

"What is that?" I asked calmly.

At that moment, she burst into tears, which couldn't have surprised me more than if she'd hopped up on my desktop and started dancing the jitterbug. I jumped up, fumbled in my desk drawer for a box of tissue and held it out to her. While she took one and held it under her mascara-streaked eyes, I sat back down across from her, stymied about what to do next.

"I'm very sorry," I said again, my words sounding feeble to my ears. I hadn't realized how truly upset she was over her friend's death. Behind my closed door, a group of men laughed, on their way to the wood shop down the hall. In the distance, the whine of a wood saw accompanied Constance's sobs. I held out the tissue box again, and she took two more.

"Constance, what happened to Pinky?" I asked in a gentle voice. I was still shocked at her uncharacteristic outburst. She'd always been one of the most self-assured, imposing, some would say controlling, people I'd ever met. Confidence in herself and her place in San Celina's society had always made her seem like nothing could ever shake her. Seeing Constance's vulnerable side was something that caught me off guard. It also made me more than a little wary. Once she regained control, I was sure she'd make me pay for glimpsing this vulnerable moment of her psyche.

She inhaled deeply, dabbed at her eyes and then straightened her spine. "They say she had a heart attack in her sleep, but I know it isn't true."

"Did Pinky have heart problems?"

Constance shot me an exasperated look. "Of course she did. That's not the point."

It seemed the whole point to me.

"She had a heart problem, but she didn't have a heart attack no matter what the doctor says. No matter what your husband says. She was murdered. She took her medicine faithfully and was feeling better than she had in years. She told me so herself. She said she had something special she was working on, something she said I'd really enjoy. We had plans to take a cruise to Italy next month. We were already planning next year's Christmas ball. She just had one hundred tulip bulbs planted! Does that sound like someone who would just up and die for no reason?"

I wanted to point out that people made plans all the time, and death intervened. Death doesn't call and make an appointment; how well I knew that.

She sat up straight, her momentary emotional outburst over. General Patton had returned. "You work for me, and since your husband won't do his job, I demand you investigate this crime."

I couldn't help it. Despite my pity for her loss, and even though her cheekbones were tinged a very familiar angry pink and in spite of the fact I knew I'd live to regret my action, I couldn't help it. I laughed.

"Investigate? Constance, I am a museum curator, not a private eye. If Gabe doesn't think there is a crime, what can I tell you? He's the expert."

"You've done it before. Found killers."

Though she was technically right—I'd been involved in a few incidents where I'd done some investigating on my own—I'd sworn to Gabe I would stay away from playing detective. And, frankly, after what had taken place less than a month ago with the hostage situation, I was more than happy to leave the bad guys to my husband and his officers.

"Yes, I have," I said. "But those incidents were all accidental."

"But you solved them when the police couldn't."

That was true. It was also the reason I was determined to stay away from this disagreement she had with the police about her friend's death. My and Gabe's marriage had enough problems without me getting involved with something like this. Not to mention his mother was coming to town in—I glanced up at the schoolhouse clock on the wall—seven hours.

"Constance," I said, looking directly into her red-rimmed eyes. "I am truly sorry about your friend, but I can't go against Gabe's decision. I assure you that he and his detectives are very good at their jobs, and if they say that there was nothing suspicious about your friend's—"

"They are wrong," she interrupted. "I'll pay you overtime. All your expenses, gas and meals and whatever equipment you need to solve the case. Isn't that what you do with private detectives?"

"I wouldn't know because I'm not a private detective." I took a deep breath, working particularly hard at keeping my voice from sounding irritable. After all, she'd just lost a close friend, and perhaps this was her way of working it out. Besides, I reasoned, it was good practice for the next two weeks with Kathryn who, I was willing to bet, could give Constance a run for the roses in the intimidation department.

"Benni, please." Her normally commanding voice sounded odd saying those words. "I'll do anything. I'll pay anything."

I looked at her a long moment, wishing like anything that I'd called in sick this morning. "I wish I could help you, but if Gabe says there's nothing suspicious about Pinky's death, why would you doubt him?"

"Because I know what I know." She wagged a long, elegant finger at me. It sounded like something my gramma Dove would say.

"C'mon, Constance," I said, finally getting frustrated enough to nip this in the bud. I had too many things to do today. "Who would possibly want to murder your friend?"

Her triumphant smile told me immediately that my question was the wrong one to ask. She opened up her purse and took out a folded sheet of paper.

"I have a list," she said.

Of course she did. I groaned out loud. "I didn't mean I actually wanted to know—"

She slapped the paper into my hand. "There are three names on there, the women who are next in line for 49 Club membership. One of them did it."

I stared at her like she was a fire-breathing dragon come to life. "The 49 Club? You think someone killed Pinky to take her place in the 49 Club?" The idea was so outlandish, I couldn't even laugh.

"I *know* it."

The 49 Club was San Celina's most exclusive female-only society club. Formed seventy-five years ago, faithful to its name, it was comprised of only forty-nine members. They were the elite of the elite, and a woman could only become a member after one of the forty-nine died and then only by a unanimous vote of the other forty-eight members. They put on an invitation-only Christmas Ball and Silent Auction every year that was the most talked-about holiday event in the county. Last year it was five thousand dollars a head and limited to three hundred people. Tony Bennett, a personal friend of one of the 49ers, attended and sang a medley of Christmas carols. All the money raised was directly donated to various charities helping women and children in the county. I'd never gone to the ball, something like that being far out of my price and social range, but Elvia attended last year with Emory and said it was even more amazing than what the newspapers reported. The club met once a week for lunch in their historical landmark clubhouse in San Celina designed for them by Julia Morgan, the architect of William Randolph Hearst's infamous castle.

I clutched the sheet of paper in my hand, fighting the temptation to read her list. "You can't be serious. I mean, I know the 49 Club is . . . well, many people are . . ." I almost said dying to join, then caught myself. "Many women would love to join, but I find it hard to believe that anyone would actually kill to become a member."

She stared at me silently for a moment, her eyes bulging with some kind of emotion. At our feet, Boo gave a little chirrup, then rolled over on his back, splaying his back legs out in a pose that would have been X-rated had he been a human.

"Please, Benni," she finally said. "Just consider my request. I have nowhere else to go."

I felt myself weakening. It was the second *please* that did it. Constance had never uttered the word please to me. She'd likely never said it to anyone in her life.

"I don't know," I said, still attempting to maintain some boundaries with my boss. "It—"

She stood up and closed her purse with a snap. "One day to look at what I've written. That's all I ask. I'll pay you five hundred dollars for a retainer. Right now."

I gave a big sigh and stood up. "I don't want your money. I'll see what I can find out from Gabe. That's the best I can offer."

She gave a sharp nod. "Fair enough. Are we set for the exhibit opening?"

"Yes, the wine arrived yesterday. I have it stacked in the storage room. The caterers are all set. I'll come in early tomorrow to make sure everything is in order."

"What about the painting?"

"It arrived this morning and is probably in Gabe's office right now. I called him the minute it came. D-Daddy's waiting for the alarm people today to double-check the system. I'll bring it to the museum and hang it tomorrow."

"Good. We want this event to be special. Maybe Miss Finch will tell some of her artist connections, and the museum will receive even more donations."

"I'll do my best to make sure everything's perfect."

"See that you do." She brushed past me without even a good-bye, the familiar autocratic Constance returned. Had I just imagined the sobbing and vulnerable Constance of a half hour ago?

"Okay, my little Bugaboo," I said, waking the puppy up. "Let's get you fed, and then let's go visit your Uncle Gabe. We have to run this whole thing by him before we become involved."

Boo, unaware of the hullabaloo he'd just entered, pounced at my loose shoelace, capturing it with a triumphant bark.

CHAPTER 3

$\mathcal{W}$HEN I WENT OUT TO MY TRUCK TO DIG THROUGH Boo's stuff, I found a note stuck to my windshield. It was from Hud.

"Hey, ranch girl," it read. "I realized I forgot to give you Boo's schedule, his likes, dislikes, etc. He's sort of house-trained, ha-ha. (Sorry.) I'll donate five hundred bucks to the folk art museum if you can accomplish that. When I came back inside the museum, your door was closed. It sounded like there was some kind of emotional crisis going on, so I decided not to disturb you. Call my cell or the ranch if you have any questions about Boudin. Thanks again. You're a stand-up broad. Your buddy, Hud."

So, I thought, the going rate for finding a killer and potty-training a puppy seemed to be the same in San

Celina. I wasn't sure which one would be harder.

"Okay," I said to Boo, who was now scampering about my feet, playing with a dandelion sprouting from the gravel, "according to your schedule you are due for lunch. But I suspected that." I looked at my watch. "Then it's time to meet *perro grande*, and I don't mean Scout. Be on your cutest behavior, because I'm not sure how he's going to take sharing his home with a semi-housetrained corgi."

Boo yapped, then chased a bee. I found his food and a black and red ceramic dish that had Yummers! printed on the bottom. I fed him, then took him to the side of the building to do his business. I put him in the pickup's bed while I struggled to secure his padded car seat with the passenger seat belt. I recaptured him, slipped his tiny halter on and hooked him into his fancy car seat.

"You know," I said, starting my truck. "Traveling with Scout is a whole lot easier." After introducing Boo to Gabe, I was going to spend some of that thousand-dollar retainer at All Paws on Board. He'd be in expert and loving hands with Suann, the day care's owner and head dog wrangler.

At the police station, it took me twenty minutes to maneuver the short walk to Gabe's office. There was something about a puppy that softened the eyes of even the most hardened street cop, cynical detective or seen-it-all dispatcher. Before I made it to Gabe's office I heard three long-winded memories of a special dog in someone's life. Gabe's oak door was closed when I walked up to his assistant's desk. Maggie, a fellow rancher and dog lover, had to spend her requisite minutes fawning over Boo and telling me about a corgi-beagle mix her grandfather once owned.

"Is Gabe in?" I asked.

"Yes," she said, cuddling Boo to her chest. "But he's only got fifteen minutes to spare before he has a meeting."

"More important, is he in a good mood?" He had been when he left this morning, but being a police chief, that could change in a flash-bang.

"Reasonably so. He's excited about his mama coming out for Christmas." She grinned at me. "Said you were excited about it too."

I grinned back. Maggie knew me too well to believe that. "More like anxiously anticipating. Kathryn and I came to something of a truce when I visited Kansas a few years ago. Except for three or four short phone conversations, we haven't talked since."

Maggie rubbed her cheek against Boo's head. "The only advice I have is that a person can fake anything for two weeks."

"I certainly intend to try."

The door opened as soon as the words came out of my mouth.

"Try what?" Gabe asked.

I looked away from Maggie, afraid the amused look in her shiny black eyes would cause me to start laughing. "Try to figure out how to tell my darling husband that he's the most wonderful, understanding, open-minded, caring and generous person I've ever known."

He gave a disbelieving grunt and raised his thick eyebrows. "What do you want? I'm already tempted to say no." He glanced over at Maggie. "Who's this cute little guy?" He reached over and scratched Boo under the chin with his forefinger. "Bet you can pick up fifty channels with that ear."

Maggie carefully handed Boo back to me. "That's my cue to head for the snack machine. I hear a Snickers calling my name."

The situation dawned on Gabe. He had, after all, been a detective for the LAPD for many years before he took this police chief job.

"Oh, no," he said, holding his hands up. "We're not getting a puppy." But the indulgence in his voice told me that, if a puppy was what I wanted, he wouldn't fight me on it.

"That's not what I'm asking." I followed him into his office. "Boo belongs to Hud, and he asked me to baby . . . uh . . . puppy sit for the next two weeks."

Gabe turned to study me, his jovial expression suddenly careful. He knew how Hud felt about me but had reluctantly conceded to my absolute assurance that Hud's crush would pass and that Gabe had nothing to worry about. Gabe was sympathetic to Hud and what he'd gone through last month when his daughter was held hostage and, I guessed, felt a little guilty for the part his cousin played in it.

"Hud is going with Laura Lee and Maisie to Texas for Christmas. He bought Boo for Maisie at the suggestion of their family counselor."

"Hud's going to Texas with his ex-wife," Gabe repeated, looking thoughtful.

I smiled. "I told you there was still something between them. Think of taking care of Boo as our way of helping reignite their love."

"Don't count on it," he said, ever the cynic. "But, since you'll be doing most of the work taking care of the little guy, I can't say much."

I set Boo down on the floor, where he promptly squatted and presented Gabe with a highly personal and aromatic gift.

"Stop him!" Gabe said. "The DA is meeting me here in ten minutes."

"Relax," I said, laughing. "I'm sure it won't be the first time he's smelled crap."

"Very funny." Gabe took a box of tissues from his credenza and held it out to me. "You can do the honors."

I picked Boo up and handed him to Gabe. "Keep him out of trouble while I clean this up." I picked up Boo's mess with a doggie bag I'd stuck in my back pocket. "I have something else to discuss with you."

He glanced up at the wall clock. "Can it wait?"

"It's quick, I promise." As I scrubbed the spot with some alcohol I found in Gabe's desk, I told him about my odd encounter with Constance and her belief that Pinky Edmondson was murdered.

He groaned and shifted Boo in his arms. "That woman is nuts. Her friend died of a heart attack, plain and simple. Arva Edmondson's doctor and the medical examiner both said there was absolutely no sign of foul play. The only family Mrs. Edmondson had was some distant cousins back East. They would not give permission to do an autopsy, and I don't blame them. She was cremated, and her ashes will be flown to some family crypt in Philadelphia. Case closed."

"I agree with you, but she's all over me, Friday. Did

she tell you she's convinced that one of the aspiring members to the 49 Club offed Pinky to claim her spot? She also tried to hire me to investigate."

Gabe threw back his head and laughed. "That's the craziest thing I've heard all week."

"Which statement are you referring to?"

He wisely refused to say. "Go ahead."

I cocked my head, confused. "With what?"

"Tell her you'll investigate. But don't sign anything or make a statement that says she is hiring you to investigate. You're not licensed, and that could get sticky. Call yourself an artistic consultant or something."

I opened my mouth and clutched my chest, feigning a heart attack. "Am I hearing correctly? You actually *want* me to investigate Pinky Edmondson's death?"

"I want you to keep Constance Sinclair off my back. If she thinks you're investigating, she'll leave me and my detectives alone."

I nodded my head, grinning. "I wish I could get this on tape."

"Don't look so smug." He handed Boo back to me. "If I really thought there was even a hint of truth to her story, I wouldn't ask you to do this."

"I'm just enjoying the moment. It'll probably never happen again."

"We agree on that." He leaned down and kissed me lightly on the lips. "So what do you say, Mrs. Ortiz?" His voice caressed the words. I could tell it still thrilled him that I'd officially taken his last name a month ago. "Meet me at the train station at five forty-five? The other Mrs. Ortiz's train is arriving at six."

43

The *first* Mrs. Ortiz was the unspoken statement. I wondered briefly what she would think about me finally taking her son's last name. "I'll be there. What do you think we should do for dinner? Go out or eat at home?"

"You decide."

He stuck his hand in his pants pocket and jiggled his keys. Gabe wasn't the type of person who had nervous habits. Maybe it was his time in Vietnam as a foot soldier when he learned the art of perfect stillness, or maybe it was just his guarded personality, but it was hard for people, except the few who knew him very well, to tell when he was apprehensive. Anger and frustration he had no trouble showing. Fear or anxiety, that was something else. He was obviously more nervous about his mother visiting than I realized.

"How about my beef and barley soup, a green salad, baking powder biscuits and Dove's peach cobbler?" I had all those things ready to throw together at home.

"Sounds perfect. I imagine Mom will be tired. Eating at home would be more relaxing."

"Her room is ready down to her favorite Ivory soap and Meyer lemon hand lotion."

He gave me a puzzled look. "You know her favorite soap and hand lotion?"

I shifted Boo to my other arm. "No great detective work there. I called your sister Becky. You should try it once in a while. She says you never call her back. Angel says the same thing."

"I always mean to."

I just rolled my eyes at him.

"Actually," he said, changing the subject from his lack of communication with his sisters, "what you did is exactly what a good detective would do. Check the obvious source, those closest to the . . ." He stopped, obviously not wanting to compare his mother to a homicide victim.

"I'll keep that in mind when I work on my new case."

"*Pretend* case."

I just shrugged. "Did you send someone to pick up Abe Adam Finch's painting?" I'd called Gabe as soon as it was delivered at home this morning.

"Miguel picked it up. He's the only one of my officers that Scout was likely to let in." He nodded across the room at a locked closet. "It's right there. Just let me know when you want it delivered to the museum."

"Probably tomorrow. The security people are supposed to come by today and check the system."

The intercom on his desk buzzed, and Maggie informed Gabe that the district attorney had arrived.

"See you tonight," Gabe said. "Have fun playing Nancy Drew."

"Don't kid yourself, Chief. You owe me big time for this."

On the way out to my truck, the more I thought about it, the more difficult it seemed. Would Constance fall for it? And how long did I need to keep up the charade? Maybe I needed a little coaching, so I decided my next stop would be my friend Amanda Landry's office. Though she'd been a private attorney for years, she'd recently accepted a deputy district attorney position with the county. She specialized in crimes against women and children. Maybe Amanda could give me a few tips about what I could do to make Constance believe I was really investigating this alleged crime.

I hooked Boo in his car seat and headed for the government offices downtown. It was only when I parked on the street across from the county courthouse that I realized, unlike my well-trained, adult dog, whom I could, on a cool winter day like today, leave for a half hour or so in the cab of my truck with a dish of water and the windows rolled down, I couldn't leave this little puppy for one second. And I doubted that he'd pass for a Seeing Eye or companion dog, so I couldn't take him inside the county buildings.

"You are already beginning to put a crimp in my style," I told him. He was sleeping peacefully in his padded bed. I sat there contemplating my next move when luck smiled upon me. I spotted my stepson, Sam, walking down the opposite side of the street.

I rolled down my window. "Hey, Sam! Want to make twenty bucks?"

He waved at me and called back, "Sure, I'm flat broke."

That's what I was counting on. Sam, Gabe's only child, had lived in San Celina for the last few years, most of the time out at my dad and gramma Dove's ranch. He worked as a part-time ranch hand for his room and board, and at various other jobs around town, including Elvia's bookstore, for his spending money. In between that and his extensive social life, he attended Cal Poly University. Right now, his major was culinary arts, his latest ambition to be a chef. He'd stuck with this major longer than any other and worked occasionally for a couple of the town's catering companies, so it looked like this major might be the *one*.

Sam loped across the street toward my truck. Though my husband was a handsome and distinguished-looking man, his son was magazine model material. His once short, black, shiny hair was shaggy and wild, a new, slightly artsy look for him. He wore black jeans and a red T-shirt that said, Chicks Dig a Man who Bastes. He and Gabe had an often fractious relationship, but Sam and I had hit it off from the beginning, mostly because, not ever being a mother, I didn't have any interest in mothering him.

"Who do I have to kill?" he asked when he reached me. He leaned inside the open window, resting his tanned arms on the frame. "Wow, cute puppy."

"Glad you think so. That's what I need you to do for the next hour. Take care of Boo while I investigate a murder for your father."

"Who and what?" His dark brown eyes sparkled with questions.

I gave him the quick rundown on Boo's name, his temporary visit, Constance Sinclair's assertion about her friend and Gabe's request of me.

"Man, Pinky is dead?" Sam said. "That stinks. She was a cool lady. Outstanding tipper."

"You knew Pinky Edmondson?" Today offered one surprise after another. Sam and Pinky were about a thousand miles apart on San Celina's social scale.

"Met her when I worked a couple of gigs for Jacques." Jacques of San Celina was one of the oldest caterers in the county. Many Cal Poly culinary students had learned their catering chops working for Jacques.

"Pinky liked real traditional catering," Sam said. "Stuffed mushrooms, shrimp puffs, Brie, French Chardonnay. You know, old-school finger food. She belonged to some ladies' club that we did a couple brunches for. Unlike some of the women there, not mentioning any names . . ." He raised one dark eyebrow. "She was real nice. Like I said, good tipper and didn't throw any crazy fits."

I knew he was referring to Constance, whose fits were legendary. "Pinky actually died of a heart attack, but Constance has been haranguing your dad with her absolute belief that Pinky was murdered. Your dad has passed her obsession on to me."

"Harsh," he said sympathetically. "You have to, like, fake her out?"

"Exactly. I decided to get some tips on how I could do that from my friend Amanda in the district attorney's office, but then I remembered my furry little friend here."

"No problem. I'll watch the little monster while you learn how to lie."

I grimaced at the word *lie*. "There'll be no actual lying taking place. I'm just going to . . ." I faltered.

He raised his eyebrows.

"Okay, okay," I conceded. "There might be untruths spoken, but it's in the name of harmony." That certainly didn't justify it, but it was all I had.

"Whatever," Sam said. "Tell it to your priest. No judgment here." He walked around to the passenger side and opened the door. Boo was awake now and ready for some new fun.

"Meet me back at the truck in an hour. Here's a leash and some plastic bags. Don't forget to clean up after him."

"Got it, *madrastra*." Sam stuffed the leash and bags in his pocket, then picked Boo up. "This'll be sweet," he called over his shoulder. "Women love puppies."

"An hour," I called back. "Then you get your twenty bucks."

I watched him walk down Lopez and, sure enough, before he reached the end of the block, two college-age girls had stopped him and were cooing over Boo. I had a feeling after an hour, I'd have to search him out and pry that girl-attracting puppy out of his arms.

Inside the gray concrete government buildings, I took the elevator up to the district attorney's offices on the third floor. The cool, nondescript foyer was empty. Behind the bulletproof, Plexiglas window a clerk asked me if I had an appointment with Ms. Landry.

"No," I said.

"I'll see if she's free."

I flipped through a three-month-old *Time* magazine, thinking that this bland office was a huge change from the one Amanda had leased above the Ross Department Store. Earlier in her law career she worked for the San Francisco district attorney's office. When her father, a retired Alabama judge, died and left her a small fortune, she moved to San Celina and went into private practice. She was tired of dealing with sociopaths every day, she'd told me the first time we'd had lunch when she dropped by the museum and offered her pro bono services to the museum and co-op.

"It feels like you're a cat in a roomful of mice on speed," she'd told me. "You might catch one or two, if you're lucky, but, mostly, they just jump out of your clutches. I'm just plumb tuckered out."

So it surprised me when a month ago she called to tell me that she was closing her practice and accepting a job with the district attorney's office.

"I'll keep y'all on, of course," she'd said. "But I'm just flat-out bored out of my skull drawing up trusts and fighting fencing issues. I need to feel like I'm doing something useful. Besides . . ." I could imagine her wide, Carly Simon smile. "I kinda miss them ole bad guys. Always loved growling back at them in court when they thought they could intimidate me with their high-hat prison sneers."

Amanda, almost six feet tall, with a kudzu-thick head of auburn hair that she wore, more often than not, to her shoulders in full, shoulder-length curls, was both überfeminine and strikingly Amazon-like, which fascinated and scared most of the men she met.

She was out in the lobby in minutes, pulling me up into a huge, warm Southern hug. "Benni Harper Ortiz, where have you been? I've missed you, girl. Come on in and see the hovel these people call an office. If I wasn't having such a good ole time, I'd quit this place and buy myself one of your cousin's smoked chicken franchises. I swear, it's the best chicken I've ever eaten."

I followed her through the rabbit warren of cubicles and offices. She called out greetings as she passed by open offices filled with overflowing desks. You would have thought she'd worked here two years, not two months.

"Wow, you've really settled in," I said when we reached her tiny office. "You seem to know everyone." One small window looked out over the parking lot where they loaded and unloaded prisoners.

"Have a seat," she said, pointing to the government-issue vinyl and metal visitor's chair in front of her gray metal desk. "Don't forget, I've been practicing law here in San Celina for a while. Ran across most of these folks at one point or another. Not that I had a lot of criminal cases, but I do belong to every law association in the county. Schmoozing is the one talent I inherited from my dear sweet daddy." She gave me a broad wink. "I like to think of using my talent for good rather than evil."

Her father had been a prominent and, according to her, absolutely corrupt-to-the-marrow Alabama judge. She'd once said that fifty thousand dollars' worth of psychotherapy, a fraction of the money she inherited from him, was the reason she could laugh about him today.

She folded her hands on her maroon desk blotter. "So, what can I do for you? Got any criminals you want me to persecute?"

"Don't you mean prosecute?" I said, laughing.

Her eyes twinkled. "Whatever."

"You're having fun, aren't you?"

"You bet. I'd forgotten how satisfying it is putting away bad guys."

"I won't keep you long," I said, sitting forward in my

chair. "I have a favor to ask. How do I fake investigating a homicide?"

She cocked her head, her sculpted eyebrows knit in question. "That sounds downright intriguing."

I smiled. "Don't worry, I have Gabe's permission. As a matter of fact, it's at his request."

She unfolded her hands. "The plot thickens."

I quickly filled her in on the whole Constance-Pinky dilemma. "In a nutshell, Gabe wants me to keep her busy and off his back. I think he thinks she'll eventually just move her attention to something else."

"He's probably right. She sounds as nutty as peanut butter pie."

"Maybe, but it also might be her grief talking. I can't help feeling sorry for her. If one of my friends died and I even had an inkling that something was amiss, I'd probably throw as big a hissy fit as she's doing."

I meant what I said. Though I only knew Constance as a boss and, despite having felt many times the sting of her snobbery, I still felt sympathy for her. She'd never had children and had been widowed for years. I suspected her friends were a big part of her life. Not having children myself, I could definitely relate.

"So, what do you suggest?" I asked Amanda.

"This should be easy. Like most everyone else, her ideas about how a person investigates a homicide are probably from television shows. Her reference would likely be Jessica Fletcher or that show with Dick Van Dyke. You know the routine. First, get a small notebook and one of those little portable tape recorders. You can find them at the drugstore."

I nodded. "Then what?"

"She said she thinks that one of the aspiring 49ers is the killer?"

"She's positive."

"Boy, there's a picture for you. If I were you, I'd just casually question each one using your position as curator and your background as a historian. Tell them you're thinking about writing a history of their club."

"Except that the people I'll be talking to aren't actually members of the club yet."

"Then tell them it's an article for a history magazine. Make one up. Trust me, they won't bother to check. Once you get people talking about themselves, they often won't shut up." She lifted one eyebrow. "As a matter of fact, we prosecutors count on that. Many a criminal has talked himself or herself directly into jail simply because they admired the musical sound of their own voice."

"Everything you've said was along the lines of what I was thinking about doing."

"Why the visit then?"

I stood up. "For one thing, I just wanted to say hi and see your new office. It's been too long since we've seen each other."

"You're right as rain there. What else?"

I laughed. "It won't be a lie when I tell Constance that I'm in contact with the district attorney's office about Pinky's case."

"You sly dog," she said, standing up. "It's been good seeing you. What're your plans for the upcoming holidays?"

I grimaced and gave a dramatic shudder. "Mother-in-law coming in on the train tonight. Wish me luck."

"Do you one better. I'll offer my guest room when you need a place to hide."

I went around the desk and gave her another hug. Her perfume, smelling like spring rain and sweet magnolias, reminded me of my late mother. "I might take you up on your offer. What're your plans for Christmas?"

"Got about twenty people coming for a potluck supper. Not an in-law in the bunch, though there're a few that might qualify as outlaws." She winked at me. "Friends of Eli's."

"I'm not even going to ask." Eli was her housekeeper and, for some time now, as she liked to put it, her gentleman caller.

"Best you don't," she agreed.

After tracking Sam down in front of the Tastee-Freez, where a bevy of females was spoiling my foster puppy, I asked him to stay put while I ran across the street to Longs drugstore to buy a notebook and tape recorder. Soon I was on my way back toward the folk art museum, Boo exhausted and snoozing in his car seat.

I stopped off at All Paws, told Suann my story of being Boo's foster puppy mama for the next two weeks and asked them to watch him for me.

"I'll be back in a few hours," I promised. Then it dawned on me. "Darn, I'll have to take him with me to pick up Gabe's mom." All Paws closed at seven p.m.

"He's still a little guy," Suann said. "You could carry him into the station. Usually no one will say anything. Or I can let you borrow this carrier." She pointed to a leopard-print dog carrier that resembled a piece of luggage.

"I think I'll just carry him. Or I'll wait in the car with him."

After temporarily relieving myself of my little charge, I went back to the museum, where the docent manning the gift shop gave me a large manila envelope left by a messenger. It was, of course, from Constance.

"Dear Benni," read the letter on top of the thick sheaf of papers. "Here are the backgrounds on the ladies who are applying for the open spot in the 49 Club. Please keep me informed on your progress. Also enclosed is your retainer fee. Sincerely, Constance Sinclair." Attached to the letter was her personal check for five hundred dollars. Under the memo part of the check she'd written "consulting fee."

"Well, well," I murmured as I walked back to my office. "My first money as a private detective. Maybe I should frame it." I stuck the check in my wallet, not certain if I would cash it or not. It seemed deceitful of me to accept money for what was essentially a fake investigation. Then again, I could donate the money to the co-op's Art for Kids program.

Once inside my office, I sat down and looked through the other papers. She had three women listed, all with, it appeared to me, impeccable society credentials. I couldn't imagine one of them killing to gain membership to some lame society club.

First was Dorothea St. James. Nickname was Dot. I had seen her photos frequently on the society pages of the *San Celina Tribune*. She was sixty-eight years old and the widow of a local podiatrist. She had one daughter who owned a jewelry boutique in Cambria. She'd been involved with just about every San Celina society club in her twenty-eight years living in this county. The committees she chaired and charity events she hosted at her huge house in Cambria filled three pages. Her list was neatly typed with detailed explanations of each event. She'd been on the 49 Club waiting list for twenty years, passed over twice for women who hadn't lived here as long as she. That, I thought, had to cause some resentment. What had kept her from being accepted by the 49 Club before?

Second was Frances McDonald. Called Francie by her friends. She was applying to the 49 Club for the first time. She'd only lived in San Celina County for five years since her husband, a retired federal judge, decided he wanted to spend their golden years in the Golden State. They'd lived and raised their family in Philadelphia, where she listed two very impressive pages of charitable works to recommend herself. I'd also seen her photos in the *Tribune*, though, unlike Dot, who had attended a few events for the folk art museum, I'd never seen Francie in person. Under her references there were two state senators and a congresswoman. Under the question what would she have to bring to the 49 Club, she wrote: "I have a long list of connections throughout the United States and at three Ivy League colleges that I would happily put at the disposal of the club's discretion for either personal or charitable use."

"In other words," I mumbled out loud, "you'll help anyone's kid or grandkid get into Yale or Harvard when they don't have the connections or grades to do it themselves. Dot, you might get shut out again."

"Did you say something?" asked Janet, one of our docents, standing in the open doorway of my office.

"Just talking to myself," I said, realizing it might be prudent to keep my sarcastic remarks to myself.

"I hear you," she said, smiling. "Sometimes, in my house, I'm the only one who'll listen when I talk." She had four sons, fourteen to nineteen, all still at home. "D-Daddy sent me to tell you the exhibit's ready for your final inspection. The only thing missing is Mr. Finch's painting. I can't wait to see it."

"I've only seen photos of it myself. It came wrapped up, and I didn't want to unwrap it until I got it here. Tell D-Daddy I'll come check out the exhibit in a minute. I want to finish reading these papers."

"More grant proposals?" she asked, knowing from my past whining that writing proposals begging for money was a never-ending job for me.

"Umm," I said, noncommittally. After she left, I speed-read through the third candidate's application, the only person I actually knew.

Roberta "Bobbie" Everette was one of the biggest landowners in San Celina County. Her family went back as far as Constance Sinclair's, to the time when California was still a part of Mexico. The Everette family owned a ranch that abutted the northeast section of my dad's ranch. They'd always been good neighbors, and we'd never had a negative fencing issue with them. Their family ran primarily Black Angus and even owned a restaurant on Interstate 5 in the Central Valley that was a popular stopping place for thousands of tourists traveling up that long road through the center of California. I knew Bobbie from the Cattlewomen's Association, where she'd been voted president an unprecedented four times.

Everyone loved Bobbie. She was one of those women, I'd venture to say, who could be president of the United States if she set her mind to it. Both men and women liked her, and she managed to fit in wherever she was. Not only was she intelligent and practical, she also knew how to have a good time, had never met a stranger and was interested and knowledgeable on a wide variety of subjects. She was a longtime, though not particularly active, member of the historical society, a frequent and generous contributor to the folk art museum simply out of her love for the art form. No strings were ever attached to her donations, and she was the major contributor as well as instigator of the new San Celina Humane Society building. She owned six dogs herself, all rescues. She donated time and money to more charities than any of the other candidates and belonged to every club of note in San Celina. Which made me wonder why in the world she'd apply for membership to the 49 Club. She was sixty-seven years old, had money, influence, popularity and not enough time for one more club. Why did she care about adding the 49 Club? I had to admit, that made me a little curious. Though I could imagine Bobbie shooting a poacher or cattle rustler, or even strangling with her bare hands someone she caught mistreating an animal, I couldn't imagine her killing one of her peers just to add one more stuffy club to her résumé.

I sat back in my chair, contemplating the three women, a bit chagrined at myself. I was going over their backgrounds as if they actually were suspects. I needed to get my mind off that and on to how I'd chat with them long enough to fool Constance but not make the women suspicious.

Talking to Bobbie would be easy enough because we ran in some of the same circles. The others would call for a cover just like Amanda suggested. An article for a fictional history magazine would be good, though I wouldn't put it past any of these women to check out whether my magazine existed. It would have to be a real magazine. Emory could help me with that. He'd worked for the *Tribune* when he first moved to California, so I was certain he'd acquired connections with the various county magazines. There was *San Celina Today* and a new tourist-oriented magazine, *Central Coast News*. Maybe I could use one of them as a cover. Or, even better, maybe I could actually get an assignment to write about the 49 Club. It was county history, and both of those magazines had articles every month about some small segment of San Celina history.

I wrote "ask Emory about magazine contact" on my list. I'd probably see him either tomorrow at the Christmas parade or Sunday at the traditional Santa Maria–style barbecue that Dove had planned to welcome Kathryn to San Celina. That reminded me to call Dove and ask her if there was anything I could bring to the barbecue.

She wasn't at home, so I tried her cell phone. She hadn't had it long but had already declared that she didn't know how she'd gotten along without the darn thing.

"Hello!" she yelled, causing me to hold the phone away from my ear. "Let me step outside!" I heard rustling and voices, telling me she was moving toward a quieter place. She still believed that cell phones were not much above the tin-can-and-kite-string method of communication, but she was always polite enough to not make anyone except the person calling her suffer with her loud conversations.

"Okay," she yelled. "I'm out in the historical society's garden now. Can you hear me now?"

"I can hear you fine. Don't strain your voice."

"I'm talking perfectly normal," she yelled.

"Okay," I answered, giving up. "Do you need me to bring anything for the barbecue Sunday?"

"Got it covered. You pick up Kathryn yet?"

"Not until six o'clock. We're having soup at home," I told her before she could ask. "Also baking powder biscuits and a green salad. And your peach cobbler."

"Perfect. I can't wait to see Kathryn again. What did you get her for Christmas?"

"Still looking. Elvia promised to help me." I was stymied about what to give my mother-in-law. The last few years we'd sent her various packages from Harry and David's, Wolferman's Bagels, See's Candy and magazine subscriptions to *Real Simple* and *National Geographic*. All suggestions from Gabe's sisters, Becky and Angel, because, unlike their brother, I called them once a month. This year, since she'd be here, I wanted to buy her something really thoughtful. I'd been shopping three times and come home with nothing. Gabe was no help, no surprise there.

"How about a gift certificate?" he'd suggested.

"We can't give her a gift certificate."

"Why not?"

"Because it's not personal enough."

"So, ask my sisters."

"I want to do it myself this time."

He shrugged. "Well, spare no expense. Buy her something nice."

But no amount of money was helping me come up with something that I thought would impress her. One more thing to try to fit into the dwindling days before Christmas.

"I made her a lap quilt," Dove said. "Rocky Road to Kansas pattern."

"Sounds great," I said, wishing I'd thought of it. Then again, I already had four unfinished quilts in the closet. Dove was much better than me at finishing the quilts she started. How did she get so much accomplished in a day? It remained a mystery to me.

"You'll think of something," she said. "Guess you'll be out early tomorrow to help your daddy tack up the horses for the parade." The parade this year was at ten a.m., something Gabe pushed through the city council because it cut down on the students' drinking and made it more of a family affair.

"Tell him I'll be there by six a.m." Normally, I'd go out to the ranch tonight and spend the night, but it seemed rude to do that on Kathryn's first night here. Then again, she probably would have loved having her son to herself. At least my early morning date with my dad would give me a valid excuse for going to bed early. I'd only have to be convivial for a few hours.

"Oh, no," I said, glancing at the clock, which now showed almost five p.m. I suddenly remembered that my life was not entirely my own right now. What would I do with Boo tomorrow morning? I couldn't leave him for Gabe to care for, since he'd probably want to show his mother around town. All Paws wasn't open on the weekends. I'd have to think of something.

"What?" Dove yelled.

"Nothing," I said. "I'll tell you tomorrow." I knew she'd be up early too, being a true ranchwoman and not a layabout, as she liked to call me these days. I'd beg her to watch Boo while I helped Daddy, then I'd figure out something for during the parade.

I headed for the museum's main gallery. We had two galleries, with a third one being considered in part of the stables that the co-op currently used to store supplies. We were looking into either buying a shed for supplies or having D-Daddy build one. The main gallery, the largest room, always held our current exhibit as well as a section for our few permanent pieces. The upstairs gallery, half the size of the main, was used for smaller exhibits. Right now we were showing an exhibit of antique toys on loan from a sister museum in Ohio. That exhibit would be here for one more month. Then I was considering having D-Daddy do some renovation upstairs before we used the space again.

This California Outsider Art exhibit was a first for us. When we put out a call for outsider artists who lived or worked in California or used the state as a subject in their art to send in photos of their work for possible inclusion in our show, the response had been overwhelming. Outsider art had always been popular and prolific in the Southern and Southwestern states, but it was, I thought, not as common on the left coast. In reality, there was a large semisecret cache of California artists whose work could be considered outsider. I had so many submissions, we were forced to form a committee to help decide who qualified and then decide who to include in the exhibit.

We finally settled on twenty-five artists, the most our main gallery could accommodate. We sent a letter to the others telling them if this show was successful, we might do another outsider exhibit in the spring. We tried to include an array of art forms that represented the many manifestations that outsider art could encompass: painting, sculpture, fabric arts, kinetic art, woodworking and my favorite, art made from only found objects, the ultimate in recycling. Those pieces told a particularly unique story about twentieth-century life in California.

The centerpiece of the exhibit would be Abe Adam Finch's painting, even though, technically, he wasn't a California artist. It was said he lived in Nevada, though no one knew for sure. When his niece, Nola Maxwell Finch, said he wanted to donate a painting to our museum now that she lived here in San Celina County, it only took our committee ten seconds to decide he was sort of an honorary Californian. At least that's what I explained to the co-op artists who complained to me about Mr. Finch's inclusion in the exhibit. It was a weak argument, I was the first to admit, but I said that I felt we didn't have a choice if we wanted this exhibit to garner media interest outside of our own county, something that Abe Adam Finch's celebrity could accomplish. Newspaper articles in Los Angeles and San Francisco newspapers brought tourists, which brought potential buyers of their art. After I pointed that out, there wasn't too much of a protest. We all understood the economic need for celebrity endorsement.

Though there were rumors that the reclusive artist might show up to the opening, they were just that, rumors. To be honest, no one except his niece would know if he showed up, since there wasn't a clear picture of him to be found. One of the few interviews I'd found of him, apparently one done through the mail, stated that he preferred to let his work speak for itself.

"Pretentious snob," I'd overheard one of the co-op artists say to a colleague at the downtown gift shop recently. Both women were putting in their requisite volunteer hours manning the cash register. I'd been taking inventory of the quilted items so I could let the quilters know if we needed more table runners or coasters.

"Now, Lilah," the other artist said, mildly protesting. "Maybe he's agoraphobic."

Lilah, a painter who favored bold, abstract birds in her paintings, snorted. Her work hadn't been accepted for the exhibit. "I daresay he keeps himself scarce just to triple the price of his paintings."

The other artist laughed and shook her head.

A part of me sympathized with Lilah. It was true that often the odd personality or unique background of an artist gave that person's art an aura of significance that it sometimes didn't deserve. As with all the arts, sometimes it wasn't the most talented artist who succeeded, but it was just a matter of being in the right place at the right time and having someone with influence single out your work. Even worse, sometimes it was just a matter of being born in the right family.

According to his official biography, Abe Adam Finch's work had been discovered ten years ago by a famous San Francisco collector, Lionel Bachman, on a trip with friends to Las Vegas. The story went that he'd seen one of Abe's paintings for sale in the back of a funky souvenir shop downtown. It was of a walnut tree with tiny faces painted into the hundreds of walnuts hanging on the branches. The name of the painting was *Family Nut Tree*. He bought it for twenty-five dollars, took it back to San Francisco and hung it in his living room. Six months later, a spread in *Architectural Digest* showing the collector's living room made Abe Adam Finch *the* outsider artist to collect. Mr. Bachman died last year, and that same painting was auctioned off for twenty-eight thousand dollars.

I walked through the exhibit amazed at the complexity of many of the pieces, the attention to detail that is often very apparent in outsider art as well as the messages that many were unafraid to present. Unlike a lot of highly educated, marketing-savvy fine artists, the majority of outsider artists never expected to make a living with their art, often didn't even think about selling it unless they needed the money for food or rent. Many, I'd read and been told by the collectors I'd met, were so happy someone liked what they did that they often tried to give it away. Having an exhibit like this was the epitome of what I'd hoped this museum would be: a combination of art and history, a place where artists and those who appreciated their art could meet on equal ground, where it didn't matter where they went to school or who their parents were. There was only the fact that something compelled them to make art, to communicate with paint and clay and fabric and words to represent what was wonderful and terrible about this one particular speck of time we lived in.

These thoughts were part of a talk I was scheduled to give on this very topic of outsider art and how it was similar to oral history. My talk would take place at the opening of the exhibit this Wednesday night. Nola Maxwell Finch, Mr. Finch's great-niece, would be there to officially present his painting to the museum. I'd not met her yet and, to say the least, I was nervous. There wasn't a lot of information available on her uncle, and I didn't want to say anything about him that wasn't absolutely true.

But I had miles to go before making that speech, and right now I needed to go pick up my pudgy little charge and figure out what I should do with him so that I could make it to the train station in time.

I drove to All Paws and found the place a bit more quiet than when I dropped Boo off a few hours ago. Only Henry, a beagle not much bigger than Boo, and a perky little Chihuahua named Peanut, were left.

"How'd he do?" I asked Suann, who was sitting in the front office. You could see the rooms where the dogs played through a clever porthole window behind the front desk.

"Oh, he's a little knucklehead, but he fit in fine," she said, laughing.

"What did he do?" I asked, feeling a twinge of anxiety, as if he were a child who didn't fit in at preschool.

"He already loves the sound of his own voice," she said ruefully. "He and Henry really enjoy their little barking contests."

"I'm sorry," I said, something I don't think I've ever had to say about anything involving Scout. Then again, he was grown and trained by the time he came into my life.

She waved her hand. "It's part of the job."

I glanced up at the boat-shaped clock behind her head. I had an hour before the train arrived, time enough to go home, introduce Boo to Scout and see if either of my neighbors, Beebs and Millee, were home. I knew they'd watch Boo for the time it took for me to go to the train station.

Luck was on my side in both cases. Scout, as I expected, accepted Boo with a noblesse oblige that any royal prince should envy and emulate. After a few sniffs, Scout allowed Boo to dance around his sturdy legs, nipping at them. He seemed to even give a doggie smile at Boo's high little puppy barks.

Only Beebs was home when I called, but she happily agreed to puppy sit. I was feeding Boo on the front porch when she arrived bearing a macaroni and artichoke salad for us to enjoy with our soup.

"Thanks, Beebs," I said, hugging her. "If nothing else will impress my mother-in-law, your macaroni salad will."

"She'd be nuts not to adore you like we do," Beebs said, her silvery hair catching the glow of the fading sun. The sky, ragged with clouds, was painted turquoise and gold, carmine and tangerine, one of those breathtaking California winter sunsets that caused people to sell their homes in Kansas and Michigan and move to our already overcrowded Golden State. I hoped Kathryn was taking a nap right at this moment.

"I did pretty much ruin any chance of her baby boy ever going home to Kansas to live," I said, walking back into the house. "Not that he would have anyway. I think I just didn't make a great impression when we first met."

"You're on your home turf now," Beebs said, picking up Boo and gently scratching him underneath his chin. He yawned, showing sharp little puppy teeth. "She'll see you in a whole different light."

"I hope so," I said, putting a bouquet of mixed flowers in a Mason jar and setting it in the middle of the table. "Darn, I really need to get some good vases."

"I have plenty I could loan you," she said.

"No time. As always, I think of stuff like that at the last minute. Maybe she'll see it as retro chic or something."

Beebs gave her high, distinctive laugh. "Don't worry, dear. It's only two weeks. She'll be gone before you know it. A body can suffer through anything for two weeks."

"You're the second person who's told me that."

"Must be true then. I have a pie in the oven, so if you don't mind, I'll take little Boo home with me. I'll bring him back in a few hours. Once Millee sees this handsome little guy, she's going to want to play with him."

"Be my guest. Bring him back whenever you want."

As she started out the door, Scout got up from his customary place in the hallway and followed her.

"Oh, my," Beebs said. "Looks like I'll be watching two dogs."

I laughed. "Scout's no dummy. He knows who's got the good dog treats."

"C'mon, big brother," Beebs said. "Let's go find your aunt Millee."

I made it to the train station five minutes before Kathryn was due to arrive.

"Where have you been?" Gabe asked. He paced across the shiny floor of the mission-style Amtrak train station located a mile from our house.

"Had to find a sitter for Boo. Doggie day care closes at seven p.m. Beebs is watching him until we get home."

He slipped an arm around my shoulders. I could tell he was nervous by the slight vibration in the air surrounding him.

"Don't worry, Friday," I said, circling his waist with my arm. "Your mom will have a great time." My words were full of a false bravado that would have been obvious to a six-year-old.

"I know," he said, his voice low with tension.

When the announcement of the train came over the crackly loudspeaker, we walked outside to meet it. I said a quick prayer for two weeks' worth of patience and waited for the train to roll to a stop.

I rested my hand on the small of Gabe's back as he searched the crowd for his mother's face. Minutes passed, then he saw her.

"Mom!" he called over the heads of hugging and chattering passengers.

He weaved his way through the crowd toward her

snowy-haired figure, towering over the other passengers. I'd forgotten how tall she was, that her genes were where Gabe inherited his long, lean figure. I followed him and watched him pull his mother into a hug.

Please, Lord, I prayed, glancing around her, *don't let Daphne be with her. And, please, help her focus on something else besides my inadequacy as a wife.*

Like all my prayers, it was answered, just not in the way I expected.

Gabe was so intent on hugging his mother that he failed to notice the man standing directly behind Kathryn. The man who wasn't moving toward some waiting wife or child. Not moving in that way that says, *I'm with this person.* He was tall, taller than Gabe or Kathryn, both of whom were six feet. His face was tanned the reddish brown of someone who works outdoors, and his cheekbones were gaunt to the point of reminding me of a childhood image of Ichabod Crane. He wore a hat like the kind they did in the forties. What was it called—a fedora? His suit was obviously custom-fitted for his unusually tall frame.

Though I've never claimed to be psychic, it didn't take a great premonitory talent to sense that something big was about to happen. I forced myself to smile and walked up to Gabe and Kathryn.

"I'm so glad to see you, Mom," Gabe was saying, reaching down to pick up the plaid overnight bag at her feet. "I bet you're starved."

The man behind Kathryn took a step closer. In that moment, he caught my eye. They were the bright blue of a California winter sky. He smiled and gave me an amused wink.

"We *are* starved," Kathryn said, smiling at me. "We waited to eat because I was sure Benni had something wonderful planned."

"Soup's on," I said, glancing at her, then back at the man standing behind her. "And I mean that literally."

My husband's police-trained nature finally kicked in when he heard the word *we*, and his gaze settled on the man standing behind Kathryn. Had I been the recipient of that look, I would have hopped back onto that idling train and ridden it clear to Canada. This man, obviously comfortable in his own skin, just smiled.

Gabe looked back at his mother. "We?"

She smiled at him, not a bit afraid, even though he wore his most suspicious, stern police chief face. Then again, this was the woman who changed his diapers and taught him how to brush his teeth.

"Gabe, honey, this is Ray. My husband."

CHAPTER 4

OF COURSE, THAT WOULD BE THE MOMENT WHEN MY cell phone started singing "Happy Trails."

"That's me," I said, fumbling through my purse. I gave his mother and her new husband an apologetic look.

Gabe just stood there, staring at his mother like she'd suddenly said that, by the way, son, I just robbed Wells Fargo. Could you please hold this bag of money?

I glanced at my phone's screen. Constance. Of course it had to be her. Anyone else I'd just ignore and call back. But Constance was as persistent as a toothache. She'd redial and redial until I answered.

"Excuse me," I said, looking straight at Kathryn. "I

really should answer this. It might be a crisis at the museum."

"Oh, dear," Kathryn said, the face I distinctly remembered as stern and unyielding now soft and sympathetic. "Of course you must. And you probably need your privacy. Gabe and Ray can fetch our luggage, and we'll meet you at the car."

"Uh, okay, thanks," I said, stepping over to her, not certain whether I should offer her my hand or a hug. The phone sang out again.

She deftly solved my dilemma by reaching over and patting me on the shoulder. "We'll have plenty of time to catch up after your crisis, Benni."

Relieved, I glanced over at Gabe. His face was in its unreadable mode now. Trouble was definitely brewing. I walked over to a quiet corner of the train station and answered my phone. "Hello?"

"What took you so long?" Constance barked. "I have your interviews all set up for tomorrow afternoon. Your cover is that you're doing a chapter for the Historical Society's San Celina history book. The subject is charitable clubs of San Celina. Your first interview is with Bobbie Everette at one p.m."

"Tomorrow? But I'm riding in the parade—"

"That's over by noon. Plenty of time to meet Bobbie. Then you have Francie. Dot is last. She was the hardest to pin down. That woman's middle name is busy."

Their names sounded even funnier when she listed them, like characters in a Frankie Avalon–Annette Funicello beach blanket movie.

"Okay," I said, knowing there was no way I could wiggle out of it. I was tempted to ask her if she'd step up to the plate and help me untack my horses, wipe them down, pick their feet. "But first I have to—"

She jumped in before I could finish my sentence. "Bobbie said she will meet you downstairs at Blind Harry's at one p.m. Francie will meet you at Miss Christine's Tea and Sympathy at two. Dot at the historical museum at three."

I inhaled a slow breath, trying not to sound as irritable as I felt. "I absolutely have to be done by five o'clock. My mother-in-law just arrived from Kansas and will be here two weeks. I have to make dinner. I have to spend some time with her."

"I hope she won't interfere with your work too much," Constance said, her voice sharp and demanding.

I didn't answer. I'd found that ignoring her self-centered comments was the most prudent way to react. As much as I was sympathetic to her feelings of loss for Pinky, it annoyed me that she was completely oblivious to the fact that other people had lives.

"I want a full report as soon as possible," she said. "Call me at home if you have to."

"I'll be in touch." It was another thing I'd learned with Constance: to be as vague as possible. "Gotta go." I hit End, then immediately turned off my cell phone. If she tried to call back, she'd get voice mail. I'd pay for that, but right now I had my own family crisis.

Walking toward the car, it occurred to me how similar this situation was to how Gabe and I got married. I was fairly certain not even her daughters knew about it because I'd just talked to Becky two days ago, and I knew she'd never be able to keep something like this from me. She'd mentioned that Kathryn had been "seeing" someone, but she hadn't elaborated. It seemed so inconsequential that I hadn't even mentioned it to Gabe. When had she gotten married? Had she been keeping it a secret from everyone?

At the car, I found Gabe and his mother casually discussing Gabe's city-issued car as Ray silently worked at fitting luggage into the gray four-door sedan's large trunk.

"I still have Dad's truck," Gabe said to Kathryn. "And the Corvette. Benni drives her little Ford Ranger. But I needed a car for work, so the city is providing this." He deliberately ignored Ray. What had happened in the few minutes I'd been gone? Had it been resolved? Ha, in my dreams.

"It's very nice, son," she said. "It'll be good to see your dad's old truck again. We must go for a ride in it."

"Sure," Gabe said, glancing over at Ray. I could almost see my husband's thoughts: *We're not bringing* him, *are we?* Again, I was dying to know what took place between the three of them the five minutes I was gone.

When Ray finally maneuvered all the luggage into the trunk, we drove home with, at my suggestion, Kathryn riding in the front seat next to Gabe and me sharing the backseat with Ray.

"So," I said, as we settled down for the short ride. "How did you two meet?"

"We were domino competitors at the senior center," he said, smiling.

"Ray's an engineer," Kathryn said, her voice proud and a bit strained.

"Was," he said amicably.

"Really? What kind?" I said. "Software? Electrical? Aerospace?"

"Choo-choo," he answered, his voice solemn.

Kathryn gave a high little laugh. "He loves doing that to people."

"Wow," I said. "A real engineer? That is so cool. I mean, you don't really think about people doing that anymore. I've never met an engineer. Isn't that an interesting profession, Gabe?"

"Sure." His voice from the front seat was noncommittal. He didn't even turn to look when his mom laughed. Remembering how hard it was when my gramma Dove first met my stepgrandpa, Isaac, and how much I mistrusted him, I shut up. Gabe would have to get comfortable with this in his own time, and me trying to smooth the way would likely make it harder.

I sat back in the leather seat. I was on pins and needles wanting to ask when they tied the knot, but since everyone else was talking around the elephant in the room, I took the cue and also avoided the subject. "So, Ray, have you ever been to California?"

"Had a route here for a few years, Kansas City to Los Angeles. That's a beautiful building, L.A.'s Union Station. Haven't been here in twenty years, though."

"Our part of California isn't quite as crowded, though we are starting to get our share of congestion and big city woes. Gabe could tell you about that. He was an L.A. cop for a long time before he came up here."

"So Kathryn told me," Ray said. He directed a question to the back of Gabe's head. "Do you ever miss the excitement of the big city, Gabe?"

"Not really," Gabe said.

Kathryn glanced sharply at her son's cool tone. I could tell she was a little annoyed at him, which made me annoyed with her. What did she expect, surprising Gabe with something this big? And doing it in such a public place?

Sure, we sort of did the same thing to her, calling her after we got back from Las Vegas and telling her we just got married. And, like she did to Gabe, he also hadn't told her he was dating me. This smelled suspiciously like payback. I sighed and turned my head to stare out the window. Gabe and I could have really used a fun, easy holiday after what we'd gone through a month ago. Surely his mother would have understood that?

I turned back to Ray. "How long did you drive a train?"

"Worked for Union Pacific for thirty-nine years. Miss it every day of my life."

"It must be an interesting place to view life. Sitting in the front of a locomotive."

"It is at that. I wish I were a painter or a photographer. The sights I have seen were worth recording."

"My stepgrandpa is a photographer. I bet he'd envy you that view."

"I am a big fan of Isaac Lyons's work," he said, rubbing the side of his eagle beak nose. "I'm most eager to meet him."

"You will Sunday afternoon. My gramma Dove's

having a barbecue for you two. You'll meet the whole clan."

"I'm so looking forward to seeing Dove again," Kathryn said, giving me another big smile. I smiled back, sort of liking this new, more easygoing Kathryn, but I was still hesitant. There was this surprise marriage that would be the center of attention for the whole visit, I was sure. How was that going to affect her and Gabe's relationship?

At home, Gabe started the soup heating while I showed Kathryn and Ray the downstairs guest room. While we chatted about the plans we had for their visit, I added more towels in the downstairs bathroom.

"Everything is lovely, Benni," Kathryn said, gazing around at the room I'd decorated in deep green and navy blue, a Ship at Sea quilt on the queen-sized bed. The furniture, a cherry-colored mission style, was similar to the new furniture in my and Gabe's room. The custom-made lamps, a housewarming gift from Emory and Elvia, were Tiffany-style glass with a Friendship Star quilt pattern.

"Thank you," I said. "Take your time getting settled in. We'll have dinner in about a half hour, unless you need more time."

"That's perfect," Kathryn said, sitting down in the rocking chair next to a window overlooking our side yard. I'd planted an array of flowers there last weekend— mums, impatiens, daisies—and put in a hummingbird feeder made from a gourd, one of the big sellers at the folk art museum's gift shops.

"The sooner the better for me," Ray said, standing next

to Kathryn, his hands in his pockets, softly jingling his change.

"Okay, then," I said. "I'll see you in the kitchen. It's where we eat all our meals. We haven't bought a dining room set yet and mostly use that room as a library. There're only bookcases in it so far."

"Add a comfortable chair, and I'll not trouble you for two weeks," Ray said.

I smiled. "That can be arranged." Ray certainly would be an easy guest. I started out the door, then stopped, remembering my other guest. "Oh, dear, one more thing. I hope you're not allergic to dogs, Ray."

"Daphne loves him," Kathryn said. "Ray's great with animals. Kids too."

"Never had any of my own," Ray said, still jingling his coins softly. "Kids, I mean. Have been owned by a whole array of canines in my life, though I've actually sort of been dog-shared with my neighbor, Bob."

I cocked my head. "Dog-shared?"

"Like a racehorse," he said, smiling, his hands still now. They came out of his pockets to gesture as he talked. "I was gone for long periods of time. One of my next-door neighbors was a widower, like me. He was a cop who also worked odd hours, so we shared dogs. Three of them, all rescues. The dogs had beds, water dishes, food dishes, toy baskets at both houses. We cut an opening in the fence between our yards. The dogs learned to check both back doors, whichever one was open, that was where they spent the night. It gave two old farts something to talk about."

"What a wonderful idea," I said.

Scout, always the perfect canine, picked that moment to trot into the guest room. He must have seen us arrive home and crossed the street from Beebs and Millee's house. He came up to me for a quick neck rub.

"Kathryn said you had a dog. He's a nice looking Lab."

"Yes, Scout is a darling, but I can't take any credit for that. He was trained before I inherited him. And besides you two, I have another guest these next two weeks. He's a little doll, but not quite as well-trained as Scout. As a matter of fact, you might have to be careful where you walk, as he is still in the midst of potty training."

"You have a puppy?" Kathryn said. Her blue-gray eyes, so like my husband's, lit up.

"Only for two weeks. A friend of mine went with his family to Texas for the holidays and left him with me."

"What kind is he?" Kathryn asked.

"Corgi. A Pembroke. That's the kind with no tail."

"They're great dogs," Ray said. "So smart. What's his name?"

"Boo. Right now he's across the street at my neighbors'. I'll go get him before we have dinner."

I left them alone to settle in and joined Gabe in the kitchen. He already had the soup heating and the biscuits warming in the oven. There was something to be said for irritation getting a man to work.

"Are you okay?" I asked, opening the refrigerator and taking out the butter dish. "What happened when I answered Constance's phone call? Did your mom tell you when she got married? And where? Why?"

"I'm fine," he said, his voice stiff. "They made a

detour to Las Vegas two days ago. As for why, I couldn't begin to guess."

I was without words for a moment, not certain what I should say. "It's odd," I finally commented. "I mean, that they sort of did the same thing we did."

"What's that supposed to mean?" His tone became a little snappish.

I set the butter dish down on the table. "Whoa, pull back on the reins. I was just saying that we didn't exactly give anyone the heads-up about our wedding either."

He glared at me. "It's entirely different."

How? I wanted to ask, but decided that it would definitely be wiser for me to keep that question to myself, at least for right now. This was obviously something that he and his mother would have to duke out.

"Okay," I said, keeping my voice soft. "Let's just get through the next few hours, and we can talk about it upstairs."

He took a deep breath, ran a large brown hand over his face. When he looked at me again, his face was no longer angry, just sad.

"Oh, Gabe," I said, going over to him and putting my arms around his waist. "It'll be all right. I know it's a shock, but Ray seems like a nice guy."

He rested his lips on the top of my head, brushing them back and forth. "We'll see. But, you're right, we just need to get through the next few hours."

"Good," I said, hugging his waist. "Now, I have to go across the street and fetch Boo. I'll be back in two seconds."

When I returned carrying Boo, Kathryn and Ray were in the kitchen helping Gabe set the table.

After the requisite few minutes of puppy fawning, I gave Boo and Scout a biscuit, then put Boo in his downstairs crate and closed the metal door. When Boo started to whimper, I told Scout to stay. Like the perfect dog he was, Scout lay right next to the crate with his nose touching Boo's nose through the gate.

"Scout is a miracle dog," I said, sitting down. "He already has taken his big brother relationship to heart."

Dinner was more than slightly uneasy. We avoided the real thing we wanted to talk about and discussed Gabe's sisters, their kids and the activities we had planned for Christmas here in San Celina. Then we all retired to the living room.

"Would anyone like coffee or tea?" I asked.

"No, actually, I'd like to take a walk with my son," Kathryn said. "If you don't mind."

"Of course not," I said. "Take a jacket, though. I know it's not Kansas, but it can get kind of nippy here after dark."

"Brought one with me," she said, standing up. "Let's walk, son. I'd like to see your neighborhood Christmas lights."

"Take her downtown, Gabe. The Christmas window contest is being judged tonight."

"Sounds delightful," she said.

It was obvious that she wanted to talk to Gabe privately about Ray. More power to her. Straighten this out right off so we could all relax.

After they were gone, I fed the dogs, then Ray took me up on that coffee. We took our cups out on the front porch, where we watched the dogs have one last playtime before bed. When we settled down in the green wicker chairs, I decided to quit beating around the bush and ask Ray about their marriage.

"Were you and Kathryn engaged long?"

He cleared his throat and looked me straight in the eyes. "Benni, I know I was a huge shock to Gabe. I wanted to call from Las Vegas, but Kathryn insisted that it would be better to surprise him. He's her son, so I couldn't very well argue with that."

I sipped my coffee, contemplating his words. Her actions seemed pretty passive-aggressive to me, but what did I really know or understand about Gabe's relationship with his mother? She probably did know him better than anyone.

"She might be right," I reluctantly conceded. "As hard as it is on him to be surprised, if he'd known twenty-four hours ago, he might have really worked himself up into a snit." The minute I said it, I felt guilty, like I was being disloyal to my husband with this virtual stranger. "Not that Gabe isn't a really accepting and friendly person. He is, it's just that . . ."

Ray gave a slow smile, causing the deep wrinkles in his face to shift. It occurred to me then who he really reminded me of. The scarecrow in *The Wizard of Oz*. Or rather the man who played the scarecrow. Ray Bolger. Ray, I thought. That's funny, they had the same first name.

"I understand," Ray said. "He's a police officer. Suspicion comes with the job. No doubt, he'll have me checked out as soon as he can to make sure I'm not some con man trying to take his mother for her pension and savings. I would think less of him if he didn't use all his resources to investigate me."

I sighed in relief, because I knew that's exactly what Gabe would do. If he wasn't on a walk with his mother now, he probably would have excused himself with the pretense of going to the bathroom and instead called one of his friends who'd left the force and was working as a private detective. Gabe wouldn't do anything illegal to find out about Ray, but this was his *mother*. He'd find out about the man she married one way or another.

"Question," I said.

"Feel free."

"Do Becky and Angel know?"

"We called them last night. We were actually married on Wednesday. Kathryn wanted to wait a day before she called anyone."

"Why?" I asked.

He shrugged. "I love Kathryn, Benni, but I can't pretend that I understand her."

"Welcome to my world. How did the girls take it?"

"A little better than Gabe, because I've actually known them for a few months."

"How long have you and Kathryn been seeing each other?"

He thought for a moment. "About six months."

He must be the guy that Gabe's sister Becky said Kathryn was "seeing." But apparently even she hadn't realized how serious it had turned. Great, so I sort of knew about Ray and didn't mention it to Gabe. I wondered if there was a way I could never let him know that.

Oh, well, I'd worry about that later. "You know, I don't even know your last name. And what your kids think of your marriage."

"Austin. Like the Texas capital. Never was blessed with children. I'm just a cranky old widower."

I laughed. "You don't seem a bit cranky to me. So, did Kathryn take your name?" It was something I would not have the nerve to ask her.

"Actually, she did. Though she kept Ortiz as her middle name. I didn't ask her to take my name and didn't expect it. It's nice, though. A man likes marking what's his."

I was taken aback a moment by his borderline sexist remark. Had I read this guy wrong? Was he really a creep? Then one of his watery eyes gave a slow wink, telling me he was pulling my leg.

I shook my head and laughed. "You remind me of my daddy. I don't always know when he's teasing. I'm going to have to really keep on my toes around you."

"People have been known to grow muscular calves when being around me too long."

I shook my head again. "Well, Mr. Ray Austin, you must be tired. I have to get up early to help Daddy tack up our horses for the Christmas parade tomorrow, so if you'll forgive me, I need to get ready for bed."

"I am a bit weary myself," he said. "I think I'll turn in too."

"Rest well, Ray."

"You too, Miss Benni. I'll see you tomorrow."

I took Boo out for one last potty break, then went upstairs to my bedroom to made a quick call to Dove.

Though I'd see her first thing tomorrow morning, I knew she'd throttle me if I didn't tell her about Kathryn's new husband as soon as I could.

"I was just settling down in bed with my favorite man," Dove said.

"I thought Isaac was gone until tomorrow night." He was speaking at a photography convention in Monterey.

"I meant Father Brown." Her laugh, a cheerful cackle, reminded me of her chickens when they were complaining at her to be fed. Dove had reread G. K. Chesterton's Father Brown mysteries probably a dozen times.

"I'll save you some time; the butler did it," I said, putting Boo in his crate and closing the metal door.

"Not a butler to be seen in this one," she said. "How did it go with Kathryn? Did your house pass the white-glove inspection?" She knew how worried I'd been and had teased me about it, telling me that no amount of lemon Pledge or homemade biscuits could make up for the fact that I flat-out stole this woman's only son.

"It's been great," I said, smug in the fact that I had information that would shock her, something hard to do with my gramma, who claimed she had seen everything there was to see in human nature in her seventy-seven years. "She didn't look twice at the house. She's been gracious, kind, loving and actually seems glad to be here." I took a breath, ready to spring my big news.

"Lord, have mercy," Dove said. "She got married, didn't she?"

CHAPTER 5

"D O-OO-VE." I STRETCHED HER NAME INTO THREE syllables. "That was my big news." How did she *know* these things?

"What's his name?" Dove asked. "Is he nice? What does he do? Who's his family?"

"I didn't find out much, but he seems like a nice man. His name is Ray Austin. He's a retired engineer of the choo-choo variety."

"Good retirement benefits," Dove said, her voice approving. "He's probably dependable and has strong nerves."

"Gabe and Kathryn went for a walk after supper, and Ray and I were able to talk for about a half hour. After his wife died, he dog-shared three dogs with his next-door neighbor, who was a cop, so he's an animal lover. He's retired. Scout likes him. So does Boo, though Boo is still sort of indiscriminate in his tastes in people."

"I still can't believe you volunteered to babysit a puppy," Dove said. "Don't be expecting me to relieve you. I'm busier than a boll weevil in high cotton."

It didn't surprise me that she already knew about my four-legged guest. There wasn't much that happened in my life in San Celina that didn't find its way to her doorstep, usually within the hour.

"What could I tell Hud? He went to Texas with Laura Lee to her grandmother's ninety-fifth birthday. Think of it as my way of trying to help reunite a broken family."

"That boy will never settle down for long. I still think you need to watch him like a hungry coyote."

"I won't have to the next two weeks, and I won't ask you to take care of Boo, except—"

She didn't let me finish. "I know, I know, you need someone to watch him during the parade. Lucky for you, missy, I'm feeling gimpy and not riding in the parade this year."

I tickled Boo's nose through the door of his upstairs crate. "I promise that most of the time I'll be in charge of his care. I will gratefully appreciate some help for tomorrow, though."

"So, how is Gabe reacting to his new stepdaddy?"

"The jury's still out on that one. He seems quiet and a bit standoffish, but that's Gabe whenever he first meets someone. I'll find out more when he gets home from his walk with Kathryn. I'll update you tomorrow morning on the new marriage and my murder investigation." I hoped to surprise her with the last part of my statement.

"I heard about that," Dove said. "Who do you think sent Pinky Edmondson to sleep with the fishes?"

"How could you have possibly heard about that?"

"Constance mentioned her suspicions to Lorraine, Dr. Olson's nurse, who told her daughter, Sylvie, who told her husband and was overheard by her daughter, Heather, who works at the Tastee-Freez, where she told Sissy Brownmiller's granddaughter, Autumn, who told Sissy, who couldn't wait to call me with the gory details, which I had to pretend to already know because you never call me and tell me anything."

"Give me a break. Constance told me less than twelve hours ago."

"Which gave you eleven hours and thirty minutes in which to call and tell me so I wouldn't be humiliated in front of the town's biggest gossip."

"I thought you said you pretended you knew about it."

"That didn't fool her for a minute, and you know it," Dove grumbled.

"So, did you hear that my own husband asked me to investigate?"

I could hear her perk up over the phone. "No, Sissy didn't mention that."

"That's because she doesn't know it."

"Details," she demanded.

"Gabe is asking me to keep Constance off his back by pretending to investigate. He thinks she's crazy, that Pinky died of heart failure, just like her doctor and the medical examiner concluded. But you can't tell anyone about this. Gabe just wants Constance to think I'm looking into it."

"Oh," Dove said, disappointment obvious in her voice.

"It's really just one more chore I have to do this next week, pretend I'm interviewing the candidates for the 49 Club to find out which one is dying . . . or rather killing . . . to get in. That's who she suspects."

"Better you than me. I've got pies to bake and baskets to fill." Dove, as usual, was in charge of the San Celina Farm Bureau's holiday baskets drive. Our goal this year was four hundred gift baskets to deliver on Christmas Eve to families in crisis.

"I've got a bunch of stuff collected in the bin at the folk art museum. I'll bring it on Sunday, and we can work on them next week."

I'd taken my shower and was reading a book by a folklorist who had interviewed dozens of artists in the South, when I heard voices downstairs. Minutes later, Gabe was in the bedroom unbuttoning his shirt.

"How was your walk?" I asked, setting aside my book.

"Fine," he said, tossing his shirt on the top of Boo's crate.

Boo had fallen asleep a half hour ago, and even Gabe's entry into the room hadn't disturbed his deep, puppy sleep. I glanced over at my alarm clock. Ten thirty p.m. I'd set it for two a.m. There was no way a puppy this age could make it through the night without a potty break. I resigned myself to broken sleep patterns for the next two weeks.

"Fine isn't enough information, Friday," I said, crawling out from under the down comforter. "What did you two talk about?"

He shrugged, pulled off his jeans and underwear. "Family and things. Just caught up."

I admit, I was distracted for a moment by his muscular thighs, then looked back up at his face. "I want details. I want to know about why she decided to just up and get married. Did you two talk about that at all?"

"Let me take a shower first. Then you can grill me."

After he was finished with his steamy shower and settled next to me in bed, I started in. "C'mon, Chief, tell me everything your mother said, or I'll be forced to use thumbscrews."

He settled more deeply into his two down pillows. "There's not much to tell. She met him at the senior center in Wichita. He was born in North Dakota but has lived in Kansas since World War II. He was in the navy, then worked for the railroad. Widowed, no children."

"Did you ask her why they got married without telling anyone?" I sat up, eager to dish about his mom's new husband.

"No."

"She wouldn't tell you?"

"Didn't ask."

"What? You didn't ask? Why in the world not?"

"Doesn't matter. What's done is done."

I stared at his face. His expression was enigmatic, but I didn't believe for a moment that this didn't bother him. "You're not mad?"

He shrugged; a flash of some kind of emotion crossed his face and was gone. "I don't feel like talking about it."

I lay back down and turned on my side, facing him. "I have a confession to make."

He looked over at me, his face neutral. "Don't tell me you knew about this, because if that is true, I'll . . ." He left it open, knowing my imagination would fill in the blanks with something worse than he'd actually do.

"No, not exactly."

"Elaborate."

"Your sister Becky sort of told me your mom was seeing somebody, but she didn't say it was serious." I reached across the bed and stroked his forearm. "To be honest, I don't think she knew it was serious, either. Ray told me they called your sisters and told them."

He stared at me a long moment, considering this new information. "Mom called the girls? When?"

I hesitated, wishing now I hadn't been the one to mention that. "Uh, I think, yesterday?"

"Fine." He rolled over, turning his back to me.

"Oh, Gabe, don't be mad. Maybe your mom was just afraid to tell you. You know, like you . . ." Then I shut up, realizing that pointing out how afraid he'd been to tell his mother about our quickie marriage might not be the best thing to say right now.

He rolled back over on his back and stared up at the ceiling. "I'm not. I'm just . . ." He paused for a moment, and I thought he might reveal what he was actually feeling. "Forget it. Let's just deal with this tomorrow." He took my hand, kissed the palm, and turned out his bedside light.

"Sounds good," I agreed and turned out my light. I lay back on my pillows, uneasy about how quickly he calmed down. To be honest, I almost wished there had been a huge blowup between him and his mother tonight. It would have cleared the air, gotten everything out in the open, settled things. That's what Dove and I would have done. Then again, she wasn't my mother. I knew from watching my friends and even the relationship that Dove had with my father that conflicts like this weren't always dealt with as directly and quickly as Dove and I resolved things. It seemed that having that extra generation between two people helped lighten the animosity.

"Dream sweet, *querida*," my husband whispered to me.

I tried to discern his mood, anticipate what might happen between him and his mother in the next few weeks, but I only heard his normal voice, a little sad, but normal.

"You too, Friday."

❖

FIVE A.M. CAME TOO QUICKLY. BOO'S MIDDLE-OF-THE-night bathroom breaks were going to be the death of me. Any desire I'd ever had about riding in the Christmas parade was long gone. Would Daddy totally kill me if I called and begged off? Probably, since I'd talked him into riding in the parade in the first place.

"Hud owes me big time," I muttered, setting the table for the breakfast I wouldn't be sharing with Gabe, Kathryn and Ray.

"What was that?" Ray asked, coming into the kitchen already dressed for the day. He wore a red plaid flannel shirt and blue Dickie work pants.

"Good morning," I said, glancing down at my faded sweats. I thought I'd be out of the house before anyone woke up.

"Sorry I'm up so early," he said. "Once I retired, I couldn't break the habit of getting up at four a.m. I've never needed more than six hours' sleep. Less now that I'm older."

I poured him a cup of coffee. "No apologies necessary. Feel free to do whatever you like here. This coffee is the real stuff, if that's okay."

"Absolutely. I only drink the kid stuff at night." He took the mug and nodded his thanks. "Why don't you go on to the ranch? I imagine you have a lot to do today with the parade and all. I know a fork from a spoon. I can set the table."

"I can't let you do that," I said, though I was sorely tempted. "My gramma Dove would kill me."

He touched a finger to his lips. "It'll be our secret."

With that, I took him up on his offer and was out the door in less than a half hour, lugging Boo under one arm. The fancy Western clothes I'd wear in the parade were already cleaned and ready at the ranch. I settled him into his car seat and headed for the ranch.

"He is a cute little guy," Dove said, taking Boo from my arms, her peach-colored face softening. "Just leave him in here with me." I knew once she saw him she'd be a goner. She had never been able to resist babies of any kind.

"Boo's travel bed is already hooked up in my truck, so why don't you just drive that into town? You can go home with Daddy. I have his leash, a travel carrier and poopy bags in the bag." I handed her the green and white L.L.Bean bag with his name on it. "His puppy treats and food are in there. He eats three times a day, and I have it portioned off in baggies. He likes—"

She waved a hand at me and set him down on the kitchen floor. "Get out to the barn and help your daddy. I was taking care of babies a million years before you was born."

"Yes, ma'am," I said, smiling with relief. "After the parade Constance set up interviews for me with her three suspects. Could you—?"

"I'll take him back to your house and visit with Kathryn. Give me a chance to meet her new husband. I need to be at the airport by five p.m. though. That's when Isaac arrives. He left his car at the airport. He can take me home."

"No problem. Gabe or I will drive you to the airport. Kathryn will love seeing you. There's tons of stuff in the freezer for lunch."

She waved me away again without stating the obvious, that she'd also been feeding people years before I was born. I went into her bedroom, put on a tomato-red cowboy shirt and black Wranglers, brushed off my black felt cowboy hat and stuck it on. On the way out to the barn, I grabbed a freshly baked cinnamon roll and a mug of coffee. The frost-covered grass crunched like corn flakes under my feet. I opened the barn door and heard my father talking to the horses while he tacked them up.

"Hey, Daddy," I said, walking up beside him.

"Hey, pipsqueak," he answered, straightening his favorite silver-trimmed saddle on his big old bay mare,

Apple. He always rode Apple in parades because a bomb could explode in front of her and Apple would just blink her eyes. "Heard Kathryn got herself hitched. Your horse is all ready to go." He nodded over at Mustard, another longtime ranch horse with nerves of steel.

"Almost shocked Gabe out of his britches," I said, stroking Mustard's neck. Mustard loved parades. I swear his chest puffed up a little when we passed by cheering crowds, even though there was nothing spectacular about his plain brown looks. Maybe during parades in his mind he became the Black Stallion. "Ray seems like a nice man. He's an engineer."

"So I heard. Got to be pretty steady to control a train."

"Gabe didn't intimidate him. That says a lot."

Daddy raised his white eyebrows. "He married Gabe's mama. Kathryn's not too short on the intimidation ruler herself."

I nodded and led Mustard over to the four-horse trailer hooked up to Daddy's one-ton Ford pickup. "Gee, you're all ready. Did you get up at three?"

"Figured you'd take your time getting here," he said, his voice still holding a trace of his native Arkansan drawl. "Someone had to get it done."

"Hey, I got up at five. That's early."

He grinned at me. "Done a day's work by then."

"Huh, you'd best watch out, Daddy. You're the last one not married now. Your turn is coming."

He shook his head and whistled for Spud, the corgi he'd bought a while back. The dog, female despite her name, dashed around the corner, her muzzle dripping water, and slid to a stop in front of Daddy, her face expectant. "Spud's the only woman I need in my life."

"For now. I'm thinking about signing you up on one of those Internet dating services. Ladies will be lining up at the end of the driveway."

"I'll hide in the hills till they're gone. Get up in that cab and buckle yourself in. We've got a parade to get to."

By the time we got to the staging area for the parade, the sun was bright, but the air still had a winter chill to it, perfect weather for a parade. Daddy and I were riding twelfth in a parade that had, from what I heard, sixty entrants.

"It's a record number of entries," said Bev Adams, San Celina High School's FFA advisor. She and I had been in FFA together back when we were in high school.

"I think last year proved that having it during the day makes a big difference," I said, combing my fingers through Mustard's brown mane. I wished now I'd taken the time to braid and decorate it with silk flowers.

"I think you're right," she said, climbing up on the crepe paper and pine bough decorated truck that proclaimed, Happy Holly Days from Future Farmers of America! "I'm sure glad Gabe got it changed last year."

Traditionally, the Christmas parade had been after dark. But in the last seven to eight years, with the influx of so many out-of-town students as compared to students whose families lived here, drunk and disorderly arrests had skyrocketed. Last year Gabe, with the wholehearted approval of the city council, suggested a daytime parade in an attempt to bring it back to being a family affair. Granted, the floats probably weren't as pretty since using lights didn't do much good during the day, but, as Gabe predicted, the number of drunk and disorderly arrests had fallen 60 percent, a statistic that couldn't be disputed. I certainly liked riding in it better without the worry of some ignorant, city-raised student tossing a bottle of beer at my horse just because he wanted to see it rear up like the Lone Ranger's Silver.

Daddy and I were riding with the San Celina Cattlemen's and Cattlewomen's Association group, twenty of us in all. By earlier agreement, the women all wore red shirts and black Wranglers. The men wore dark green shirts and black Wranglers. Everyone wore their best hats and fanciest silver belt buckles, and rode on their most elaborately decorated saddles.

"There's so much silver here, I do believe we'll blind some folks," said Bobbie Everette, riding up on a glossy black gelding with a slightly off-center white star on his forehead. She wore a red and green elaborately embroidered cowboy shirt that I was sure cost ten times what my cotton one did.

"Hi, Bobbie," I said, catching her eye, then looking away. I was already feeling guilty about my upcoming fake interview with her. "Beautiful shirt."

"Thanks," she said. "Like most of my clothes, I've had it for thirty years. Bought it in Houston at the stock show. Guess that would make it vintage now, wouldn't it?"

"Guess so," I said, forcing myself to look her in the eye. Her face was red-cheeked, wind-roughened and honest as a newborn calf. Her gray hair was pulled back in a neat bun, and her smile was made whiter by her bright red lipstick, the only makeup she wore.

"Benni, don't be acting all weird on me now," she said,

throwing back her head and giving a hearty, masculine laugh. "I know Constance has you interviewing me to find out if I killed ole Pinky Edmondson. I'll answer any questions you have to the best of my ability. But, please, don't get all stressed out. I promise you, I didn't murder Pinky, though, heaven knows, there were times when I wanted to. And I wasn't the only one." Her horse did a little crow hop and started dancing nervously in place. "Whoa, there, Blackstrap. Whoa, now." She tightened the reins and brought the horse back in control.

"You . . . you know?" I stammered, almost dropping my reins in surprise.

She gave another full-throated laugh, sidled her horse next to mine and said in a low voice, "Sweetie, there's not a club on earth I'd kill to get into, though there's a few I might consider killing to get out of." She looked around to see if anyone heard, then grimaced and shook her head. "Forgive me, that was tacky, considering poor Pinky's remains are hardly cold in the ground. Hard as it might be for Constance to understand, I don't even care about being in the 49 Club. I'm only applying to be a member because it was something I promised my mother on her deathbed ten years ago. I have hoped like heck that all those old biddies would live to be a hundred and ten. I'd take myself off the list, but I promised Mother I'd really try. She was one of the club's founding members, bless her heart."

"Oh," I managed to get out. It sounded like a mouse squeaking.

"Look," she said. "I'll meet you at Blind Harry's at one, just like Constance said. We'll have a cup of coffee, a scone or two and you can mark me off your list. How about that?"

I nodded, not knowing what else to do. "I do have some questions. I mean, ones that I would ask someone if I really were going to write an article." I smiled at her. "Who knows, maybe I actually will. At least it will give me something to show Constance." I shrugged, moved Mustard into line. "I mean, if you don't mind. Just to keep her happy."

"Don't mind at all. Constance Sinclair is crazy as a doodle bug, so I don't envy your position one bit." She gave me a sideways glance. "I just wanted to make sure you understood that I know exactly what is going on."

"Yes, ma'am. There's absolutely no doubt in my mind."

She chuckled. "Don't you ma'am me. I'm only thirty years older than you. Old enough to be your . . . older sister."

"Yes—" I started, then said, "You bet."

"I'm going on ahead and ride with Pete Fitzgerald. We're seeing each other, you know. See you after the parade." She touched her horse's flank with the back of her heel and moved up to the front row where Pete was riding his palomino.

Pete Fitzgerald and Bobbie Everette dating? I was surprised that Dove hadn't told me about it, since both Pete and Bobbie were very involved politically in San Celina's ag community, which seemed to be getting smaller and smaller every year as more ranches turned into housing developments. Maybe their relationship was new. They'd known each other for decades and had both been widowed in the last few years, so it wasn't a totally surprising connection.

Up ahead, we heard the sound of the bullhorn telling us the parade had started. Our group was lined up four abreast, with a total of twenty horses and riders. The idea was to be red/green/red/green. I ended up being between Daddy and Bert, one of his cracker-barrel cronies from the Farm Supply.

"Hey, Daddy," I said. "Ready to ride?"

"I'm ready for this to be done so I can get me a nice plate of scrambled eggs and sausage over at Liddie's," he grumbled.

Bert's grin was as wide as a jack-o'-lantern's. "Ah, don't listen to him, Benni. He's been primping for this parade all week."

I laughed while they tossed insults and jokes across me like Ping-Pong balls. Bert knew Daddy well. He liked to moan and groan about things like the Christmas parade, but Daddy actually enjoyed being in the thick of the action. And he especially enjoyed reliving it for weeks with his buddies at Liddie's or in the back room at the Farm Supply.

"Hey, did you guys know that Bobbie Everette and Pete Fitzgerald are a hot item?" I asked.

Daddy glanced over at Bert, a secretive look on his face. I glanced at Bert, who grinned again and shrugged.

"What's going on?" I asked as we started our horses walking. We were behind the Miss San Celina—Past and Present float. It was an array of red, green and, oddly, purple crepe paper flowers and streamers decorating a long platform pulled by a red Peterbilt truck cab. The current Miss San Celina was dressed like Mrs. Santa Claus. That is, if Mrs. Claus was eighteen and wearing a fake fur-trimmed miniskirt. They threw candy to the crowd, which caused my dad to grumble under his breath when he had to pull Apple up short when a child ran in front of him to grab an errant candy cane.

When we'd settled back to a quiet walk, I tried again. "What's the deal with Pete and Bobbie?" I asked, looking at Daddy, then Bert.

Bert nodded at Daddy. "Your girl's asking you a question, Ben."

"You know I hate to gossip," Daddy said.

"Oh, please," I replied. "All you guys do at the Farm Supply is gossip. You know more about what goes on in the community than Dove's quilting circle at church."

"We don't gossip," Daddy said, his sunburned face indignant.

"That's right," Bert said, chuckling. "We discuss important issues."

"Okay, so what's the discussion about Bobbie and Pete?" I asked, kneeing Mustard to the left to avoid the pile of manure left by one of the horses in front. It was the job of the street cleaners behind our entourage to rush in and clean up the horse pies. They were members of the Junior Cattlemen and Women of San Celina. I'd paid my dues doing that job myself many years before I was allowed to ride in a parade.

Bert winked at me. "Heard they're thinking about getting hitched and that both sets of kids are none too pleased."

"Why?" I asked, spotting Gabe and Kathryn in the

crowd as we passed by Blind Harry's Bookstore. I gave an enthusiastic wave. Ray was nowhere to be seen. That didn't feel good to me. I turned to Daddy. "Both Bobbie and Pete have known each other forever. Why would their kids object?"

"Land," Daddy said, his voice matter-of-fact.

"Of course," I said.

It was always about land with the old ranching families. Either it was easements or fencing issues or grazing rights or some animal or tree that an environmental group was claiming to be endangered. And the developers. Always the developers. Many of the old ranching families had children and grandchildren who were not raised in the rural life, who only knew the ranch as someplace where they occasionally visited Grandma and Grandpa on the way to their "real" vacation in Hawaii or Mammoth. They didn't have a personal connection to the land that had been in their family for a hundred years or more. When Grandma and Grandpa died, it was just expensive real estate that would either assure their free ride to Yale or Cornell or buy them a condo in Orange or Marin County.

Bert gave a loud sniff. "Kids on both sides are against them marrying, especially because both Pete and Bobbie are considering setting up conservation easements with the Nature Conservancy."

I nodded. "So their families can't sell it carte blanche to real estate developers once Pete and Bobbie are gone."

"Heard they recently turned down a huge chunk of change for their properties over by Santa Rosa Creek."

"I know the property. It's over by the Linn's Fruit Bin Farmstore. Beautiful land."

Linn's was a San Celina tradition. It was located on a small, winding road outside of Cambria and was popular with tourists, college kids and senior citizens. They specialized in olallieberry pies, jams and syrups but were also known for their pot pies and baking mixes. The olallieberry was a hybrid cross of a loganberry and a youngberry. It looked like a blackberry but tasted like a slightly tart raspberry.

"That's the one," Bert said. "They both own a big patch of land over there that's connected by Pinky Edmondson's place. Don't know what's going to happen now that Pinky's passed away."

"What?" Hearing Pinky's name suddenly thrown into the mix of Pete and Bobbie's easement issues surprised me. Without thinking, I pulled Mustard to a stop. It threw off Bert and Daddy's horses and caused a bit of a ruckus.

"Let's keep it going," Daddy said. "We're in a parade, not a pasture."

I clucked, urging Mustard forward. "Sorry, I was just surprised for a moment."

"Why?" Bert asked, looking confused.

I shrugged and avoided answering directly. "I shouldn't be. All us ranching families eventually crisscross in one way or another."

Daddy nodded, easing Apple around another horse pie. The cleanup crew behind us was getting a good workout. "I heard that Pinky was holding up the works, wasn't sure if she wanted to commit her land's future to a bunch of greenies."

"Her land was necessary for the easement?" I asked.

"From what I hear, it was the land that connected Pete's and Bobbie's. They could do it without her, but Pinky's part had the easiest public access, though Bobbie's has the creek. Hear they were thinking about making it a public park, even considering on deeding it to the city with the stipulation that it couldn't ever be developed for housing or commercial use."

"Wow, then Pinky's death puts them back at square one," I said. All of a sudden, my upcoming interview with Bobbie took on a different tone.

The Miss San Celina float ahead of us halted in front of the grandstands that held the mayor, float judges and other various San Celina VIPs.

"Looks that way," Daddy said. "Then again, we don't know all the ins and outs. Just ask Bobbie. I'm sure she'd be glad to fill you in."

I glanced at my watch. Twelve thirty-five. In less than a half hour, I'd do just that.

CHAPTER 6

WHEN THE PARADE WAS OVER AND WE WERE BACK AT the staging grounds in San Celina City Park, Daddy took Mustard's reins. "You get goin' to your meetin'."

I'd told him I had an important appointment at one p.m. He didn't ask me what or who, and I didn't offer any information. I'd have time to tell him about it tomorrow at the ranch.

"Thanks, Daddy," I said, giving Mustard a vigorous scratch on the withers. "Thanks for a great ride, old boy. I owe you an apple."

I kissed Daddy's cheek, said I'd see him tomorrow and headed for Blind Harry's. I'd not seen Dove and Boo in the parade crowd, so I couldn't help wondering if everything was okay. For five seconds I contemplated calling her on her cell, then decided against it. I didn't have time to get into a long discussion about anything. I wanted to beat Bobbie to Blind Harry's so I could have a few minutes to absorb this new information about her and Pinky and figure a way to entice her to talk about it. Why? I didn't exactly know, except that it was appearing that things with Pinky Edmondson weren't as innocent as they first appeared.

Lopez Street was still crowded with parade watchers. It looked like they were shopping and eating at the downtown businesses, which was also part of the city council's plan when they changed the parade to a daytime event. There was a long line out the door of Boone's Good Eatin' Chicken, something that would make my cousin Emory happy. He'd hated giving up his job at the *San Celina Tribune* to try to expand his father's Arkansas-based smoked chicken business here on the West Coast, but he was also practical. He now had a wife who liked the finer things in life and a baby on the way.

Blind Harry's was bustling, something that would make my best friend ecstatic. She'd first worked at the bookstore her sophomore year in college and continued working there once she graduated with a business degree. She eventually became manager and in the process made Blind Harry's one of the premier independent bookstores in California. It became hers when my cousin, the sweetest guy on earth, bought her the store for a wedding present.

I pushed past the crowd around the bookstore's prizewinning window display, a tiny replica of San Celina that claimed to show every house in the city limits. A tiny Santa Claus in a sleigh dangled over the miniature town.

Inside the bookstore it was a madhouse. I, not Constance, should have made the appointments to interview the three possible 49ers. Blind Harry's, especially on the Saturday of the Christmas parade, was not the most quiet or discreet place to conduct an interview. But it would have to do. I contemplated going upstairs and asking Elvia if I could borrow her office but thought better of it. Bobbie might reveal more if I didn't make this interview such a big deal.

Listen to yourself, I thought as I walked down the wooden stairs to the coffeehouse. Reveal more about what? So Bobbie, Pete and Pinky were thinking about going together on an environmental easement. Pinky's death might make it more complicated, since they'd have to deal with her heirs now, but that was all the more reason why Bobbie *wouldn't* want Pinky dead, not the other way around. The fact that they were involved was just a coincidence. But I'd been around Gabe too long, and I was vaguely suspicious about the connection.

When I reached the bottom step, I spotted Ray over in a corner, perusing the bookshelves that lined the coffeehouse. Elvia had a system that, when she first set it up, people declared would put her out of business. It was take a used book, leave one in its place. Sales in the coffeehouse doubled in one week.

Ray was leafing through a copy of *The Wizard of Oz*.

"I love that book," I said, coming up beside him. "Almost as much as the movie."

He looked up and smiled. "You know, I've been told I bear a striking resemblance to the scarecrow."

I laughed, feeling my face flush. "Really?"

He winked at me and closed the book. "Did you think I haven't noticed the physical similarities?" He sang softly, "If I only had a brain . . ."

"I bet you hate that song."

"Only when my buddies sang it. Usually when I did something dumb at work." He slipped the book back onto the shelf. "How was the parade?"

"Didn't you watch it? I saw Kathryn and Gabe, but not you."

He shrugged. "I started to, then I got to talking with one of the kids who designed Blind Harry's window. He offered to show me the computer program they used to design it. It's amazing."

"Yes, every year Blind Harry's outdoes itself."

"So, what're you up to now?"

Just as he asked, I saw Bobbie come down the wooden steps. After catching her eye, I gave her a quick wave. "I have an interview with one of the women who is applying for membership in a local club . . ." I shook my head. "It's a long, complicated story. I'll tell you all about it to-night."

"It's a date," he said.

Bobbie went over to the counter and started talking to the barista.

"What're you going to do the rest of the day?" I asked.

He shrugged. "Wander around the town, I suppose. I think Gabe and Kathryn are still catching up on things. Don't want to be a burden."

For a moment, I felt slightly irritated at Gabe. I knew how he could subtly make a person feel like they were a fifth wheel. Ray seemed like a nice man, and Gabe should give him a chance, despite the way his mother sprang this marriage so abruptly on him.

Then again, I could understand his hesitancy in accepting Ray right away. I remembered my own half-fearful, half-annoyed feelings about Isaac when he first became interested in Dove. I'd instantly pegged him for someone who was out to use my gramma and instead he became one of the best things that had happened to her in years. And I now loved him like he'd been my grandpa from the get-go.

"He'll come around," I said, laying a hand on Ray's forearm. "Gabe's a tad overly protective of all his women. He can't help himself."

Ray's eyes crinkled in a smile. "I'll be fine. Don't forget, I'm pretty used to being alone. Lost my Cecilia almost twenty years ago. I'm just grateful for whatever time Kathryn and I have together." His eyes seemed to turn sad for a moment.

"I'll see you at supper," I said. But before then, I was definitely going to find Gabe and tactfully suggest that he include Ray a little more. Though I wasn't always the most accurate judge of people, Ray truly seemed to be a good man who genuinely cared for Kathryn.

Bobbie had already found a table in the corner and had ordered a Mexican hot chocolate for me.

"Thanks, Bobbie," I said, sitting down. "That looks delicious."

"Figured you were probably as chilled as me being out there in the parade."

"I wore long underwear, but it didn't help my hands or face." I tasted the cinnamon-sprinkled whipped cream then took a long drink. The warmth down my throat felt good, and the sugary chocolate gave me confidence.

Bobbie sipped at her own hot chocolate. "Okay, shoot."

I unzipped my leather purse and pulled out a small notebook. "I hope you don't mind if I take notes. I was serious when I said I thought this actually might make a good article for one of the local magazines."

"No problem," Bobbie said. "Just make sure and spell my name right." She sat back in the old ladder-back wooden library chair.

I thought for a moment, then said, "Why don't you start by telling me again why you want to be in the 49 Club?"

She crossed her leg, ankle to knee, and picked at a piece of dirt clinging to the heel of her red and black boot. "Like I told you, it was my mother's dream. She was one of the founding members of the club. I'll be up front about this. My mother, though I loved her dearly and she had many, many good qualities, was a flat-out snob. She and the rest of the founding members were all snobs. It's nuts, don't you think? I mean, a club where they blackball people is so 1950s. Frankly, I hope I'm shut out. If there's one thing I don't need, it's another set of social engagements I have to figure out a way to ditch." She shook her head, her expression bemused.

I watched her as I sipped my drink, trying to discern if she was blowing smoke. Was it a matter of actually not caring or pretending not to care? I understand deathbed promises, but her mother had been gone a long time and, frankly, how would she know if Bobbie was trying to get into the 49 Club or not? I was more curious about the joint easement situation between Bobbie, Pete and Pinky.

"Frankly, Bobbie," I said, wrapping my hands around my warm mug. "I don't think you had anything to do with Pinky's death. I don't think any of the potential members did. I think Pinky just had a heart attack, plain and simple. This is probably just Constance's way of coping."

Bobbie raised her eyebrows. "Hard on you."

I shrugged and touched a finger to my drink's melting whipped cream. After licking it off, I said, "It's my job. I do have a question, just to assuage my own curiosity. How did you know she was having the potential members investigated?"

Bobbie uncrossed her leg and set her boot down hard on the concrete floor. "Oldest way in the book. She confides in her housekeeper. Her housekeeper knows my housekeeper. And you know they know *everything* about us."

I nodded in agreement. That was exactly the reason why I never wanted to have one.

Bobbie shook her head. "I swear, Constance has gone completely batty. As if you don't have better things to do with your time."

"It's okay; I can handle her. Let me just get enough to pad out this investigative report so I have something to tell Constance."

Bobbie's expression made it clear what she wanted to tell Constance.

"So, where were you last Saturday night between . . ." I checked my notebook. ". . . eight p.m. and midnight?"

"That's when Pinky died?"

I nodded. "According to the medical examiner's report. December seventh. Constance told me that Pinky's housekeeper . . ." I checked my notes again. "May Heinz last saw Pinky on Saturday night December seventh at eight p.m. when she made up Pinky's customary tray of Lady Grey tea and butter cookies. Ms. Heinz lives in a guesthouse behind Pinky's house. May found her the next morning at six a.m. when she brought Pinky her breakfast coffee. The medical examiner said Pinky likely died somewhere between nine and midnight."

"Not a bad way to go," Bobbie said. "Sleeping in your own bed after tea and cookies. We should all be so lucky."

I didn't mention that the tea and cookies hadn't been touched, something that was also in the report. "I suppose."

"Saturday night, you say?"

I nodded.

"If I remember right, I was helping Pete at his ranch. About midnight I'd say we were in the middle of pulling a calf. We have had a mess of problems these last few weeks. Pete bred some of his new heifers to a Brangus bull. Paid a pretty penny for the bull at a Dallas auction. But it was a real mistake. Calves are just too dang big."

"I know what you mean." I'd done my share of pulling oversized calves from frightened heifers. Daddy and I were real careful now about which bull impregnated which heifer. I looked back down at my notebook, pen poised.

I looked up from my notebook. "Okay, I do have a question that does concern Pinky. Is it true you and Pete were going in with her on an agriculture easement on your properties over by Santa Rosa Creek?"

Her eyes started blinking rapidly. "Where'd you hear that?"

I shrugged, not about to give Daddy and Bert up.

Her red lips narrowed into a flat line. "Cracker-barrel gang, most likely. Well, it's not exactly a secret. I'm sure our kids have complained hither and yon about it."

"They're not happy about it?"

"Not in the least. That's why they're against Pete and me getting married. That's the *only* thing the two families can agree on." She gave a mischievous smile. Then her face turned serious. "You know, she was thinking about pulling out, even though she'd given us a verbal agreement. We *heard* she received an offer on her land that she couldn't refuse."

"Who told you?"

Her face grew secretive. "Does it matter?"

I wanted to say, *Yes, it does.* But I also knew I'd be pressing my luck. "Did you ever ask her about it?"

She shook her head no. "Just heard about it a few days ago, and we hadn't had a chance to call and ask her about it." Her lips turned up into a half smile. "Does this make me and Pete prime suspects?"

I gave a forced laugh. "Not hardly. I mean, unless either of you inherit her land."

"No such luck. From what I remember her saying, her closest relatives are some cousins back East. That land will be ranchettes in no time."

I glanced up at the wall clock and closed my notebook. "Whoa, I'm running late. I have another appointment."

Bobbie stood up, pushed her Wranglers down over her boots. "Your next suspect?"

"Thanks so much for humoring me, Bobbie," I said, not answering her.

"You're welcome. If it would help set Constance's mind at ease, I'd be happy to pull out of the running for Pinky's spot."

I stood up, grabbed her mug and mine and started for the counter. "I'm sure that's not necessary. I think Constance will come to her senses soon and see that she's chasing fireflies."

"Don't count on it," Bobbie said, following me. "Good luck to you."

"Thanks, again." I waved and ran up the stairs.

Less than ten minutes later, my side aching from running the four blocks to Miss Christine's Tea and Sympathy, I stood in the doorway and surveyed the crowd of chattering ladies. The parade and the holiday season had brought both locals and tourists downtown. Since one p.m. almost constituted the beginning of tea time, Miss Christine's was doing a brisk business.

I spotted Frances "Francie" McDonald on the far side of the flower-scented room. Though Francie and I had never formally met, I recognized her from her many pictures in the *Tribune*'s society pages. In the five years she'd lived in our county, she'd managed to get invited to all the most important parties and charity functions. It made sense that she wanted to be a part of the most prestigious women's club in San Celina County.

I inhaled, trying to slow down my labored breathing, and wove my way through the crowded tearoom. From what I could see, at least half the customers were indulging in Miss Christine's specialty, the chocolate tea. The pastries and cookies, not to mention the chocolate-flavored tea, looked delicious, even though I'd just finished a huge Mexican hot chocolate.

"Mrs. McDonald?" I asked, walking up to the corner table. She'd already ordered a pot of tea and was drinking from a thin china cup painted with green holly and red berries. A twin of her cup was waiting for me. "I'm Benni Ortiz."

"Please, call me Francie," she said, gesturing for me to take a seat. She was dainty-looking, like someone who hadn't eaten a good solid meal in twenty years. Her skin was a translucent peach shade that seemed enhanced, rather than marred, by tiny spiderweb age lines. Though Constance's notes said Francie was sixty-nine years old, she could have passed for fifty-five.

"It's so nice to finally meet you," she said, pouring my tea. "I've seen you around town and read about your . . ." She smiled, not certain how to delicately bring up that my frequent mentions in the paper usually had to do with a murder. That is, if I wasn't being held hostage.

"*Escapades* might be a good word," I said, smiling as I pulled out the silk-upholstered chair. "I do manage to get around. Not always into places that my husband approves of."

She sipped her tea, then patted both corners of her pale lips with her pink linen napkin, politely not answering. She was the kind of woman who actually looked natural in a tea parlor.

"But we're not here to talk about me," I said, pouring a small amount of cream into my tea. "I'm sure Constance told you that I'm doing a chapter for a book on San

Celina history. She said you wouldn't mind being interviewed, since you are one of the ladies in the running for the 49 Club's open spot."

I watched as a proper expression of genteel dismay changed the countenance of her soft features. It was like watching someone at an acting class be told, "Now, show sadness," and they do.

"Such a tragedy," she murmured, bringing her napkin up to the corner of her mouth again. "Though I do desire to join the 49 Club, it troubles me that . . ." She stopped in the middle of her sentence, pressing her lips together.

"That someone has to die for it to happen?" I finished for her.

I wanted to add that it wouldn't be a problem if the club would just open up its membership roll to whomever wanted to join. But, then, someone like Francie McDonald might not find belonging to it quite as appealing.

"Yes, I suppose that's it," she said, her voice without any emotion that I could discern. "I only knew Pinky Edmondson on a casual basis, but she seemed a lovely lady."

I pulled my notebook out of my shirt pocket. "I don't want to keep you long, so I'll get right to my questions. What makes the 49 Club so appealing to someone like you?"

She placed her cup so softly into its saucer that I didn't hear a sound. "Whatever do you mean, someone like me?"

I tried not to sound impatient. I still had one more interview and another dinner with my mother-in-law to get through before I could crawl into my warm bed to-night, so I wasn't in the mood to treat this privileged woman with mink-lined gloves. I softened my words with a smile and an upturned palm. "I mean, someone who is as popular and connected as you. Constance told me about the many things you've accomplished in your life, and I've read about a lot of them in the society pages of the *Tribune*. You don't need to prove anything to anyone, so why is the 49 Club something you want to add to your already prestigious résumé?"

Her lips didn't return my smile, which told me my blatant flattery hadn't fooled her one minute. "The 49 Club is important in San Celina. This is my home now, and I want to be with my . . ." She paused a moment, her neck flushing a rosy color.

I was tempted to say "peeps" but I wasn't sure if she'd understand the Hollywood term for people she felt comfortable around. Her *equals* was what she meant to say, I was sure. When she didn't finish her sentence, I filled in the blank. "Your friends."

"Exactly." Her expression was grateful for two seconds. "But more importantly, they do some of the best charity work in the county, and I think my expertise in raising money would be a good addition to their group."

"Absolutely," I said, wanting to tell her that her stump speech was wasted on me. I had no vote in the matter. "Okay, I'll put in the article that, like all the other 49 Club members, you place great importance on giving back to your community, and you feel that the 49 Club would help you give even more." That overblown sentence rated me another two-second look of gratitude.

"Exactly," she said again. "But if the members decide again that I'm not acceptable, I'm taking myself off the list." She narrowed her diamond-hard blue eyes at me. "That, my dear, is off the record."

I felt myself tremble, like Scout when he knows he's talked me into throwing the ball for him. Again? That means she'd been blackballed before. Why hadn't Constance informed me of that little piece of information?

"Absolutely," I said, closing my notebook, implying that what she was telling me was not going into the article. I wasn't really lying, because there wasn't actually going to be an article. "Do you have any idea who might have . . . objected to your membership?"

Her face went suddenly hard. "You can call it what it was: being blackballed. I don't know for sure, but I know that—" She abruptly stopped and put a thin-fingered hand up to her mouth.

I waited a moment for her to continue. When she didn't, I prompted, "You know that . . . ?"

"Never mind, it doesn't matter. What kind of article did you say this was? I'd better not be made to look the fool, young lady, or there'll be a severe price to be paid."

"It's a small chapter," I assured her. "Part of the history of the 49 Club and its possible future. You and the other prospective members will be profiled as the type of high-quality people the club aspires to attract." I tried to make my smile genuine. "I think I have enough. Anything you'd like to say about the 49 Club?"

She shook her head and stood up. "I've paid for our tea already. Please feel free to enjoy the rest of it, but I must get to an appointment."

Before I could say boo, she was walking toward the door, her back as straight as one of Dove's quilting seams. Our tea sandwiches and scones arrived just as she was walking out the door.

"Where is Mrs. McDonald going?" asked Christine, the owner of the teahouse, rumored to have once been a Vegas showgirl. Today she was wearing a flowing dress adorned with sparkling teacups and a headband with feathers that recalled the roaring twenties.

"She had another appointment," I said, grabbing one of the teahouse's signature cashew chicken salad sandwiches. "That's okay, this is actually just enough for me." Each sandwich was one bite, one of my biggest complaints about teahouses. Every time I went to one I had to go to Taco Bell afterward to assuage my hunger.

"So," Christine said, sitting down in Francie's vacated chair. "What case are you working on?"

"What do you mean?" I asked, popping another tiny sandwich in my mouth.

She wagged a red-nailed finger at me. "Don't try to fool me, Benni Harper Ortiz. You only frequent my establishment under duress of work or someone's wedding or baby shower. What's cooking with Mrs. Francie McDonald?"

I smiled. "Okay, you got me. And you reminded me of something. I need to start planning Elvia's baby shower."

"Call me after Christmas, and we'll talk," she said. "Baby's not due until the summer, right?"

"July first. I want her to have it on July fourth. That way, every year on her or his birthday, there'll be fireworks."

Christine shook her head and smiled. "With Emory as a daddy, that little child's going to get fireworks every day of its life." She leaned closer to me. "So, what's the scoop on Francie?"

I knew Christine was the soul of discretion, so I filled her in on Constance's new job for me. I left out the part about Gabe asking me to fake an investigation. He'd be in a large vat of hot water if that ever got out.

Miss Christine shook her head, her lips pursed. "It is a shame about Pinky—she was a good customer—but I think Constance has a head full of bumblebees flying around in that champagne-blonde head of hers."

I nodded in agreement. I glanced down at my watch, then picked up one more peach and almond scone. "I gotta go. I have to meet my last suspect at the historical museum. Dorothea St. James."

Miss Christine looked both ways, then scooted her chair a little closer to mine. "There's something you should know about Francie."

My ears immediately perked up. "What's that?"

"She was blackballed by Pinky three years ago, the first time she applied for membership in the 49 Club. I was told it had to do with Francie making fun of some artist that Pinky loved."

I stopped chewing my scone and stared at Christine. Some investigator I was. While I was stuffing my face, a nugget of information just fell into my lap, like an overripe apple. "How do you know it was Pinky who blackballed her?"

Christine just placed a long, elegant finger to her lips. She was keeping that to herself.

"Any other little tidbit you might want to share?" I asked, brushing the crumbs off my fingers onto my flowery china plate.

"That's all I have for now," she said, glancing over my shoulder at someone coming into the tea parlor. A sudden burst of cold air caused the crystal chandelier in the middle of the room to tinkle. It was dramatic enough to cause a ripple of laugher to flow through the crowded room like a wave.

"Nola!" Christine stood up and, like an elegant yacht, sailed across the room toward the thin, elegant woman standing in the parlor's doorway. "Thank you for gracing my establishment with your lovely presence."

While I watched Christine weave her way through the tables, I quickly assessed the woman who'd donated the museum's now most prestigious acquisition. Though she'd lived in Cambria over a year now, I'd never met her in person. She apparently spent a lot of time traveling, speaking about and promoting her uncle's work. We'd spoken by phone a few times concerning the security of her uncle's painting before it was officially shown at the museum. I'd assumed I would meet her at the opening, but it appeared it would happen sooner.

The photographs I'd seen of Nola Maxwell Finch didn't do her justice. In a word, she was gorgeous. With wavy, shoulder-length hair the color of apricots and wide-set, chambray-blue eyes, she was the type of woman that caused men to act courtly and other women to feel like bull moose. She was thin with an almost flat chest and features that were just this side of sharp, though not unattractively so. She was dressed in tailored, camel-colored slacks and an icy blue sweater set.

Christine said a few words to her, then turned to point at me. Then she gestured at me to come to her.

"Benni Ortiz?" Nola Finch said when I reached them. Her complexion was almost transparent, with a light sprinkling of pale orange freckles.

"Yes," I replied. "It's so nice to finally meet you." I held out my hand and was surprised by the firmness of her grip.

"Nola Maxwell Finch," Christine said. "It is an honor to welcome you again to my humble establishment. The town is just thrilled about your generous donation to our beloved folk art museum."

I smiled at Nola, who seemed a bit taken aback by Christine's enthusiasm. "I second that wholeheartedly," I said. "Everyone's really looking forward to your presentation at the California Outsider Art exhibit on Wednesday evening."

"So am I," Nola said, her voice soft and cultured, with just the touch of a Chicago accent. "My uncle is thrilled to be giving your museum one of his paintings."

"There's a reporter from the *Los Angeles Times* coming up to cover it." I couldn't help the pride in my voice. It took quite a bit of finagling on my part to convince the arts and leisure editor that this event was worth covering. That and Emory's generous offer to pay for the reporter's two-night stay in San Celina's best bed-and-breakfast.

"That's wonderful," she said. "I'd love to come by the museum and see where you've hung his painting."

"Absolutely," I said, reaching into my backpack and finding a business card. "The museum's number is on the card, and so is my cell phone. If you'll call me, we can set up a time, and I can meet you there. I'll give you the two-dollar tour."

"I'll do that," she said, taking the card and slipping it into her small leather clutch. Her eyes flickered, looking at someone behind me. "I think I see my lunch date. I'll call you."

"I'll look forward to it," I said, stepping aside.

"What a delightful woman," Christine said. "Such a nice addition to our town. So generous."

"Yes," I agreed. "I have another appointment, so I have to boogie. I'll call you soon about a baby shower for Elvia."

Christine clasped her hands together. "I have some wonderful ideas already brewing."

Fortunately, it was a short walk to the historical museum for my last interview with Dorothea St. James. On the way, I called Constance on my cell phone to find out why she hadn't told me about Francie being black-balled by Pinky. Constance's phone rang six times before her housekeeper answered.

"I'm sorry, but Miss Constance is resting right now," she said.

"It's an emergency. Don't worry, I'll take full respon-sibility for disturbing her. I'll tell her that I harassed you into it."

A huge sigh came over the phone telling me that my words didn't hold much water. "I'm sorry, but she said she is exhausted and absolutely must not be disturbed."

I felt like giving a Tarzan yell into the phone, except that the person who deserved to hear it was peacefully snoozing the afternoon away. "All right, then would you please ask her to call me the minute she wakes up?"

"I'll tell her you called." Her long experience with Constance had clearly taught her not to promise anything. Her tone told me it was doubtful that Constance would call me back.

I growled at my cell phone. "I will track you down sooner or later, old woman. And I'm going to cash that check as soon as the bank opens on Monday. And buy dog toys with it."

Dog toys. Yikes, I'd completely forgotten about Boo. I was going to owe Dove big time for watching him for me. What kind of puppy godmother was I? I hadn't even checked on him. Before I could dial home, the phone rang.

"Hello?"

"Benni? It's Hud."

"What a coincidence. I was just going to call and see how Boo is doing."

"Where is he? At All Paws?"

"Not today. Dove is watching him while I do a little . . ." I paused, not wanting to go into this with Hud. "Work for the museum. I'm interviewing some society ladies for an article. How's Texas?"

"Big," he said, laughing. "We're having a great time, though Maisie misses Boo. And I have to confess, I miss the little peckerwood myself. How's he doing?"

"Just fine. You really owe me for this one, Clouseau. I won't be getting a full night's sleep until you get back.

Earlene Fowler

Next time, make sure you potty train a dog before you leave him with someone."

"Ah, what fun would that be, ranch girl? But you're right, I do owe you a Texas-size favor. But I have one more tiny thing to beg of you."

I groaned out loud. "What?"

"I need to have you take Boo to see Santa."

"What?"

"I said . . ."

"I heard what you said, I just can't believe it."

"I promised Maisie that Boo would go see Santa and have his picture taken. It's killing her that he's spending his first Christmas away from us, so this was my way of appeasing her. I'll wash your truck. I'll massage your feet. I'll pay extra."

"Leave my truck and feet out of this. I'll settle for a generous donation to the folk art museum."

"As soon as I get back. Be sure to get pictures. Maisie needs to believe that Boo actually saw Santa."

"I cannot believe I'm agreeing to this. If you knew how busy I am . . ."

"I'm writing the check now," he interrupted. "Josiah Sinclair Folk Art Museum. Five hundred? Six hundred? A thousand?"

"All of the above. Now, go back and do whatever it is people do when they go to Texas."

"You're my hero. Kiss the Booster for me."

Dorothea St. James, aka Dot, arrived at the front doors of the San Celina Historical Museum at the same time as me.

"Benni!" she exclaimed in a voice that always said a

person's name as if they were the exact person she wanted to see at that exact moment.

"Hi, Dot," I said, opening the heavy wooden door of the old redbrick Carnegie Library. "Shall we go inside out of this cold wind?" As happens so often in San Celina, one moment you are toasty warm, peeling off your layers, the next moment a cold, damp wind descends upon you, chilling your bones.

"Good idea!" she said with as much enthusiasm as if I'd said, hey, what do you think about using mold to make a medicine that will cure life-threatening infections? I'd met Dot many times at different historical society functions. She was one of San Celina's most beloved and respected society ladies. She was tiny and fast and had the biggest wardrobe of St. John's knits in three counties. That last bit of information was given to me by Elvia, who was impressed, and that was saying something about my clotheshorse best friend.

Dot never seemed to stop moving. Her husband, a local doctor, was respected and admired in San Celina. Her children turned out well, something that can't be said for many of the affluent members of San Celina society. Her son followed in his father's footsteps and was a local podiatrist who also raised wine grapes, and her daughter owned a boutique in Cambria and was active in local charities. A genuinely nice woman with impeccable credentials, I couldn't help but wonder why she hadn't been elected a member of the 49 Club a long time ago. Did she have something in her past like Francie did that irritated one of the 49 Club members enough to blackball her? If she did, I just couldn't imagine what it might be.

Serving the wrong kind of finger sandwiches at a charity tea, not bidding enough at a charity auction, wearing white shoes after Labor Day?

"Let's go see if the downstairs meeting room is empty," I said. "It might be a bit cool, but at least it will be private."

"Let's just go into the volunteer break room. I could use a hot cup of tea. How about you?"

I was about hot-drinked out, but I gamely agreed, and we went down the wooden stairs to the small room used for the volunteers to take a break or work on some project. Luckily, it was empty for the moment, though we couldn't be sure when someone would walk in.

After fixing herself a cup of tea, she sat down across from me at the communal table. "Constance said you're writing some kind of article about the 49 Club. I can't imagine why she'd want you to speak to me. I'm not even a member."

I shifted in the folding wooden chair, causing it to squeak. "She told me you were up for the empty spot, and I thought it would be interesting to not only interview members, but soon-to-be members."

Her face brightened. "Have you heard something?"

I felt my neck grow hot. "Actually, no, that was . . . just a figure of speech."

"Oh." Her lips turned down slightly in what was the closest she'd probably ever come to a grimace. She sat up straight and smiled. "Of course *you* wouldn't know anything. You were just trying to be diplomatic. You know, I'm sure, that I've missed being asked twice."

"Oh," I said, not knowing what else to say. "That must

be . . ." I almost said painful, but for crying out loud, it was just a silly little club. Why in the world did these intelligent, successful women care one iota about being asked to join? And why didn't the club just open up the membership and change the doggone name to the *Infinity* Club?

Because, honeybun, I could hear my gramma Dove's voice say, *that would make it entirely too democratic and equal and not nearly as much fun for those crazy old snobs.*

"I'm sure I'll be chosen this time," Dot said, waving her hand. "What would you like to know?"

I pulled out my notebook and pretended to read through my notes. "I guess I'm curious . . . and your readers would be curious about what is so special about the 49 Club as compared to other clubs you are associated with."

I hoped I'd flatter her with the phrase, *your readers.* She started rambling on about the uniqueness and quality of the 49 Club and its members, how making it exclusive kept up the quality of the work they did, how the quality and dedication of the members made the club more successful. I let her talk while I pretended to take notes. If she said anything that sounded suspicious, I was sure I'd catch it. After about twenty minutes, I closed my notebook and said, "I think I have enough. Thank you so much for taking time out of your busy schedule to talk to me." If I heard the word "quality" one more time, I'd blow my top.

She stood up, brushed down the front of her tailored blue skirt. "You'll send me a copy when it's finished? My secretary keeps a file of my clippings."

"Uh, sure. Constance has your address, right?"

"Yes, she does." Dot gave me a sparkling smile. "Give Constance my best. Tell her I'll see her at Pinky's memorial service."

"When is that?" I knew that real investigators often went to the funerals of victims to see who attends. It might be beneficial for me to go to Pinky's memorial service. Oh, for cryin' out loud, I said to myself. You're acting like this is a *real* investigation.

"I'm not sure," Dot admitted. "But I'll attend if it's not private, of course. I know how close she and Constance were. I truly admired Pinky Edmondson."

I noticed that she used the word admired, rather than liked. Was that significant? Did any of these society ladies who spent so much of their time together on charity committees truly like each other? It was probably like the ag community; some people you served with you liked, others you tolerated, some you flat-out avoided.

"I'm sure Constance will let people know when or if there is a service," I said, even though I didn't have a clue if she would or not. "I think all of Pinky's family lives out of town, so I'm not sure what the plans are."

On my walk back to my truck, I mulled over the three interviews. Frankly, I felt like I'd wasted an afternoon that I could have spent doing something useful. I didn't find out one thing about these women that wasn't pretty much common knowledge. Still, the reason I was doing this was to humor Constance, so once I made my report to her and to my husband, I was through. There was nothing that led me to believe any of those three women wanted the spot in the 49 Club so bad they would kill for it. As far as I was concerned, I'd done my due diligence, and the case was closed. But I should have known better. Few things in my life have ever turned out to be what they initially appeared to be.

CHAPTER 7

WHEN I WALKED INTO MY HOUSE, I IMMEDIATELY smelled something was up. Supper, to be exact. Dove's chicken and dumplings, if my nose served me right. No one greeted me at the door, but I could hear the sound of laughter coming from the kitchen.

Inside the warm, butter-scented room I found Dove, Kathryn, both dogs and Ray. Dove stood in front of the stove dropping her homemade dumplings in one of my six-quart pots, while Kathryn tore lettuce for a salad. Ray was teaching Boo to play tug of war with someone's athletic sock.

"Thanks a lot, Ray," I said, smiling at the tiny growl coming from Boo's fuzzy little body. Scout lay in the corner watching the game with a huge doggie grin on his face. "You know he'll start thinking all socks are toys now. But since he's not my dog, I actually don't care."

"My dogs always loved a good sock tug," he said. "Seems a small doggie sin to possess."

"I agree. But, like I said, 'taint my dog." I walked over to Dove and laid my head on her shoulder, stooping slightly to do so. It felt like an arrow in my heart; she seemed to be shrinking before my eyes. "Thank you, Gramma, from the bottom of my wicked, but contrite heart. Today was definitely a chicken and dumplings day." It was my ultimate comfort food, and no one made this dish like Dove. "Hey, aren't we supposed to go to the airport to pick up Isaac?"

Dove shook her head. "He came in early. He's already at the ranch. Ben picked him up."

"Do you know when Gabe is coming home?" Kathryn asked.

I turned to face her. "I haven't seen him all day. I thought he was with you."

She looked back down at the lettuce head she was tearing, her face neutral. "Gabe and I had some words this afternoon."

I glanced over at Ray, who didn't look up from his tug-of-war with Boo. I turned to Dove, who just shrugged and went back to dropping dumplings.

"Has anyone called him?" I asked.

"He said he was going for a drive," Kathryn said. She turned to Dove. "Didn't you mention you brought some tomatoes from the ranch?"

Dove wiped her hands on the towel she had stuck in front of her jeans for a makeshift apron. "They're out in the truck."

"I'll get them," I said. It would give me a chance to call Gabe and see what was going on.

Outside, I called his cell phone. He answered the second ring.

"Ortiz, here."

"Ortiz here too. Where are you?"

"I'm about two miles out of town. My ETA is about five minutes."

"Good. Dove's making chicken and dumplings. By the way, what did you and your mom fight about?"

There was a long silence on the line. In the background I could hear Etta James playing on his Corvette's tape player. He only played Etta when he was very agitated. "What did she say?"

"She said you two had words. Care to elaborate?"

"No."

I didn't answer for a minute. "Okay, we'll talk about this later. Are you and she going to be able to get along through dinner?"

"We've been faking it all my life. What's one more night?"

"I'll see you soon," I said, not wanting to delve into this any deeper at the moment. Right now, just getting through dinner looked like it was going to take a gargantuan effort.

I was washing the tomatoes when Gabe opened the front door. Ray had taken Boo outside, since he'd just been fed, to try to coax him to do his business in the yard and not on my new carpet. Kathryn was setting the table, and Dove was checking the progress of her baking powder biscuits.

"Supper will be ready in five minutes," Dove said. "Better tell Gabe to wash up."

He was halfway up the stairs when I came out of the kitchen. I followed him into the bedroom, where he was pulling off his navy blue sweatshirt. I sat on the bed and watched him go through his dresser drawers picking out and discarding one T-shirt after another. He finally settled on a plain black one.

"Supper's almost ready," I said.

"Okay," he replied without turning around.

"Gabe—" I started.

He held up a hand for me to stop, causing my hackles to rise. There was no gesture that I found more condescending. It took every ounce of self-control I had not to smack him in the back of the head.

"Fine," I said, standing up. "See you downstairs."

Throughout the meal, Gabe and his mother pointedly talked to everyone but each other. We discussed the Christmas parade, the decorations downtown and the place where Gabe and Kathryn had eaten lunch, Carlos by the Creek. It was a new Mexican restaurant whose building straddled San Celina Creek, which wove through the center of town like a drunken snake.

"Speaking of decorations," Dove said. "When are you going to get your Christmas tree? It's only eleven days to Christmas."

I glanced over at Gabe, who shrugged and went back to eating. "We were waiting for Kathryn and Ray to get here so we could decorate it together," I said.

Actually, we had been waiting for Kathryn. We hadn't even known about Ray, but I'd had this great idea about

135

having a tree trimming party while Kathryn was here and inviting some of our friends so Kathryn could meet them. Now, it didn't seem like such a good idea. It didn't appear as if Gabe and Kathryn were in the mood for a party.

"Tomorrow," I said, making an executive decision. "We'll buy it on the way home from the ranch. We can decorate it Monday night."

Dove nodded, then smiled at Ray. "Hope you like beef, Ray. There'll be a lot of it tomorrow. Not to mention a little bull."

Ray smiled at Dove. "I've always been a little partial to both. I'm looking forward to a day at your ranch."

After another uncomfortable half hour of making conversation, Gabe excused himself and went upstairs. I glanced over at his mother, whose face looked stricken and old. I stared after him, trying to decide if I should follow, then concluded it would be more sensible to let him be alone for a while. I'd help Dove clean up and then go talk to him.

"Let me help," Kathryn said, as I picked up her plate.

"Not a chance," I said. "You already helped make dinner. You're probably tired. I'm sure the time change is working a number on your body clock."

She sighed deeply; her blue-gray eyes seemed to sink into her face. Her sharp cheekbones, the bone structure she'd passed down to my husband, stretched tight across her pale skin. "You're right, Benni. I am rather weary. Maybe I'll make it an early night."

"I think I'll take a walk," Ray said. "Give you some time for your nightly ablution."

"I love a man with a good vocabulary," Dove said, eliciting a smile from both Ray and Kathryn.

After they left the kitchen, I turned on the hot water, started rinsing the dinner dishes and arranging them in the dishwasher. At the same time, I began a game of ball to keep Boo occupied. His favorite toy was a large fabric ball covered with colorful tags. I'd kick it across the kitchen floor, and he'd scamper after it, his tiny toenails clicking across the tile floor. Scout, obviously tired from his day with the puppy, lay on his side next to the back door, content to let me entertain Boo.

"I'll do the stockpot by hand," Dove said. "Takes up too much room in the dishwasher."

I murmured agreement and kept rinsing dishes. When I finished, I turned on the dishwasher and sat down on a chair. "Gabe and his mom had a fight."

"I figured it was something like that," Dove said, wiping the kitchen table.

I picked up Boo and settled him in my lap, scratching the back of his downy neck, trying to calm him down enough to go to sleep. "What am I going to do?"

Dove scrubbed at a stubborn spot on the table. The hum of the dishwasher vibrated the floor of my kitchen. An occasional clink of a dish not fit in properly echoed through the kitchen. It was the kind of thing that I could ignore and would drive Gabe crazy. He'd turn off the dishwasher and reorganize the dishes. I'd leave the room. Funny, I thought, just exactly the opposite of how we handle emotional problems. In that case, he's always the one to leave the room.

"What can you do?" Dove said. "Whatever is going on

between them started a long time before you and Gabe met. Just stand out of the way, and let them work it out. You can't be a referee in this game. You'll only get hurt."

Of course she was right. I repeated it to myself as I drove her home, kissed her good night and drove back to my house. I mentally reiterated her words as I took Boo out for his last constitutional, settled him into his crate, gave Scout his nightly dog biscuit and while I took a long, warm shower.

Gabe was in bed reading the latest James Lee Burke book whose character, Dave Robicheaux, a Vietnam vet like Gabe, both delighted and irritated him.

"Anyone who took that many punches would be in a wheelchair permanently," he'd always say to me while he devoured Mr. Burke's latest book. "And he's always pissing off the bad guys and getting his women killed."

"I truly appreciate that you don't do that," I'd tell him every time he said it. But he still always bought Mr. Burke's latest book in hardback.

"How's this one?" I asked, turning over on my side and propping my head up with my hand.

He peered at me over his gold-rimmed reading glasses. "Robicheaux's pissed off some psycho, and he's after Robicheaux's daughter."

"So," I said, throwing all my good intentions to the wind. "What's the deal between you and your mama?"

He looked back down at his book. "It's nothing. Don't worry about it."

I stuck my head over the page he was reading. "Good try, Friday, but we're going to discuss this, so you may as well give in. You know I'm as persistent as a mole."

He raised his head to look at me. There was just the slightest shadow under his chameleon blue eyes, eyes that never failed to make my heart beat a little faster. "I don't want to talk about my mother right now. Let's just get through her visit with as little conflict as possible. We can talk about it after she's gone."

I held his gaze, not convinced by his words. "I would agree to that, except I've been married to you long enough to know that she'll leave, and then you won't want to talk about her because then it doesn't matter; she's gone. I think we've been married long enough now that you can open up a little bit to me about your mom. Obviously, you two had an argument, and it would help me get through her visit if I had a little hint about what it was about."

He lay his book down, not bothering to save his spot. "Why would you knowing what my mother and I argued about make her visit easier for you?"

I hated it when he turned homicide investigator on me, not answering my questions but posing questions of his own. I leaned over and poked a finger in the middle of his chest. "Look, mister, you're not going to sleep tonight until you talk to me."

He grabbed my hand and brought it up to his mouth, resting his lips on it. "*Querida*, please, I just can't do it right now. My mother and I have lots of history, some of it good, some bad. Like all parents and children. She surprised me with this sudden marriage, and I told her so. She got a little huffy. I got a little huffy. By tomorrow, it'll all blow over. Trust me on that. She and I have danced this dance many, many times."

I pulled my hand out of his and laid it on his scratchy cheek. I suspected there was more to it than just the normal conflict between mother and son. There was some painful history between the two of them. When Gabe's father died, Gabe had only been sixteen, a particularly hard age for a boy to lose his father. The only part of the story I knew was that he'd gotten into some trouble back in Kansas. His mother, probably reeling from the shock of her husband dying from a heart condition they didn't know existed, trying to keep working as a teacher, caring for Gabe's ten-year-old twin sisters and dealing with her own grief, did what I was sure she thought was the best thing for Gabe. She sent him to live with his dad's older brother, Antonio, in Santa Ana, California. Uncle Tony had been a police officer in the Santa Ana police department, had four sons of his own and didn't hesitate for a moment when Kathryn asked him to let Gabe finish out his high school years with his family.

Gabe loved and admired his father's older brother and often gave his uncle credit for Gabe's success both in the marines and in police work. The one thing Gabe never spoke about was what he felt about being sent away from home only months after his father died. Like his time in Vietnam, his feelings about those years were in an emotional room that he kept closed and padlocked. I had a feeling that between those long-buried feelings about his father's death, the tragedy involving his cousin Luis, and his mother's unexpected marriage, something was going to explode. I thought talking about it would ease some of the pressure. He obviously thought the opposite.

I thought all this as I caressed his cheek, the roughness

of his evening beard tickling my hand. "You know I love you."

"I know." He pulled me to him, and I laid my head on his chest, listening to the thumping of his heart. I couldn't remember exactly the age his father had been when he died of a heart attack, but I fretted about Gabe's heart. He'd had all the tests, was given a clear bill of heart health so far, but I couldn't help worrying that something lurked under his coppery skin, a clot or genetic flaw that would take him from me in an instant.

"I'll be here for you," I said. "When you need to talk."

"I know," he said again, stroking my hair.

I admit, as much as his vulnerability touched me, I was still a little annoyed that he'd managed to turn the conversation around so that none of my questions were answered. I felt his lips on the top of my head.

"Change of subject," he said, deftly closing the door on any more discussion about his mother. "What's happening with Constance?"

I pulled away from him and sat up. "That rat! She never called me back!"

"She was supposed to call you?"

"After I interviewed the three potential 49 Club members, I called her because I wanted to verify some information I discovered. She was taking a nap and not accepting phone calls. I told her housekeeper to have her call me as soon as she got up." I crossed my arms over my chest. "I swear, I'm going to shoot that woman."

"Please, not in the next two weeks," he said, a half smile softening his tired expression. "I've got enough on my plate at work."

"Don't worry, I'll make sure not to leave any clues. I think I could murder someone without getting caught."

"Oh, you do, do you?" He pulled me back to him and kissed me hard on the lips. As he was so good at doing, his kiss made me forget his mother, forget Constance Sinclair and probably, if asked, forget my own name, for a few minutes. When he slipped his warm hands underneath my T-shirt, I pulled away from him, scooting to the other side of the bed.

"No way, Friday. Not until your mama leaves."

"You're kidding," he said, giving a low, dramatic moan. "It's the holidays!"

"That's the dumbest reasoning I've ever heard," I said, laughing. "Besides, don't you want to hear about my investigation?"

"Not particularly," he said, reaching over and stroking my bare thigh.

I swatted at his hand. "They are leaving the day after Christmas. You can just wait."

He tossed his book on the floor next to the bed, causing Scout to lift his head from a dead sleep. "Okay, if I can't have sex, then go ahead and tell me about Constance. That should cool my jets."

"It's okay, Scooby-Doo," I called softly to my dog. "Go back to sleep." Then to Gabe I said, "Well, she failed to tell me one little thing about Francie McDonald, that she'd been blackballed the last time she was up for a place in the 49 Club. By none other than Pinky Edmondson."

Gabe slipped down under the down comforter and turned out his bedside light. "So?"

"So, that might be a motive."

"Except for one thing."

I cocked my head. "What?"

"This isn't a real investigation, remember? Pinky Edmondson was not murdered. She died of a heart attack."

I set my alarm clock for two a.m. and turned out my own light. "I know that, but I don't have to tell you that people have killed for a lot dumber things than getting into an exclusive club."

"It's not real, Benni," he repeated. "Am I going to have to take you off the case?"

"How can you take me off a case that's not a case to begin with?" I reached over and started rubbing his stomach. It was a big house, and his mother was all the way on the other side of it.

"Don't start something you don't intend to finish."

"I never do, Friday."

CHAPTER 8

*T*HOUGH I DON'T KNOW HOW THEY DID IT, THE NEXT
morning Gabe and his mother were laughing and acting
like nothing had happened. Well, I knew why Gabe was
in a relaxed mood, and I took a little credit for that.

But I was more than a little bleary-eyed when I walked
into the kitchen at seven a.m. carrying Boo and wearing
the kelly green cashmere bathrobe my cousin Emory
bought me for my birthday this year.

"Cashmere and puppy," Gabe commented as he
scrambled eggs. "Probably not the wisest combination."

His mother was sitting at the kitchen table dressed
in knife-pressed khaki slacks and a red sweater. She
was drinking a cup of tea and hulling some fresh
strawberries.

"Good morning, Kathryn," I said, attempting a smile. "Eat dirt, Chief." I softened my comment by patting him on the butt as I walked past him toward the back door. After Boo watered the grass and we were both back in the warm kitchen, Kathryn motioned at me to take a seat.

"Let me pour you some coffee," she said. "Or would you rather have tea?"

"Coffee, thank you. What's cookin', Friday?"

"My special scrambled eggs and whole wheat–pecan pancakes."

I wrinkled my nose. I liked his scrambled eggs, full of cheese and onions and green peppers and topped with sour cream. But his whole wheat pancakes were too bumpy-lumpy, organically good for you for my taste.

"I saw that," Gabe said, without turning around. "Don't wrinkle your nose. My pancakes are delicious."

I stuck my tongue out at his back, then grinned at Kathryn. "The pecans are good."

He just laughed and said, "Go ahead, have one of your ubiquitous Pop-Tarts. At least I have some people at the table who'll appreciate my culinary expertise."

"Oh, quit showing off in front of your mom. Ubiquitous isn't even the exact right word. I often run out of Pop-Tarts and happily switch to Lucky Charms or Cap'n Crunch."

Gabe shook his head and laughed, stirring his eggs.

"Sounds like you two have been married for twenty years," Kathryn said, smiling.

"Feels like it sometimes," I quipped. Then I added quickly, "Though in a good way." Though she was being good-natured, I wasn't sure how far I could push my joking.

"Don't believe her for a minute, Mom," Gabe said, pouring the first set of pancakes. "I've tried her patience more than once or twice in the last few years."

"I can well imagine," she replied.

Though she said it in the most bland way, not meaning, I was certain, for her words to harbor any sort of undertone, I could see Gabe's back stiffen.

Let it go, I sent a mental message to my husband.

Maybe it was my psychic message or maybe his own good sense, but in a few seconds his back relaxed, and he didn't answer her. Fortunately, Ray walked into the kitchen at that moment whistling Steve Goodman's "The City of New Orleans."

"Hey, Ray," I said. "That's one of my favorite songs. Have you ever actually ridden on that train?"

"I have," he said, going over to Kathryn and kissing her cheek. "Good morning, Katie-do."

Gabe turned around to look at Ray, his eyes surprised, then annoyed. It threw me too. Katie-do? I couldn't imagine a less appropriate nickname for his very proper Midwestern mother. I imagine Gabe was thinking the same thing. I wondered briefly what his father used to call her.

"Good morning, Gabe," Ray said evenly, not at all flustered by Gabe's less than hospitable look. "Something smells delicious."

Gabe murmured something and turned back to his pancakes. I glanced at Kathryn, whose face showed the same annoyance that her son's held, though hers was directed at his broad back.

We stuck to neutral subjects while we ate, and again I noticed that Gabe never actually spoke to Ray. It was going to be a long day. Forget that, it was going to be a long holiday season. After breakfast, we coordinated plans for going out to the ranch at noon. Gabe would take Kathryn and Ray in his comfortable city-issue car; I would take the dogs in my truck. It would be a tight fit in the front seat of the truck for me, Scout and Boo in his car seat, but we'd manage.

As we dressed, I told Gabe I was going to take Boo and Scout for a walk down to Elvia and Emory's house to try to burn off some of Boo's puppy energy. "I'll use the time to call Constance, see what she says about not telling me about Francie being blackballed."

Gabe, to his credit, didn't reiterate what he said last night about this investigation being fake. He just shrugged, his mind on something else. Should I say something to him about the way he was treating Ray? I decided to keep quiet. It would just be better if we all walked on eggshells around each other until this awkward visit was over. A big blowup was something no one needed right now, least of all my husband, who'd been on edge since his cousin died last month.

"In case you're gone by the time I get back, see you at the ranch." I stood on tiptoe and kissed the bottom of his chin.

On my, Boo and Scout's very slow amble to Elvia and Emory's house—I'd forgotten how easily puppies were distracted by every little flower or bug—I dialed Constance's number. Fortunately for both her and me, she answered.

"Hi, Constance, it's Benni. You never called me back." I didn't try to hide the irritation in my voice.

"I wasn't feeling well last night," she said, her high voice thin and, indeed, sick-sounding. "One of my migraines. I'm still feeling woozy. What did you want?"

"Why didn't you tell me that Frances McDonald had been blackballed once already by the 49 Club?"

"What difference does that make?"

"A big difference, Constance!"

"How did *you* find out about it? Our membership vote is supposed to be private."

"You don't really believe that, do you? One of the things Dove always says is that the only way something is kept secret is if it is between you and God and no one else."

"The 49 Club members are different," she said, her voice haughty. "We take an *oath*."

"Whatever," I said, unwilling to waste time arguing about this. I was almost at Elvia's house. "Are there any more little secrets about these three ladies that you forgot to tell me?"

"I didn't *forget* to tell you about Francie. I just didn't think it had any bearing on the subject."

That last statement just about did me in. Tired, I did not have time for this pseudo-investigation, nor time to pander to Constance, no matter how bad I felt about her losing her friend. "Honestly, Constance, I found nothing that led me to believe that any of those women would murder Pinky. Bobbie doesn't really care about being in the club. Both Francie and Dot do, but I doubt that either would slit their wrists if they weren't chosen. Are you absolutely certain you want me to continue with this?"

I'd reached Elvia's house and wanted to cut our conversation short. I meant what I said. Though each of the ladies had a bit of troubled history with Pinky, none of them was capable of killing someone. I was certain of it. Well, almost certain. I'd also been surprised enough by people in life to never state unequivocally that someone was innocent.

"You need to come to the 49 Club Christmas tea this Wednesday," she replied. "Maybe you can find out some more information then."

"Constance, there's nothing to find out. I'm really, really sorry that Pinky died, but I think you are searching for something that doesn't exist." I waved at Emory, who'd come out on his front porch holding a dark blue mug and wearing an expensive-looking navy blue jogging suit. He gestured at his mug, asking me if I wanted coffee. I nodded yes, and he disappeared back into his house.

"I need you at the tea," Constance said, her voice just this side of pleading. "I would consider it a great favor."

That gave me pause. Having Constance owe me was not something to sneeze at. "All right, I'll come. But I still think you should let this obsession about Pinky go." I couldn't believe how nervy I was being. Then again, what did I have to lose? Right now, I'd gladly turn my curator job and the constant care of Madame Sinclair over to anyone who'd take it.

"Thank you," she said, garbling the words as if they were ones she was not familiar with pronouncing, which probably wasn't far from the truth. "I'll call you with the details."

"Okay." I turned off my cell phone, slipped it into my pocket, scooped Boo up and climbed the wooden stairs to my cousin's wide front porch. Scout followed, flopping down on one of their hand-braided rugs. My cousin stood at the top step with a cup of hot coffee, creamed and double sugared just how I like it.

"Didn't anyone tell you that Sunday is a day of rest?" he asked, handing me a mug of steaming coffee. I reciprocated by handing him Boo.

"Make yourself useful. I don't want the Booster falling down these steep stairs." I sat down on one of the hickory rocking chairs Emory bought from an Appalachian artisan in West Virginia. It made a soft, homey-sounding squeak with every rock.

Boo licked Emory's hands and settled down in his arms as if he were meant to be there. Emory stroked Boo's silky head. "Looks like I made myself a friend."

"Don't get too proud," I said, inhaling the nutty smell of my coffee. "He likes everyone, especially if you have a treat in your pocket."

"Don't burst my bubble, sweetcakes," he said, sitting down on a rocker that was a twin of mine. "How's life in the Ortiz household?"

I grimaced and shook my head. "Awkward as heck. Gabe and his mother bounce between not speaking and pretending to be a fifties television mother and son, and Gabe hasn't said two complete sentences to Ray since they arrived. I tried to talk to him about it last night, but he sweet-talked his way around me, basically telling me to mind my own beeswax."

Emory massaged Boo's neck absentmindedly, and I

could see the puppy's eyes start to close. Maybe I could talk my cousin into taking Boo for an overnighter, convince him that getting up in the middle of the night for potty patrol would be good practice for those two a.m. feedings that were in his near future.

"I can't help you there, cuz," he said. "You know my mama died too early for me to go through that resentful, adolescent stage. But I've had enough friends stuck in a time warp relationship with their mamas to know that it's always a lot more complicated than it appears. And with Kathryn springing her new husband on Gabe with no warning, I'd say that's just the last onion on a truckload of old resentments that are sitting there idling away. Keep in mind, it's not your job to unload the truck."

I sipped my coffee and rocked slowly back and forth, comforted by the motion. He was right. But like a truck idling outside your motel window at five in the morning, it was irritating, and there would be no way I'd get any sleep or peace until they resolved their conflict . . . or Kathryn left. It would more than likely be the latter.

"You're right, Emory. You really should have stuck with that psychology major in college. You'd make a good therapist."

He shifted Boo in his arms, and the puppy let out a little chirp of disapproval. "Sorry, young fella, my arm was getting tired. I'll be needing a therapist my own self, sweetcakes, before this child of mine is born. I don't think I'm going to make it through this pregnancy. I'm about ready to go nuts."

I laughed. "Don't be cryin' in my soup. You were just as much responsible for bringing this baby into the world as Elvia, and she's the one suffering the most. But you listened to my woes, so I'll do you the favor back, what's going on?"

So I listened to his complaints about Elvia's up and down emotions, her crying jags, her morning, noon and night sickness, his dashing out in the middle of the night for crazy food cravings. Cracker Jacks was the latest.

"Not caramel corn, mind you, but Cracker Jacks. It had to be Cracker Jacks. Do you know how hard it is to find Cracker Jacks anymore? And she ate them while drinking tomato juice. I tell you, Benni, I had to leave the room before *I* threw up!"

I nodded sympathetically, giving up my plan to have Boo stay over. It looked like Emory already had his hands full.

"So," I said, when he stopped to catch his breath. "Are you guys coming out to the ranch today? I know Kathryn would love to meet you."

"I'll have to ask the admiral. It depends on how the smell of barbecuing meat is affecting her these days." He leaned closer to me. "Tell me, does it get any better?"

I shrugged. "Emory, you're asking the wrong person. Remember, I've never been . . . never had a baby."

I almost said I'd never been pregnant, something that wasn't entirely true. Once, during my first marriage to Jack, I'd been pregnant, for two months. We were so excited, had lain in the dark at night watching the shadows dance across the ceiling and discussed names, wondered what it would be like to be parents, talked about the whole amazing thing of our genetics mixing to make another human being. We didn't tell anyone, and when I lost the baby, we were glad we hadn't. It was something that happened so long ago, I felt sad but distant from it. Like my life with Jack often felt, it was like the incident happened to another person.

Emory's face grew concerned. "Is this . . . is us having a baby . . . are you . . . ?" His face flushed pink as he struggled to articulate his feelings.

I reached over and placed my hand on my cousin's forearm. "I'm fine, Emory. I'm so happy for you and Elvia. I don't know if it's in the cards for me and Gabe to have children and, you know, I'm surprisingly okay with that."

As I said the words to him, I knew them to be true. It was something I'd thought a lot about, prayed about, something I'd only talked to Gabe about, this strange but certain feeling that if we never had children, I would be fine. Though we did nothing to prevent it, I had no intention of going through the barrage of tests and infertility treatments other people choose to go through. I just couldn't stand the thought of all the poking and prodding, the loss of privacy. Maybe I just didn't want a baby badly enough. I loved other people's babies, just didn't feel this overwhelming urge for one myself. Did that make me a horrible person, an emotionally sick person like some would say? I didn't think so. What was so great was Gabe didn't think so either. One of the things I loved the most about him was he didn't find it odd, didn't say *I* was odd, for feeling the way I did.

"No one knows your own heart better than you, *querida*," he'd said, the last time we talked about it. "And, children or no, I will love you till I die."

"Good," Emory said, obviously relieved. "I've been wanting to say something. Elvia too. We just didn't know how to bring it up."

"You nut. I can't believe you've worried about this. It's me, Benni, your best friend. Elvia's best friend. I mean, what more could a girl ask for than her two best friends marrying each other and having a baby? I feel like little *niño* or *niña* Aragon-Littleton is partly my baby too."

"We want you and Gabe to be godparents."

"I'd punch your lights out if you asked anyone else." I stood up and scratched Boo under the chin. "Could you watch him for a few more minutes? I want to say hi to Elvia. Then I need to get out to the ranch and help Dove."

"Sure, I'll watch the pup."

Inside, I found Elvia in her clothes room again, tossing pants left and right, leaving them in blue, gray and tan piles around the shiny wooden floor. I groaned inwardly. Another clothing meltdown.

"Need any help?" A pair of navy wool slacks flew past me.

"I have *nothing* to wear to the ranch." She glared at her reflection in the mirror. She was wearing a beautiful gray silky nightgown with matching robe, trimmed in ecru lace. I could see her little baby mound under the thin fabric.

"Just wear one of your baggier dresses. You'll be inside the house all day anyway. It's not like you'll be rustling any cattle."

She closed her eyes and, I was guessing, said Hail Marys or whatever it is Catholics pray when they are upset. Maybe it was like that oh-so-common Baptist prayer: Grant me patience, Lord, and give it to me right now!

Elvia opened her eyes and took a deep breath. "Tomorrow. Two o'clock. Meet me in my office. We're going shopping."

I knew better than to argue with her. I didn't mention that I'd be virtually no help when it came to shopping, seeing as I did most of my own clothes shopping at the Farm Supply or with a Cabela's or L.L.Bean catalog. I'd go along for emotional support, to hold her handbag and water bottle, to tell her everything looked great. "Okay, just wanted to see how you were doing. Kathryn's looking forward to meeting you."

Elvia turned around to look at me, her makeup-free face concerned. "How's her visit going?"

"Up and down. You can hear the details from Emory, but I think that Gabe and his mama have a lot of things they need to get off their respective chests. Unlike my crazy Southern family who, except for Daddy, believes that no emotion or opinion, no matter how trivial, is worth keeping to yourself, Gabe and Kathryn are being consummate, good-mannered Midwesterners. They pretend like nothing is wrong except when they are shooting invisible arrows at each other's backs."

For the first time in weeks, I saw Elvia smile. "Do you think a confrontation is coming?"

"Probably not, though I think one would certainly clear the air and help everyone feel better. I think they'll just snipe back and forth and Kathryn will go home and life will get back to normal." I leaned against her eggshell-colored wall. "Frankly, I was hoping her visit would make him feel better, maybe help him open up some. Since his cousin was killed, he's been so wound up. It worries me."

Gabe's cousin Luis had sadly initiated a hostage situation that resulted in his death. There were suspicions that it was suicide, *suicide by cop* was the term, and Gabe felt responsible for his cousin's death, even though it appeared that Luis knew exactly what he was doing. Gabe and I had danced around the subject, with me willing to talk and him avoiding it. Typical of our relationship.

"You were traumatized too," she said, reaching over to touch my cheek. Elvia was normally not a very demonstrative person, but since being pregnant and me being held hostage, she'd taken to touching, hugging, even kissing cheeks occasionally.

"I'm doing fine. I've talked to Pastor Mac about it and the Big Guy upstairs. And I have Dove. And you and Emory. See, I have lots of support."

"We're there for Gabe too," Elvia said.

"I know, but we aren't his family. I mean, his blood family. He can barely speak to *me* about it. I was hoping that he could talk to his mother. If he doesn't, once she leaves, I'm going to try to get him to see someone."

"Gabe talk to a psychiatrist?" Elvia gave a soft, unbelieving laugh. "That is almost as hard to imagine as my own papa going to one."

"Yeah, I know," I said wryly. "But there's always Father Mark. He has a degree in psychology, so it's sort of the same thing, or maybe Mac. He really likes Mac."

She impulsively hugged me, enveloping me in her . . . Jean Naté?

I pulled back, aghast. "Is that Jean Naté cologne you're wearing?" My label-conscious friend would never be caught dead wearing that traditional drugstore cologne of grammas and great-aunts everywhere. Ralph Lauren and Armani were more her style.

"I know, I know," she moaned. "It's the only scent that doesn't make me throw up. I've had to ask Emory to stop wearing cologne completely. All his colognes make me gag."

"Boy, will you have a lot to hold over this child's head someday," I said, laughing. "And that doesn't even count labor."

She laughed too, and the rosy bloom in my best friend's cheeks, her obvious happiness, made my heart hurt with gladness.

"I gotta hit the road," I said. "This will be my last fun day for the next week. I've got a full schedule including my fake investigation, and Boo isn't going to make things any easier."

"Fake investigation?" Elvia's face was confused. "Boo?"

"I guess I haven't talked to you since *so* much in my life has changed. Follow me downstairs, and I'll introduce you to my new godson."

"Your what? Who had a baby? Who names their baby Boo?"

While she cooed and got all maternal over my foster puppy, again shocking me, this woman who loved pictures of baby animals more than the real thing, I filled her in on how he came into my life and what Constance was asking me to do. Emory excused himself to go inside to start dressing for the barbecue.

"Gabe actually *asked* you to investigate?" she asked, her black eyebrows raised in perfect sideways commas.

"Pretend to investigate," I corrected. "As much as it sounds like a blast to someone as nosy as me, it's turning into a big pain in the butt. I do feel sorry for Constance. I'd go completely bonkers if I lost either of my best friends." I smiled at her as she cuddled Boo in her arms. "But I really don't think Pinky Edmondson was murdered."

"Pinky Edmondson was one of my best customers. She probably spent five hundred dollars a month on books."

"Wow," I said. My investigator antenna immediately perked up. "I don't suppose you keep records of what your customers buy."

"No, I don't, but I'll tell you what she bought since I can't imagine that it would matter much. They were mostly art books."

"No surprise there," I said. "She loved art and was a very generous sponsor of the folk art museum." I took Boo from a surprisingly reluctant Elvia. "See you at the ranch."

The day ended up being a pleasant one. Again, Gabe didn't speak to Ray, but Daddy and Isaac took up the slack and entertained Ray. Isaac, an internationally renowned photographer who swore he was retired, was already making tentative plans to join Ray on a train trip from an engineer's front seat point of view. Though retired, Ray still had many connections with the railroad and said he'd be more than happy to help Isaac with this new project.

The food, as always, was superb. Daddy and Sam, Gabe's son, barbecued tri-tip steak and chicken. Spicy pinquito beans, homemade salsa, sourdough garlic bread and green salad rounded out our Santa Maria–style barbecue, the traditional meal served at rancheros back in the time when California was still a part of Mexico. Of course, Dove added her own Southern touches with sweet potato casserole, pecan pie and fried green tomatoes, a particular favorite of Gabe's.

Boo was in heaven because Daddy's sable and white corgi, Spud, from an earlier litter sired by Boo's own daddy, was willing and ready to dart around the house playing catch-me-if-you-can corgi games. Scout, appearing relieved that his high-energy young charge was temporarily occupied, settled down for a nap in front of the family room fire. I sat next to him and gave him a well-deserved neck massage and ear rub.

Later on, when the day was starting to wind down and everyone had, at Dove's urging, gone out to the front porch to watch the crimson and gold sunset, I took that time to sneak back into the family room for a little peace and quiet. Spud was out in the barn with my dad, who was feeding some pregnant heifers. Boo was exhausted, lying next to Scout, his little black nose tucked into Scout's warm neck. I worried briefly that the dogs were getting too attached to each other. How would they react when Hud came back and took Boo home? That modern phrase, *doggie play date*, started running uneasily through my head.

"What's going on in that evil little mind of yours?" asked Emory, flopping down beside me on the leather sofa, cradling a white bowl holding a huge piece of pecan pie topped with vanilla bean ice cream.

"Keep eating like that, cousin dear, and your son or daughter will be calling you Big Daddy Littleton."

He stuck his spoon deep into the bowl and smiled at me. "Then share it with me, and tell Big Daddy what's got you looking so worried."

I looked at him in mock horror. "I meant that Big Daddy as a joke. I will not call you that. It's a little too *Splendor in the Grass*."

"I think you mean *Cat on a Hot Tin Roof*, but go ahead, what's up?" He spooned a bite of pie and ice cream into his mouth, then offered me the bowl.

Before I could answer, Ray and Kathryn walked into the den.

"Your sunsets out here are almost as pretty as the ones in Kansas," Ray said, teasing me. They sat down across from us on a matching sofa.

"Oh, Ray," Kathryn said, playfully squeezing his upper arm.

"You're right," I agreed. "There is nothing like a Kansas sunset. It's probably something about the reflection off those amber waves of grain."

At that moment, Gabe walked into the room. "Hey, Mom, want a piece of Dove's pecan pie? There's peach too."

It fascinated me to watch my husband talk to his

mother. There were moments when his manner and voice reverted to a much younger Gabe, when he spoke with almost a teenager's teasing tone.

"No, thank you, Gabe," she said, smiling. "I'm so full I could burst." She looked over at the pie and ice cream Emory and I were sharing. "Although that does look very good."

"It is," I said around a mouthful of pie.

She smiled. "Maybe just a little then . . ."

"Gabe, sit down with your mother," Ray said, jumping up and motioning his long-fingered hand at his place on the sofa. "I'll get you both some. Peach or pecan? À la mode or straight up?"

Gabe didn't turn his head, deliberately ignoring Ray's offer. He continued looking at his mother. She glanced at Ray, then back at her son.

"Mom, would you like me to get you some pie?" Gabe asked again.

"Not now, son," she said, obviously deciding that the whole pie issue was becoming a bit too fraught with emotion.

I glanced over at Emory, who raised one eyebrow a fraction of an inch.

"Suit yourself," Gabe said. "I think I'll go back out on the porch." IIe left the room without a backward glance.

I stared after my husband, debating whether I should run after him and whup him upside the head like he deserved or wait and give him what-for later.

Gabe's mother, her long, pale face tinted a soft pink now, gave Ray an uneasy glance. Then she rose slowly, faltering a moment. Ray caught her elbow and steadied her.

"You're tired," he said, his deep voice gentle.

"Yes." She closed her eyes slowly, leaving them shut for a moment, as if she were gathering strength. "Maybe we should head back home."

"Sit back down and wait here. Let me get your sweater," I said, standing up. Before they could protest, I was out of the room.

After finding Kathryn's sweater, I went into the kitchen to tell Dove that Kathryn and Ray were leaving. She was cutting another pie. I'd already decided that I was going to drive them home in Gabe's car. That seemed the best thing for everyone right now.

"I'm driving Kathryn and Ray home," I said, going over to hug her. "She's kind of tired. Thanks for another great meal."

"Is she okay?" Dove asked.

"I think so. Gabe's been acting like an adolescent around her every time Ray comes into the room, so maybe it's starting to wear on her. Honestly, I'm about ready to smack him silly."

Dove just smiled to herself and kept cutting slices of peach pie.

"I know, I know," I said, bumping her with my hip. "I was just as bad when you were dating Isaac. But he should have learned from my mistakes."

"You know it doesn't work like that. Don't worry, Gabe and his mama will work this out."

"I suppose," I said, leaning against the tiled countertop. I reached over, snatched a piece of flaky piecrust and popped it into my mouth.

"Maybe not as quickly as we did," Dove continued.

"And likely not in the same way we did. But they'll work it out in a way that suits them. Those two have a lot of sad history they've not yet resolved. Might have been wiser if they'd taken care of it before she remarried. Then again, it might not have been addressed at all without this change in their relationship." She took the empty pie tin and placed it in the sink behind her. "Sometimes you need a little rhubarb with your strawberry to give it snap."

"In other words, strawberry-rhubarb pie."

Dove turned and smiled at me. "Always a crowd pleaser."

"And Gabe's favorite," I added. "I'm going out to tell him that I think I should drive his mom and stepfather home and he should drive home in the truck with the dogs. Wish me luck."

"You don't need luck," she said. "You need an armored car."

I laughed uneasily. She was kidding, but she also knew Gabe. "If I'm not back in five minutes, call the police. No, wait, that won't help."

She handed me a piece of peach pie. "Here, take this to Gabe before you leave. Manna to soothe the savage beast."

Gabe wasn't on the porch with Elvia, Sam, Sam's girlfriend Teresa and Isaac.

"I think he went to the barn," said Sam.

I actually found him in the backyard, sitting on a wooden Adirondack chair staring out at the almost-dark hills. He was barely illuminated by the sliver of light coming from the barn fifty yards away where I could hear Daddy talking to Spud.

"Hey, Friday," I said, placing the pie down on the table beside him. I perched on the chair's wide arm and rested my hand on his shoulder. I tried to make my voice light and casual. "Your mama's getting kinda tired, so I told them I'd take them home. You can come later and bring the dogs." I gently ran my fingers through his thick, citrus-scented hair.

He didn't answer. After a minute or so, I said, "Want to give me your car keys?"

He reached into the pocket of his jeans and held them up to me, continuing his thousand-yard stare.

"Gabe," I said, taking the keys. "I don't mean to interfere—"

"Then don't," he said, cutting me off.

I fingered the keys in my hand, trying to maintain my composure. "Okay, I do mean to interfere. You're acting like a big baby. Why don't you cut Ray and your mother some slack?"

"Why don't you just take my mother and her husband home and leave it at that?"

I gave an audible sigh, hoping that would influence his cranky mood. Not to my surprise, it didn't help. It would do no good to argue with him. But I also knew if this kept up, he and I were headed for a blowup even if he and his mother didn't have one.

Kathryn and Ray didn't question why I was driving them home rather than Gabe. It was pretty obvious that he was in a snit. I had to admit, as much as I loved my husband, I was a bit embarrassed by his childish behavior, not that I should be throwing stones. I'd be the first to admit that. Dove was right. Sometimes things just had to play themselves out.

Pleading fatigue, Kathryn and Ray excused themselves the minute we got home. It was about seven thirty. My mother-in-law did look tired and, it seemed to me, a bit hopeless. I felt sad for her and Gabe. Her marriage didn't have to be such a painful thing. In reality, Gabe should have been glad his mother had found love again, that she would not spend the remainder of her life alone. It was complex, the mother-son relationship, a warp-woof of emotions that made up the fabric of their connected lives. Even with someone as open as Dove, there were times when communication between her and Daddy either broke down or became intricately knotted, and they had barely been able to speak to each other.

Gabe came home about an hour later. While changing for bed, we talked of minor things, what the weather was supposed to be like tomorrow, when we would get our Christmas tree.

"I can go by Wingfield's Christmas Tree Farm tomorrow and buy one," I said. "We could have a small decorating party, maybe invite Beebs and Millee and Emory and Elvia. That would be fun."

"Whatever," he said, sounding like a petulant teenager.

"I still haven't found a present for your mom yet. And I need to get something for Ray. Not to mention buying them a wedding present."

"Why?" He pulled off his sweatshirt and threw it on the floor, an action that was so unlike my Marine Corps–trained, neat-as-new-shoes husband that I just stared at him, openmouthed.

"That's enough," I finally said. "I'm trying to be understanding here, but you are acting like a spoiled brat."

"Get him whatever you want," he said, going into the bathroom and turning on the shower. "Buy him a new car. Shoot, give him the house. I don't give a shit." Then he shut the bathroom door.

I stared at the door for a moment, tempted to fling it open and let him have the full brunt of my temper. *Let it go*, a voice inside me whispered, sounding suspiciously like Dove's. *Let him work this out on his own.*

So I heeded the voice and didn't say a thing when Gabe walked out of the steamy bathroom. I took my own shower, carried Boo downstairs for one last outside break before our two a.m. rendezvous and joined Gabe in bed. We kissed, and I touched his cheek with the tips of my fingers, looking deep into his turbulent-ocean eyes.

"I love you, Friday," I said.

"Te querido," he answered, looking so sad I felt like crying.

"Are you okay?"

"Sure." He kissed me again, then turned over. "See you mañana."

I lay awake in the dark a long time, listening to his breathing slow down and finally settle into the even rhythm that meant he was asleep. I wanted to help him through this, but I didn't know how, didn't know what he needed. Maybe *I'd* go see Father Mark tomorrow. He seemed to understand Gabe better than anyone. Surely he'd have some words of wisdom for me.

The alarm went off at two a.m., waking both Gabe and me.

"Puppy run," I whispered, patting the growling bulldog tattoo on Gabe's warm back.

"Mmmm," he murmured and went back to sleep.

I pulled on my cashmere robe, opened Boo's crate and pulled a reluctant, sleepy puppy out. His little body was toasty as a freshly baked muffin, and his yawn ended with a little squeak.

"I know, Doodleboo," I said, carrying him downstairs. "This is a drag, but your little bladder can't make it through the night. We don't want you to pee in your crate."

After he was done, we were coming back through the kitchen, lit only by the automatic nightlight, when I ran into Ray, who was filling a mug of water from the tap. He was dressed in plaid flannel pajamas and a dark blue robe.

"Oh, hi," I said, surprised. "We have bottled water if you'd prefer it."

"This is fine," he said. "I'm making some herbal tea for Kathryn." On his long face, the foothills of his wrinkles were shadowed in the semidarkness. "She's having a little . . . insomnia."

"Is she okay?" There was something in his voice, a hesitation, a split-second break, that made me ask again. "Ray, is Kathryn all right?"

He turned his back to me and carefully placed the mug in the microwave. "Yes, Benni, she is. For now."

CHAPTER 9

*O*F COURSE I WANTED TO PRESS RAY FOR MORE EXPLA-
nation, but this moment wasn't the time for it. Was
something going on with Kathryn, something she was not
telling her son, and Ray was subtly letting me know?

"See you tomorrow," I just replied and carried Boo
back up to bed. Whatever it was, surely it had to come out
before she went home. At least I hoped so. I said a quick
prayer that it wasn't something serious.

The next morning, the sun shining through our pale
curtains woke me with a jolt. I sat up, panicked. I'd slept
right through Boo's early morning bathroom break. I
looked over at his open kennel and gave a sigh of relief.
Obviously Gabe covered for me and let me sleep.

Downstairs everyone was already having breakfast

and perusing the Monday edition of the *San Celina Tribune*.

"Boo's eaten, and I took him outside," Gabe said, pouring me a glass of orange juice. He was dressed for work in a white shirt, red and gray houndstooth tie and gray Brooks Brothers suit. "Mom is going to hang out at the house today. You said something about getting our Christmas tree? We'll decorate it tonight?"

"Uh, yeah, I guess." I glanced around at the domestic picture of Gabe, his mother, her new husband and the two dogs. Everyone seemed satisfied and happy. Kathryn sipped her tea, tidy and pink-cheeked. Ray smiled and gave me a little salute. The dogs chewed merrily on their pressed rawhide bones. Had I imagined the tiff between Kathryn and Gabe yesterday at the ranch? Had I imagined Ray's weary, sad voice earlier this morning?

"I need to work on my speech about Abe Adam Finch and outsider art," I said, pouring myself a cup of coffee. "I'll be at the folk art museum most of the morning. Then I'm going maternity clothes shopping with Elvia."

"What shall we do for dinner?" Gabe asked, fixing me a bowl of oatmeal and handing me the brown sugar box, knowing that I'll only eat it with lots of sugar and melted butter.

"Let me prepare supper," Kathryn said.

"Oh, no, I couldn't—" I started.

"Great idea," Ray said. "You have a full day, Benni, so this is how we can help. Besides, I'm sure Gabe would love to eat some of his mom's home cooking. That is, if you don't mind?"

"I'm always up for anyone cooking but me," I said, smiling at him. Cooking was not an arena where I worried about competing with Gabe's mother. I glanced over at Kathryn. "Gabe has been pining for your chicken verde."

Kathryn's thin mouth turned up at the corners, pleased by my remark.

"Chicken verde it is," she said. "You mentioned something about inviting your friends over to decorate the tree?"

"I thought we'd ask Beebs and Millee across the street. They don't have any family, so they've kind of adopted me and Gabe. And I'll ask Elvia and Emory and Dove, Isaac and Daddy. And, of course, Sam and Teresa."

Kathryn nodded. "Let's invite them to supper, too. It's been a long time since I've cooked for a crowd. My daughters like to do that now. Is there a grocery store within walking distance?"

"No, but there's Dad's truck," Gabe said. "The keys are on a hook in the hallway."

"I'll make a list and send Ray," his mother said.

Though I should have felt guilty, I didn't. With the outsider art exhibit opening Wednesday night, only two days away, I had a million things to do. The most important was writing my speech. I wanted to go over and hug her, though we hadn't gotten to that point in our relationship. Instead I said, "Thank you, Kathryn and Ray, from the bottom of my overly committed heart. You don't have to worry about Boo, I'll drop him off at day care. And Scout won't bother you at all."

"Then everything's set," she said, clasping her hands

together, her face looking relaxed for the first time since she arrived. "It'll be nice to be busy."

After I finished my breakfast, I walked Gabe out to the car. "I'll come by and pick up the painting today. We need to get it hung. I think D-Daddy has the alarm situation under control."

"It's in my office closet," Gabe said. "If I'm not there, ask Maggie for the key."

I kissed him quickly, touched his smooth, cool cheek. "You doing all right?"

He gave me a perplexed look and opened his car door. "Of course, why wouldn't I be?"

I just shook my head. "See you tonight."

Within the hour, I was dressed, had dropped Boo off and was in my office at the folk art museum, my books and articles on outsider art spread across my desk. Mondays were always quiet. It was the only day the museum was closed. The artists' studios were open, but not many people were working. I could hear a distant buzz coming from the woodworking room and some muffled conversation from the large room where the quilters and weavers met. I'd run into D-Daddy coming through the museum where he was painting some trim in back of the main gallery.

"Alarm people gave us the all clear," he said. "We're ready to rock and roll." He grinned at me, his bright blue eyes lively under his thick, white pompadour.

"Rock and roll?" I said, laughing. "You've been hanging around the young folks again?"

He gave me a mischievous look. "Not young people. People your age. *Young* people, they rap and roll."

171

"Ouch. Don't remind me. If anyone needs me, this old fogey will be in her office working on her speech. I can't believe we're opening on Wednesday."

"We'll be ready," he said.

"I know you'll be." I wasn't so sure about me.

"Constance already called twice today," he called after me. "I told her I didn't know when you'd be comin' in."

"Bless you," I called back.

I was determined to avoid Constance until I finished my speech. This obsession with Pinky's death was taking up too much of my time. I'd done my due diligence and "investigated." The next time we talked I vowed to put my foot down and tell Constance she needed to let her friend rest in peace.

❖

MY MAJOR AT CAL POLY SAN CELINA HAD BEEN HISTORY, so I always looked forward to the research aspect of my job. My special love had always been oral history, specifically the history of everyday people. It had always intrigued me more than the exploits and accomplishments of the famous. Outsider art was essentially the oral history equivalent in the art world. Whether it be quilts or woodcarving or weaving or pottery, it was the art of the average man and woman.

I looked through my extensive notes and flipped through the dozen or so books I'd ordered from Elvia about folk and outsider art. The area was larger than most people realized, encompassing a vast number of regions and cultures. And that was just in the United States. Folk art from other countries was a whole other, incredible world. I couldn't even begin to delve into that with this speech. I would have to restrict myself to the United States.

One of the amazing things about folk art was how a figure carved by an unschooled black man in rural Alabama was so similar to carvings found in nineteenth-century Africa. The same with quilt designs from an elderly white woman in the hills of West Virginia and the obvious pattern influence of her ancient Celtic relative two hundred years before. Had these patterns and skills been passed down through the generations? Many scholars thought it possible.

How to start? I tapped my pencil on my blank tablet for about ten minutes before deciding to just dive in. Usually, once I started writing, it came easier.

"Outsider art. What is it exactly? We might ask, what is it outside of? Who is the insider? Who came up with the term anyway?"

I put my pencil down. That sounded awful. Like something a middle school kid would write. I leaned back in my chair and stared at the ceiling. Maybe I should start with Abe Adam Finch's biography and then delve into the definition of *outsider*.

I dug out the three articles I'd found written about him. A couple of the articles speculated that he suffered from a form of agoraphobia, but it was just that, speculation. It was believed he lived somewhere in Nevada because all of his communication was done through his niece, Nola Maxwell Finch, who, before she moved to San Celina, lived in Las Vegas. All requests for face-to-face interviews were refused, though he had been known to answer questions through the mail. There was only one small photo of him, taken in profile, backlit so that his features weren't distinguishable. He appeared to be extremely thin, with a hawkish nose. In both photos he wore a fedora-style hat pulled down over his eyebrows.

"Abe Adam Finch," I wrote. "He was born in 1929, the same year the stock market fell, though he said the event didn't really affect his family, since they were already poor. He was the middle of nine children, the son of a cotton sharecropper in Mississippi. As soon as he could walk, he picked cotton, took care of cows and chickens, baled hay. He went to a local one-room schoolhouse when he could but never made it past sixth grade. He remembers liking school, especially when the teacher allowed him to sit in the back and 'draw his pictures.' He felt compelled to draw and paint from his earliest memory. In 1946, when he was seventeen, he left home, hitchhiking around the country. World War II had just ended, and the economy was starting to boom. He worked throughout the West at a large variety of manual labor jobs digging ditches, hauling bricks, laying pipe, trimming trees.

" 'I was always the one helping,' he answered one journalist's questions. 'Never the man in charge. That was okay by me. I tended to daydream a bit. My pictures, they were talking to me in my head and telling me how to paint 'em.' An unfortunate accident at a lumberyard in Oregon blinded him in one eye. He credits that incident with forcing him to start painting seriously. 'I don't know,' he said. 'Maybe it just come to me when that wood chip took my eye that life is short. You got to go where your heart leads while it is still beating. I just love to paint my trees.'

"He burst into the art world ten years ago, coming virtually from nowhere, it seemed, when Lionel Bachman, a San Francisco art collector, saw one of his paintings in a souvenir shop in Las Vegas. Critics have praised Mr. Finch's work for its use of vibrant, often unpredictable color combinations, its childlike energy and its celebration of the relationship between the animal and human world. Various critics have said his work shows an almost obsessive energy, an unpolished directness that, one critic noted, made him sense that Abe Adam Finch might well be an artistic savant."

What did the critic mean by that? That Mr. Finch was, somehow, mentally challenged? Was that the reason his niece protected his privacy so diligently? In the few places where he was quoted from questions mailed to him from journalists, he sounded like anyone else. Then again, anyone, including his niece, could have written out the answers to those questions.

I stood up and stretched. It really didn't matter. What I had ferreted out about him seemed like enough background for my talk. Most of it I took from his official biography. The articles I'd found all told the same story, gave the same quotes and then were filled in with the art journalist's critique of Abe Adam's work, speculation about why he was a recluse and sometimes their own adventures in hunting him down. All efforts to find him eventually came to a dead end. They commented on the friendliness of Nola Maxwell Finch, but her absolute dedication to keeping the public, especially journalists, away from her reclusive uncle. I contemplated calling her and asking if she could add a little something to his biography, something that would make the journalist coming from the *L.A. Times* actually write an article longer than two sentences.

As quickly as I considered it, I discarded that thought. We were lucky enough to be given this painting. I was sure she wouldn't appreciate yet another person wanting a little something more about her uncle.

I sat back down. Okay, I had the part about him ready. Now I had to get my own talk about outsider art done. I glanced at my watch. It was already ten a.m. I picked up the phone and called Elvia at the bookstore.

"Hey, little mama, ready to do some shopping?" I had to finish this speech, but right now even clothes shopping, something I didn't particularly enjoy, seemed more appealing.

"What are you trying to avoid?" Elvia asked, knowing me too well.

I groaned dramatically. "I'm trying to write my speech for the exhibit opening this Wednesday night, and everything I write sounds stupid."

"What's the problem? You've given talks before. What's so different about this one?"

I sighed, leaned back in my chair. "Nothing. I think I'm just sleep-deprived and worried about Gabe and his mother. I think there's something going on in her life."

"Like what?"

"I don't know. Ray is acting kind of strange." I told her his cryptic remark last night.

"That does sound like he's trying to tell you something. Why don't you just ask him if there's something wrong?"

"I've thought of that, but my big fear is he'll tell me. Then I'll have to make the decision about whether I should tell Gabe or let his mother tell him."

"Gabe hasn't noticed anything strange?"

I sighed. "I think Gabe is too busy throwing a pity party for himself because someone's taking his papa's place." Then I felt guilty for my snide remark. "Oh, strike that last comment. I know Gabe is going through a tough time trying to get over his cousin's death. This anger over the change with his mother's life is just a symptom. I'm going to see Father Mark, see if he can talk to Gabe."

"Or you could step back," Elvia said. "Let him deal with it when he is ready."

"Easy for you to say," I replied, cranky that she was echoing what Dove suggested. "You don't have to live right in the middle of this little drama."

She was wisely silent, obviously realizing that I didn't actually want advice but someone to listen to my whining.

"Look," she said. "I'm going to be the best friend I can and tell you we'll go shopping at one p.m. *after* you've finished your speech. You'll be much happier once you get it done. Just pretend it's a term paper."

"That doesn't help," I moaned.

"Get to work. Meet me at the store at one." Then she hung up.

"Nyah, nyah, nyah," I said to the buzzing dial tone. But she was right. I would be happier if I could mark this off my to-do list. Before I went back to my speech, I called

Beebs and Millee to invite them over for supper and tree-trimming.

"That sounds delightful," Beebs said. "What shall we bring?"

"This time, do not bring a thing. Kathryn wants to do it all."

"In that case, we'll just bring our hungry appetites."

"Always appreciated at a dinner party," I agreed.

I marked them off my list. Then I called Dove. "Hey, Gramma, what's cookin'?"

"Apple butter," she said.

"Yum. Are you busy for dinner? We're having an impromptu tree trimming supper tonight."

"Wish I could, but I have an emergency knitting club meeting."

I laughed. "What kind of emergency could a knitting club have?"

"Christmas stockings for foster kids. We were supposed to have a hundred stockings knitted, and there's only seventy-three. Emergency knit-in at Thelma's house tonight."

"Okay, I'll let you off the hook."

"Har, har," Dove said. "That would be funny if we were crocheting, not knitting."

"Kathryn's cooking, but I'll tell her you have a good excuse."

"Sorry to miss that. Tell her I'll see her Wednesday night at your museum shindig."

"Is Sam there?"

"Nope, he left early this morning. Got to get back to my apples. Over and out."

"A big ten-four, good buddy."

I hoped no one ever overheard my conversations with my gramma.

I hung up the phone and contemplated calling around to the possible four or five places Sam might be. No, that would have to take a backseat to finishing my speech. He usually worked two or three afternoons at Blind Harry's. I'd call there as soon as I finished.

I set aside my list and looked back at my half-written speech. "Oh, just get to it," I murmured and started writing.

"Outsider art is the latest label given to works of art made by non-mainstream, untrained and, until recently, unexhibited artists. It has been referred to throughout art history as folk art, self-taught art, visionary art, naive art, primitive art, intuitive art and even by the somewhat snooty-sounding term art brut." I crossed out *snooty-sounding* and inserted *academic*. Snooty-sounding seemed more accurate to me, but I didn't want to alienate part of my audience . . . at least not with my first paragraph.

"Originally, the creation of outsider art tended to be for the purposes of recording memories or made for use, such as quilts made for warmth rather than decoration, or were the revelations or expounding of religious stories and beliefs. Today's outsider art is broader. Like mainstream art, it often portrays the artist's very personal feelings about politics, consumer culture, racism, the war between social or economic classes and environmentalism, but the lines between art made to be used—craft and design—and art made to be contemplated—painting, drawing and sculpture—become blurred within the outsider art world. The art establishment and the public have been forced to consider the term *outsider* and what it implies. We might ask, outside compared to what? Is high art or fine art necessarily more *inside*, implying superior? One distinction between outsider and mainstream art has always been the economic, social or intellectual status of the artists themselves. Outsider art has often been thought of as the 'art born of adversity,' where the artist's poverty, illiteracy, incarceration or mental illness becomes as much a part of the 'outsiderness' as the art itself."

"Outsiderness?" I said out loud. "Is that even a word?"

"Sounds good to me," a voice replied, startling me.

I jerked my head around to stare at the person in the doorway, embarrassed to be caught talking to myself. When I saw it was Nola Maxwell Finch, I was absolutely mortified.

"I'm sorry," I said, standing up, my cheeks hot as a chili pepper. "I didn't think anyone was around. I'm—"

She waved her hand at me to sit back down. "Oh, no, the apology should be mine. I shouldn't have interrupted you. Mr. Boudreaux said I could find you back here."

"No, it's fine, really. I'm just working on this Wednesday's speech. Please, come in and sit down. Is there something I can do for you?"

She stepped into my office, a serene smile on her face. She wore crisply pressed black slacks and a tan turtleneck sweater. I caught a light scent of exotic flowers. She sat down in the visitor's chair and crossed her legs in a smooth, elegant gesture. "I was hoping to see where Uncle Abe's painting would be displayed."

"Absolutely," I said, sitting back down. "But the painting isn't actually here right now." The alarmed look on her face caused me to add quickly, "Don't worry, it's at a place safer than Fort Knox. It's in my husband's office at work. He's San Celina's police chief."

Her expression became calm again. "I suppose that's about as well protected as it will ever be."

I laughed nervously. "Our alarm system was being fixed. I was given the all clear this morning. I'm picking up the painting myself this afternoon. I can, however, show you where it will hang."

"That would be lovely," she said.

Sun dappled our faces as we walked under the vine-covered breezeway that led from the co-op buildings. We chatted about the cool, sunny weather we'd been having.

"I have to admit, the Central Coast's beautiful weather is what convinced me to settle down here," Nola said, turning her face up to the sun. "It was getting so crowded and smoggy in Las Vegas. Tell me, do you ever have any bad weather here?"

"Not what others across the country would call bad weather. If it rains three or four days in a row, it is the lead story on the local news. And if there's even a hint of humidity in the summer, people whine as if we lived in the tropics." I gave a rueful laugh. "I'm almost embarrassed to tell you that. My dad calls the Central Coast bovine heaven."

"People heaven too, then," she said.

"Yes, it is hard to beat, weather-wise." I glanced over at her, curiosity getting the better of me. "Will your uncle be moving here also?"

She didn't seem ruffled by my question, obviously accustomed to curiosity about her uncle. "I doubt it. He's happy where he is. His neighbors know him and take care of him. And he's not that far from me."

I noticed she never said exactly where he was. "You're his only family?" I asked, opening the heavy back door to the museum, gesturing at her to go ahead of me.

She nodded and gave a small sigh. "Yes." Her pale blue eyes looked over my shoulder, as if seeing something behind me, something that troubled her. "He's getting so frail. I'm not sure how much longer he'll be able to keep painting." She looked back at me, staring right into my eyes. "Though this is not for public consumption, I'll be honest with you, his arthritis is starting to really affect him, especially his hands."

"Oh, I'm sorry," I said, feeling flattered that she'd confide in me.

She brushed at imaginary lint on her sweater. "Well, he is getting up there in years. I think it is starting to show in his work, and I can't help but wonder if I should subtly let it be known that he is having physical problems so that when the tone of his work changes, people don't start gossiping. Also, we've had one case of a forgery, so if his signature changes slightly, I don't want people to wonder."

"A forgery? That's terrible."

She nodded. "Yes, but with many of his paintings going for almost thirty thousand dollars now, it was to be expected. People have the idea that it would be easy to forge a primitive painter like Uncle Abe. The one who was caught trying to sell one to a gallery in Santa Fe did a fairly good job mimicking my uncle's style, but he didn't do his homework. This particular gallery had a buyer who was very familiar with my uncle's painting and saw a subtle variance in the signature that tipped him off."

"Wow, lucky break for your uncle."

She folded her arms across her chest. "Yes, it was. Besides that, we have to worry about the art critics who can make or break even outsider artists these days. In that way the outsider art world has become just as political as the mainstream art world. Certain critics are biased. Collectors, unfortunately, listen."

I contemplated her statement before answering. She had a point. Art critics could be brutal, especially once you'd become one of their darlings. Some critics seemed to take an inordinate amount of pleasure and energy tearing down the artists they themselves had taken years to champion and build up. "If it helps, there is the *L.A. Times* reporter coming to the exhibit opening this Wednesday."

I wouldn't tell her what she should or shouldn't do, but if she wanted the world to know about Abe Adam Finch's physical problem, which might affect his work, an article in the *L.A. Times* was a pretty big platform.

She nodded, patting at her light red hair, though it didn't have a strand out of place. "That's something to consider."

When we reached the main gallery, I showed her where we'd be displaying her uncle's painting.

"Our security system is top-notch," I said. "And I can guarantee that any alarm that is set off here gets top priority with the police department."

"I imagine it would," she said, smiling. "It looks like a wonderful space. My uncle would be pleased and honored, I'm sure."

After assuring her it was we who were honored, I walked her out to the front of the museum to show her where his cards and prints were displayed for sale in our gift shop.

"They are also featured in the window of our new museum gift shop downtown."

"Yes, I saw it. Your window designer did a beautiful job."

"One of our new quilt artists works for Gottschalk's as a display designer. My friend Elvia owns Blind Harry's Bookstore down the street and always wins the holiday window display contests, but I think we might start giving her a run for the money."

Nola gave a cheerful laugh. "A little competition is good for the soul. Well, maybe not for the soul, but good for commerce."

"Which is good for all of us."

She nodded in agreement.

After she left, I continued work on my talk, finally finishing a first draft. I quickly typed it up on my laptop computer and printed it out to take home. I'd edit it one more time tonight after the tree-trimming party was over and everyone had gone to bed. I added some references to other famous outsider artists who critics had compared to Abe Adam Finch, such as memory painter Clementine Hunter, who depicted daily life such as picking cotton and river baptisms in the area of Melrose Plantation in Natchitoches, Louisiana, and Nellie Mae Rowe, whose colorful visionary drawings and paintings often had a surreal quality to them because she painted the faces of humans and animals unusual colors, red or blue or "whatever looked right" to her. She also made a few quilts in the style of her paintings and created some sculptures using the unusual medium of chewing gum that she painted. She created for "God's pleasure," she was often quoted. "Call Him up," she was quoted. "He'll hear you."

In personality, Abe Adam Finch was a lot like Joseph Elmer Yoakum, whose pastel drawings portrayed landscapes of places he'd visited or claimed to have visited. Mystery permeated Mr. Yoakum's work, something that he felt made his work more valuable. Though Abe Adam Finch was open with his past history but shy about meeting the public now, Mr. Yoakum was just the opposite. Before he died in 1972, he knew and influenced many now well-known artists who met him in the 1960s and 1970s while they were studying at the Art Institute of Chicago. But Mr. Yoakum liked to keep his past a mystery, claiming once that he was a black man, then another time, a full-blooded Navajo born on the reservation at Window Rock.

So, I thought, it is true sometimes that in outsider art, the biography of the artist is often so tied up in his work that it would be hard to distinguish the artist from his backstory. Then again, wasn't it like that in almost everything? Don't our backstories form who we are, actually *inform* who we are? It was true no matter who we were or what we did for a living. It was something I was seeing lived out right in front of me with Gabe and his mother. Their whole backstory was affecting what was happening between them this moment in their lives.

I sat back in my chair, contemplating how all of this was connected, the past and the present, and wondered if it was something I should even touch on in my talk. I decided to stick to the facts and not meander off into philosophy about the past.

I noted in the biography of Clementine Hunter that the quality of her paintings was uneven, that she had a tendency later in her life to repeat her earlier subject matter and that a collector could often tell a later work by the change in her signature. Her earlier, more original works were, naturally, more valuable.

Was that what Nola was worried about, that if her uncle's later work changed, it would not be as collectible?

I printed up what I'd written and stuck it in my leather backpack. I had a half hour to get to the bookstore, just enough time to call All Paws and see how my little Cajun sausage dog was doing.

"He's doing great," Suann said. "He peed on the grass for the first time!" The day care facility had little movable wooden boxes with squares of real grass for the dogs. I was amazed, wondering who in the world held the patent on that invention.

"Hud will be proud," I said. "Get a picture if you can."

Suann laughed. "He's called three times already, you know."

"Better you than me. I'll be back in a few hours."

As if by some kind of psychic radar, my cell phone rang before I could start my truck. The phone number that came up on the screen was Hud's.

"Speak of the devil," I said as I answered.

"Good afternoon to you too," Hud answered. "Talking about me?"

"I just called All Paws to check on Boo. You might have a difficult time wooing him away from Suann."

"How's he doing?"

"He's fine. I'm fine too, though exhausted. Those middle of the night bathroom runs are getting old. How's Texas?"

"Big. Grandmama Lilly's thrilled we're all here. Maisie's decided that she wants to be a cowgirl when she grows up."

"A fine ambition. You should start buying her a herd now. I have some nice-looking heifers I'm looking to sell."

"We'll see. Last week she wanted to be a fireman."

"Firefighter," I corrected.

"No, fireman," he said, laughing. "She said she was tired of being a girl and wanted to be a boy now."

"Yeah, I went through that. She'll eventually find out that girls have the most fun."

"I believe you're right, ranch girl." In the background, someone called his name. "Whoops, gotta go. We're going for a ride down by the river. Just wanted to see how Boo was doing and whether you got the Santa Claus picture."

Darn, I thought. *I knew there was something I'd forgotten.* "It's next on my list," I lied.

"Just don't forget. Maisie's counting on it."

"I won't," I promised. "Have a good ride." Then I turned off the cell phone and started my truck. Fifteen minutes later I walked into Elvia's French country–style office at the bookstore.

"Where have you been?" she asked, turning off her computer.

"The traffic here is getting as bad as L.A. Besides, Hud called and wanted to know all the details about Boo to report back to Maisie. I got off as quick as I could."

"Did you finish your speech?" she asked as we walked out the bookstore's back door. We climbed into her black Lincoln Navigator.

I sank back into the buttery leather seat. "I finished the first draft. And I had an interesting talk with Nola Maxwell Finch."

"Why was she there?" Before she started the car, she opened a Tupperware container and took a handful of cereal, popping it into her mouth.

"Is that Cap'n Crunch?" I couldn't believe it. Elvia hadn't eaten any type of children's sugary cereal since we were ten years old.

Her expression was chagrined. "I know, it's disgusting. And, actually, it tastes better if I'm eating it with a dill pickle."

"That *is* disgusting."

"Forget that, tell me why Nola Finch visited you."

I watched, fascinated, as she crammed another handful of Cap'n Crunch into her mouth. "To check out where we were hanging her uncle's painting. I told her it was still in Gabe's office. After we are done shopping, I'm going to drop by the station and pick it up. I want D-Daddy to hang it today."

"So, was she happy with what you set up?" She closed

up the plastic container and stuck it under the driver's seat.

"She seemed to be. We talked a little about her uncle. She actually confided in me a little tidbit about him." Telling my best friend didn't count in my promise that the information about Abe Adam Finch was not for public consumption.

"Really?" Elvia's dark eyes opened wider.

"It's nothing really juicy. Just that her uncle is getting older, and she's afraid his arthritis will start affecting his painting. Actually, I think she's considering telling the *L.A. Times* reporter this Wednesday so that if there is any subtle change in his work, then the critics might feel a little more sympathetic."

"Sympathetic art critics?" Elvia exhaled a noise as close to a snort as she'd ever get. A little snirt, maybe.

"All I know is I'm glad I'm not the one having to oversee a famous artist's work. It sounds exhausting." I looked out my side window. "Where are we headed? I only have a few hours. Oh, and before I forget, you and Emory are invited to a tree trimming dinner party tonight. Kathryn is cooking chicken verde. Six o'clock sharp."

"I'll let Emory know. When did you get your tree?"

"I haven't yet. That's why I only have a few hours to help you shop. I still have to buy a tree."

"Why don't you call Sam and have him do it for you? He's working at the bookstore until two today."

"Great idea, *amiga*! He and Teresa are on my list to invite anyway." I dialed the store and in five minutes took care of two things on my list. Sam agreed to buy the tree and bring it with him tonight. "Now I'm at your disposal until five o'clock when I pick up Boo. Where's our first stop?"

In three hours we managed to hit the two maternity shops in San Celina and the maternity section of Gottschalk's. For a fairly small town whose clothing tastes tended toward the two extremes of college students with smooth, young bellies and retired women who preferred easy-care sports clothes, we managed—well, Elvia managed—to put together a stylish maternity wardrobe. I did my part holding her purse, and telling her everything looked wonderful.

As we sipped our on-the-run cappuccinos, double-caf for me, no-caf for her (it's killing me, she moaned), she pulled out on Highway 1. "These clothes will hold me for a week or two until I can get over to the Bay Area or down south and do some real shopping." She looked at a book that she'd taken from the store listing all the maternity stores from San Diego to Eureka. "We have one more place to check out up in Cambria."

"Cambria? I can't imagine a more unlikely place for a maternity shop." Cambria, north of Morro Bay, was one of the most expensive places to live in San Celina County. It was mostly settled by a few longtime locals and many affluent transplants from both the Bay Area and Southern California. Cambria-in-the-Pines was its official name, though lately the city's inhabitants had been quite worried about the pines part of the equation. An infestation of pitch canker and bark beetles had many Cambrians worried about the trees surrounding their million-dollar-plus homes. It was where Constance lived, where Nola lived and also where Pinky Edmondson had lived.

We went by the small maternity boutique called Baby by the Sea, where Elvia purchased a beautiful red silk dress that she planned on wearing tonight. While she was trying it on, I called home.

"Ortiz residence," Kathryn's low, throaty voice answered.

"Hi, Kathryn. It's Benni. How are things at the old home place?"

"Everything's fine. Ray bought everything I need for dinner. I'm cooking the chicken right now. I thought we'd have a green salad and jalapeño cornbread to go with it."

"Sounds delicious. Has Scout behaved himself?" It was a rhetorical question.

"Oh, you know he has. That dog is a sweetie."

"Yes, I know. And I can't take a single bit of credit. He was trained when I inherited him. Say, I have an idea if you haven't made anything for dessert yet."

"No, I haven't. I was thinking about baking a pie, but I . . ." Her voice grew rueful, a little embarrassed-sounding. "I'm afraid I accidentally fell asleep. I think it's too late to make a pie now."

I glanced at my watch. "It's four o'clock, so I think you're right. And that works into my idea perfectly."

"What's that?"

"Elvia and I are out in Cambria finishing up her shopping, and we're only a few miles from Linn's Fruit Bin Farmstore. How about some traditional San Celina olallieberry pies for dessert? I'll pick up some vanilla bean ice cream at the grocery store, and we'll be all set for dessert." I waited, hoping it wouldn't insult her, me taking over the dessert.

"Benni, you're a sweetheart," she said, her voice relieved. "That sounds perfect." I still had a hard time reconciling this easy-to-please woman with the same stiff-backed one I met in Kansas a few years ago.

"Good. I talked Sam into getting the tree, so all I have to do is buy the pies and ice cream, pick up Boo, then I'll be home."

"Okay," she said gaily. "See you soon."

"I think an alien has swooped down and replaced my mother-in-law with Mrs. Cunningham from *Happy Days*," I said, closing my phone.

"What now?" Elvia asked.

"I'll tell you on the way to Linn's. I need to buy a couple of pies. And, hopefully, I'll also see something I can buy Kathryn for Christmas." Linn's had a small boutique stocked with local arts and crafts. We turned off Cambria's Main Street onto Santa Rosa Creek Road, a two-lane country road that led to the original Linn's. Though Linn's café and gift shop in downtown Cambria was popular, the more nostalgic people preferred the original Linn's. On the short drive we passed farmhouses and stands of oak trees that recalled San Celina County thirty years ago, the rural part of the county that was rapidly being lost to wineries, strip mall developments and retirement ranchettes for those who could afford the half-million-plus price tag. After we'd bought the pies and perused the small gift shop where I also picked up some Linn's preserves for Kathryn and Ray to take back with them to Kansas, we climbed back into her SUV to head back to San Celina.

"You know," I said to Elvia. "I think Pinky Edmondson's house is somewhere on this road."

"It is," she said. "It's about a half mile past Linn's."

I glanced at her, surprised. "How do you know that?"

She shrugged and turned on the ignition. "She used to order a lot of books from the store and didn't always have time to pick them up, so we'd either mail them or deliver them to her, depending on how quickly she wanted them. I recognize the address."

That shouldn't have surprised me. Elvia prided herself on being a more-than-full-service bookstore. She kept a file of her customers' preferences, their birth dates, if they allowed it, their personal anniversaries and whatever else she could find out that would help her to better meet their literary needs.

"Let's go by and see her house," I said, when she pulled into the road.

"Why?" She glanced at the car's clock. "Besides, it's four thirty. Don't you have to pick up Boo at five?"

"Yes, but they actually stay open until seven, so I'm covered. It'll just take five minutes. I'm curious."

"Of course you are," she said, turning right on the road rather than left, which would take us back to Cambria.

We reached her two-story Victorian house in less than five minutes. I was surprised to see a sixtyish woman was coming out of the house carrying a woven grocery bag and a cat.

"Pull in," I urged Elvia.

"What? Why?"

"Just do it!"

Like so many times in our life, starting when we were in second grade and I talked Elvia into boosting me over

193

the schoolyard fence so I could steal apples from the Beechams' tree next door, she did what I said.

We pulled up in front of the house. The woman stood still as an oak stump, staring at us with a vaguely troubled expression. Not too much taller than my five foot one, she was broader in the shoulders, had dark, short hair and blunt, rounded features. She was one of those people whose ethnicity could run the gamut of dark Irish, Spanish, Italian or Middle Eastern.

"Hello," I called, stepping down from the SUV.

"Can I help you?" she asked in a nonconfrontational yet not-friendly voice. She had no discernable accent. She set the cat down on the top step. It arched its back and wound around her legs.

"This is Pinky Edmondson's house, isn't it?"

She bent down to pet the cat, a brown and black tiger-striped with a black patch of fur over its right eye, making it appear to have one eyebrow. She stood up and gave me a long look. "Who wants to know?"

I took a few steps closer. "I'm Benni Ortiz—"

Relief flooded her face. "Constance said you'd be by, but she said you'd call first."

"Excuse me?" I answered, confused.

"Constance Sinclair. She said you'd be by to look through Mrs. Edmondson's things. I am—I mean, I was her housekeeper, May Heinz. Her lawyer, he asked me to do an inventory of her things. For her heirs back East. Chicago, I think he said. I worked for Mrs. Edmondson for thirty-seven years. No one knows her things like I do."

I was still stunned about what she claimed Constance

told her about me. "Constance Sinclair said I'd help you inventory Mrs. Edmondson's possessions?"

She shook her head. "No, I've got that almost done. I'm using the forms the lawyer gave me. He said the family trusts me." She sniffed, her dark eyes filling with tears. "She was a good woman, Mrs. Edmondson."

I stared at the woman a moment, then glanced over at Elvia. Elvia pointed to her watch. I nodded and waved a hand.

"Ms. Heinz," I said, softening my voice. "I'm really sorry about Mrs. Edmondson, but I'm not exactly clear on what Constance told you I would do."

She sniffed again, reached for a tissue tucked into the sleeve of her sweater and dabbed at her eyes. "She said you'd be by to look through Mrs. Edmondson's things to see if you could find anything suspicious."

"So you know that Constance . . ."

"Thinks Mrs. Edmondson was murdered?" She nodded vigorously. "Yes, she's told me that every time she's been here."

"What do you think?"

She tucked the crumpled tissue back up her sleeve. "I don't know. I like Mrs. Sinclair. She was a real good friend to Mrs. Edmondson. Besides me, I think she's the only one who really cares that Mrs. Edmondson's gone." She tilted her head, her nose a darker red than the rest of her skin. "But Mrs. Edmondson did have a bad heart. I live in the house in the back." She pointed to a small guesthouse to the left of the big house, about fifty yards away, I would guess. "I think I would have heard if someone came in and killed her." She picked up the cat still rubbing up against her legs. "Mrs. Sinclair's just sad and doesn't know what to do about it. I wish she liked cats. Lionel needs a home now that Mrs. Edmondson's passed on. He's only three years old. He has a long life ahead of him."

I reached over and stroked the cat, knowing that Constance couldn't stand animals of any kind. "Yes, you might be right." I turned to wave at Elvia, telling her I was almost done. "I'm sorry, but I'll have to come back. I have plans tonight. Constance . . . uh . . . forgot to tell me about this."

"She has a key," May said. "I'm about finished with the inventory. After the family looks it over, they are going to arrange for an auction." The thought of her beloved employer's possessions being auctioned off seemed to choke her up. "Mrs. Edmondson loved her things."

"I'm so sorry," I said, laying a hand on May's arm. "I'll get out here this week and look through the house, just to set Constance's mind at ease."

"Thank you," May said, grabbing my hand and squeezing it.

"What in the world was that all about?" Elvia asked when I climbed back into her car. On the ride back to the bookstore I filled her in on what May Heinz had to say about Pinky's death and Constance's obsession.

"So," she asked when we arrived at Blind Harry's, "are you going to do what Constance asked?" She helped me load the three pies—two olallieberry, one cherry—into my truck.

"She hasn't actually asked me yet," I said. "I'll call her tomorrow and tell her that this will absolutely be the last thing I do concerning Pinky Edmondson's death. It's getting creepy now."

"At least you're doing what Gabe asked you to do, keep her off his back," Elvia said.

"And he owes me big time for that." I checked my watch and groaned. "I never went by to pick up the painting at Gabe's office, and there's no time now. I have to pick up Boo and get right home. Not to mention buy the ice cream."

"Don't worry about ice cream. Emory and I will bring it. See you in about a half hour."

I arrived home toting a hungry puppy and three pies. I walked into my house greeted by the wonderful scents of chicken verde and fresh pine. Sam was already there with Teresa, stringing lights on the most beautiful blue spruce Christmas tree I'd ever seen.

"You owe me seventy bucks," Sam said from behind the tree. All I could see were his two hands pulling through the strands of white twinkly lights.

I set Boo down, and he immediately started playing with a fuzzy ball that Teresa tossed to him. She giggled and said, "Sam, the tree only cost fifty dollars."

"Twenty is my middleman fee," he said.

"Will you take a check?" I asked, winking at Teresa.

"Got two forms of ID?"

I reached around the tree and pinched his forearm. "I'll owe you forever before I beat you out of it."

His head popped up from behind the tree. "Huh?"

I laughed. "I'm buying you a slang dictionary for Christmas. Hit your dad up for the money. Watch Boo for me?"

"Sure!" Teresa said, sitting down on the floor and pulling the puppy into her lap.

In the kitchen I found Kathryn peeking into a bubbling six-quart pot and Ray tearing lettuce into my biggest salad bowl. Scout came through the dog door and immediately demanded a quick neck rub.

"How was your day, Master Scout?" I asked, massaging his neck with my hands. "Calmer than mine, no doubt."

"He was a perfect gentleman all day," Kathryn said, wiping her hands on an apron I didn't recognize and had no idea where she got. She caught me staring and said, "When I couldn't find an apron, I sent Ray across the street to your friends Beebs and Millee. They sent this over."

I looked closer at it, then laughed. It was bright red and embroidered with the face of Carmen Miranda, her towering hat of fruit and the words, Yes, We Have No Bananas.

By six thirty everyone was here and standing in line for a plate of Kathryn's chicken verde, Spanish rice and cornbread. Since our table could only hold six people at the most, we decided eating buffet style would be the easiest. After everyone ate their fill, we retired to the living room, where Sam made a big production of turning on the Christmas lights.

After our enthusiastic applause, I told everyone to get busy putting on the ornaments while I prepared the dessert. Beebs joined me in the kitchen, where she and Millee had, of course, contributed some Christmas cookies to the celebration.

"You know we can't go anywhere without bringing food," she said. "We can't help ourselves." She and Millee were dressed alike tonight in Beebs's conservative fashion choice of dark green pants and red and green hand-knitted sweaters decorated with Christmas trees. If it had been Millee's turn to pick their clothes, the pants would likely have been red and their earrings actual Christmas bulbs that twinkled when they walked.

"I know," I said, giving her a quick hug. "If we don't eat them all tonight, I'll drive Gabe nuts and eat them for breakfast."

"You're good for the boy," she said, laughing as she cut slices of olallieberry pie. "Without you, he'd be way too serious."

The tree was halfway decorated by the time Beebs and I passed around the cookies, pieces of pie à la mode and cups of hot decaf coffee. Everyone was relaxed and laughing at Boo and Sam as he teased the puppy with a strand of silvery icicle. Boo kept trying to bite at it and getting a mouthful of air.

"Sam," Kathryn said, sitting over in the corner in Gabe's leather chair. "I have something for you. I was going to wait until Christmas, but it's not really your Christmas present." She looked up at Ray, who was standing behind her chair. "Ray, honey, could you . . . ?"

He nodded, obviously knowing what she was talking about without her saying. Gabe watched Ray with a vaguely distrustful expression.

When Ray walked out of the guest room carrying a small box, Kathryn gestured at him to hand it to Sam.

I watched Sam take it from Ray, then glanced over at my husband. His face seemed frozen, but I recognized the anger burning in his eyes, gray now from the emotion.

Sam slowly opened the hinged box and took out the pocket watch, holding it up for everyone to see.

"It was your grandfather's," Kathryn said. "He always said he wanted it to go to his eldest grandson. I didn't think you were old enough until now. And so . . ." Her eyes teared up, something that surprised me. This gruff woman who had so frightened me when we'd visited Kansas a few years ago had, for some reason, softened. Then it hit me. She had some kind of horrible disease and was dying. That had to be the reason for the change in her personality. I swallowed hard; my chest tightened. How would Gabe stand it?

"Awesome," Sam said, turning the watch over in his hand. He looked up at Gabe, whose expression, if it could register on a thermometer, would definitely be below freezing. "Want to see it, Dad?"

"I've seen it," he said abruptly, then set his half-eaten pie down and walked out of the room, into the hall and out the front door. Everyone was stunned silent.

Millee suddenly jumped up. "Who wants more cookies?"

Everyone spoke at once, declaring that was just what they wanted, using the excuse to smooth over the awkward moment.

Thank you, I mouthed to Millee, then slipped out of the room to look for Gabe.

He wasn't out on the front porch, or in the backyard, or on either side of the house. Wherever he'd gone, he'd disappeared in a hurry. It had only been a few minutes between the time he left and the time I came out to search for him. I went back around the house to the front porch, where I found Ray standing with his hands shoved deep in the pockets of his khaki pants.

"Hey," I said.

He gave a silent nod.

I stood next to him on the porch and looked out over the dark, quiet street. "I don't know where Gabe went," I said, trying but not succeeding in keeping the tremor out of my voice.

I felt his hand rest on my left shoulder. It was warm and comforting, and his gentleness made me even more embarrassed by my histrionic husband. "I'm sorry—" I started to say, but Ray's hand squeezed my shoulder. In the bushes underneath us, a cricket started chirping, answered by another a few seconds later.

Ray released my shoulder and leaned against the railing, looking out to the quiet street. "My brother and I were raised by a single mom."

"Really?"

He nodded and continued to stare into the darkness. "My dad was a drunk, would just disappear for months at a time. One time for a year and a half. Mom took care of us by working in a laundry. Pressed men's pants for twelve hours a day." He inhaled deeply, letting the air out in a long sigh. "My brother was a year younger than me. When I was twelve, he died."

I turned to look at the side of his face. "I'm sorry."

"I was supposed to be taking care of him. He was more restless than me, always wanted to be moving, moving. Mom said he got that from Dad."

"What happened?" I asked, my heart beating fast, knowing it was not something good.

"He wanted to go to the river. It was summer. Hot and sticky. Our only fan had broken, but I didn't feel like walking the half mile to go swimming."

I instinctively held my breath, anticipating the ending.

"I told him to go without me, that I wanted to lie under the tree in front of our house and read. I figured I was somewhere in the middle of *Moby-Dick* when he died."

"Oh, no," I said softly.

"He hit his head diving in, they said. There were other kids there. My mom said it wouldn't have made a bit of difference if I would have gone; Billy still would have died. But, somehow, I've always thought that if I'd just put down that book and gone with him . . . I don't know, maybe it wouldn't have happened."

"It wasn't your fault," I said, touching his arm.

"Exactly," he said, turning his head to look at me. "Yet it profoundly changed who I was, how I saw life. I was never the same after that day. I've had to struggle with how much blame I would feel, how much responsibility was mine. It took a long time for me to forgive myself, even though there was not a thing I could have done to change what happened. And those feelings would . . . and still do . . . pop up on me at odd times. I'm just trying to say in my awkward way that I think I understand what Gabe is feeling, what he's going through. He's seen so much death, his dad, Vietnam, his cousin, who knows what he's seen all those years as a police officer. They see humanity at its absolute worst. Why would he be anything but suspicious of me? And why wouldn't he be the angriest man on earth?"

"I know he's been through a lot. But I don't understand why he, I don't know, can't give you a chance. You had nothing to do with the horrible things he's seen. And you make his mom happy. That should make *him* happy."

He shook his head. "You know it's never that easy, Benni. I think it's hard because his mother and I happened out of order for him. Kathryn and Gabe have never resolved the old issues between them. Me coming into the picture, especially with no warning, has pushed those unresolved emotions to the surface. Before, they could just pretend everything was okay, pretend they didn't have this old business between them. Her anger about how he acted when Rogelio died and his anger at her sending him away. I'm still hoping they can talk about it while we are here. Between you and me, I think that's really why she came. I tried to convince her to wait to get married, that it would be better if she included you kids. She said, for once, she wanted something that was just her own. She can be stubborn, my Kathryn."

I smiled at that. "I guess I know where Gabe gets it from then."

"They'll work it out," he said, his voice even. "Or not. Either way, they'll still be mother and son. Nothing can change that."

I inhaled deeply, letting out a big sigh. The air tasted of salt, a wind blowing in from the ocean, whooshing over the hills that separated San Celina from the sea, reminding us that its power and its beauty were not far away. "Ray, if I asked you something, would you tell me the truth?"

He nodded slowly, not looking at me.

"Is Kathryn dying?"

"No," he said.

CHAPTER 10

"SHE HAS MULTIPLE SCLEROSIS."

I closed my eyes slowly and took a deep breath. It was not good news, but at least she wasn't dying. I opened my eyes and stared at the two deep crevices that bracketed his mouth.

His voice became lower, a distant rumble. "Please, don't tell Gabe. She wants to tell him herself." He dropped his head, rubbing the back of his neck. "I told her I'd let her decide when to let people know, but I didn't want you to think it was something worse. And I didn't want to lie to you. I can understand why she's trying to control this, but I'm growing weary of the charades."

I knew about the disease. My friend, Oneeta Cleary, had lived with it for as long as I'd known her. She was the wife of Jim Cleary, one of Gabe's captains and his most trusted employee.

For as long as I'd known Oneeta she'd been in a wheelchair. Her mind was as bright and active as any woman I'd ever met, but her body had an agenda all its own. We'd never actually discussed her condition, but now I wondered why I hadn't asked more questions about how long she'd had it, how quickly it had progressed, was it getting any worse. It shamed me to think that I hadn't ever asked about this important aspect of her life.

"When did she find out about it?" I asked.

"About six months ago. Her condition is controlled now with shots, and most days she feels normal. She sometimes has trouble keeping her balance, and she doesn't drive anymore. We take life day to day." He turned his head to look at me, blinking slowly. "Then again, shouldn't life always be like that? Tomorrow isn't guaranteed to anyone."

I murmured agreement, my heart fluttering in my chest. How would Gabe take this troubling news? "Do the girls know?"

He nodded. "Kathryn told them right before we left with strict orders not to call Gabe. She wanted to tell him in person. There just hasn't seemed to be the right moment for it. Between you and me, I think their past might be hindering a truly intimate talk."

"I think you're right." I turned around and rested my back against the porch railing, looking into the lit house. Sam's laughter, so similar to his dad's, rang out, followed by Teresa's girlish giggle. "I should try to find Gabe."

"Maybe not," Ray said. "Though I can't presume to tell you what to do about your husband, it might be better to leave him alone for a little while. I'll talk to Kathryn and suggest that they go for a drive as soon as they can, try to talk about things." He touched an age-spotted hand to his chest. "I'm sorry if my being here makes things harder."

"Oh, Ray," I said, impulsively hugging him. "I'm *not* sorry you're here, and I'm so happy that you and Kathryn found each other. Gabe will be too, once he figures things out."

After a few minutes we went back inside and along with everyone else did the best we could to salvage the evening. Kathryn slipped me a couple of curious side glances, obviously wondering what Ray and I talked about the half hour we were out on the porch. He'd probably tell her later. Though it would be hard, I'd keep my word and not tell Gabe about his mother's condition. It seemed we were destined in our relationship to hide things from each other. Every time it happened, I wondered how much that would hurt our still-fragile relationship. Still, this wasn't my call. I would try my best to convince him, without giving anything away, that he and his mother needed a heart-to-heart talk soon.

Since it was a work night, by nine p.m. everyone had gone home. The tree was decorated beautifully, though most of it was done by Sam, Teresa, Beebs and Millee. I was sorry I missed out on one of the things I loved most about this holiday. But I was glad Ray and I talked. It gave me hope that things between Gabe and his mother could be resolved on this trip, which was more important than me hanging a few Christmas ornaments.

"Everything will be okay, sweetcakes," Emory said as I walked him and Elvia out to the sidewalk. He pulled me into a tight hug. I could feel Elvia's hand patting my back.

"I know," I mumbled into his chest. "Gabe's just going through a tough time."

"Call us if you need anything," Elvia said, hugging me after Emory.

Once everyone was gone, I shooed Kathryn and Ray to bed, telling them that what little cleaning up there was to do would relax me while I waited for Gabe. Kathryn gave me a worried look, her blue-gray eyes reminding me so much of her son's. She started to say something, then apparently changed her mind.

"Good night, Benni," she said. "Dream sweet."

Dream sweet. Those were the same words that Gabe often said to me before we went to sleep. When we were dating and were longing so much for each other every night, those were always his last words to me: "Dream sweet, *querida*." I wondered if Kathryn said them because Rogelio had said that to her. A nighttime wish for beautiful dreams passed down from husband to wife to mother to son to husband to wife.

Gabe came home about ten p.m. Boo, exhausted, had fallen asleep against a dozing Scout. Both of them lay on the floor next to the sofa where I sat in the dark, the room lit only by the Christmas tree's twinkling lights. I'd been staring at the lights for almost an hour wondering if I should go search for my husband. A cold burst of air followed him into the room.

"Hey," he said, coming into the living room. Scout lifted his head, then laid it back down again. Boo gave a little puppy chirrup and snuggled deeper into Scout's warm chest.

"Hey," I said, not getting up.

He stood in front of the flickering tree, his face a map of sad planes and crevices. He stuck his hands deep into his pockets, appearing as if he were waiting for me to say something.

I didn't. This time he would have to ask for my help. This time I wouldn't push myself or my solutions on him. Ray was right; this was Gabe's battle, and only he could punch his way out of it. After a long minute, I stood up and walked over to him, putting my arms around his waist, laying my head against his broad back. I couldn't give him solutions, but I could give him comfort.

"I'm sorry about tonight," Gabe said.

I didn't answer. I wanted so badly to tell him what to do, to go talk to his mom, that time was running out for her, for all of us. That life was too short, too fragile to let his anger and his pain steal any more of his days than they already had.

"I'll just tell everyone I had a bad day. I'll just . . ." He let his voice drift away, knowing that the remedy wasn't that simple.

My head against his back, I could feel him swallow, holding back his emotion. I couldn't help it, I had to say something. It just wasn't in me to step back from the people I loved. That was as much a part of me as Gabe's reluctance to connect with the people he loved was a part of him.

I moved around and laid my head on his chest. "I love you, Friday. Please, do me a favor. Talk to your Mom. Who knows when she'll come out again?"

"I'll try," he said, resting his cheek on the top of my head. His arms tightened around me. "I promise I'll try."

❖

THE NEXT MORNING BOTH GABE AND I HAD DRESSED AND eaten before Kathryn and Ray even stirred. Gabe was rinsing our breakfast dishes and I was taking Boo out for one more potty break before heading off to work when Ray came into the kitchen.

"Hi, Ray," Gabe said, his voice friendlier than it had been since Ray's arrival. Ray took it in stride and said good morning.

"Where's Kathryn?" I asked, trying to keep my face neutral. She'd better talk to her son fast, because I was not known for being able to keep any kind of secrets from Gabe. My expressive face combined with his ability to detect any kind of duplicity usually made it impossible. But he'd been so self-absorbed this morning, reliving, I suspected, his bratty behavior last night, that he didn't notice any strangeness in my tone.

"She's moving a little slowly this morning," Ray said, pouring himself a cup of coffee. "She'll be up and about directly."

"Is Mom okay?" Gabe asked, turning to look at Ray.

I glanced over at Ray, holding my breath. His expression didn't change one iota.

"I just think she did too much yesterday," he said, smiling at Gabe. "You know Kathryn, she never does anything halfway."

Gabe surprised me by giving Ray a small smile back. "I'll go in and say good-bye. See what she wants to do for dinner."

After he left, I asked Ray, "Is she okay this morning?"

He nodded and sat down at the kitchen table, cupping his narrow hands around his mug as if to warm them. "Nothing a day of rest wouldn't fix. It's not just the disease, you know. Kathryn and I aren't spring chickens anymore. Getting out of our routine, the weather change, the time change, plays havoc with your system."

"I hear you." I glanced over at the closed kitchen door, then said in a lowered voice, "Do you think she'll tell him today?"

He shrugged and took a long drink from his mug. "I learned early in our relationship to never try to predict what Kathryn Smith Ortiz would or would not do. Actually, it's a great deal of her charm for me."

I laughed, totally understanding what he meant. "Like mother, like son. Those Ortizes do have a way of getting under a person's skin."

"And capturing our hearts."

I picked up Boo, who was scrambling around my feet, and buried my face in his sweet-smelling puppy fur. "Well said, stepfather-in-law."

"What's well said?" Gabe asked, walking back into the room. "Mom and I are having dinner out tonight." Then, realizing, I hoped, how exclusionary that sounded, he added, "If it's okay with you two."

"Fine with me," Ray said.

"I'll take Ray to Liddie's," I said. "He can't visit San Celina without eating at Liddie's."

211

"Good idea," Gabe said. "Well, off to the salt mines. You two have a good day." He came over, kissed me quickly on top of the head and left the kitchen whistling under his breath.

"Maybe tonight will be the night," I said.

"Let's hope so," Ray said in a good-natured but resolute tone.

I was pulling into the parking lot of All Paws on Board when my cell phone rang. The screen read Constance Sinclair.

"I have a bone to pick with you," I said before she could start in on whatever it was she was going to start in on me about. "May Heinz, Pinky's housekeeper, said that you said that I was going to go to Pinky's house and look around."

"When did you hear that?" Constance demanded.

"More important," I replied, "why are you making plans and telling people about them before you contact me? I told you that I'd thoroughly investigated whether Pinky Edmondson was murdered and found that she wasn't. Constance, you have to let this go." Behind me, Boo was whining. He already knew what going to All Paws meant: playing with other dogs. "Just a minute," I whispered to him.

"What?" Constance said.

"Nothing, I was talking to the dog."

"What?"

"Nothing," I repeated. "Why do you think me going through Pinky's house would make a bit of difference? What do you think I'll find?"

"I don't know. *That's* why I want you to investigate.

Don't forget, Benni, you took my check. You haven't finished the job."

I inhaled deeply, physically holding my lips together to stifle the scream about to spew out. I didn't want to scare the puppy. "Constance . . ." I started.

Then I exhaled. *Give it up.* It would just be easier to do as she asked, at least until the holidays were over. "Okay, I'll go by later on this afternoon. Can you please make sure that someone is there to let me in?"

"A key is in your mailbox at the museum," she said, triumph in her voice. "Call me as soon as you're done. I'd meet you there and help you, but with the 49 Club Christmas luncheon tomorrow, I don't have a spare minute."

She hung up before I could toss in that I had very few minutes to spare myself. I was handing Boo over to Suann at All Paws when my phone rang again. How was it that cell phones were supposed to make our lives easier?

"Hey, ranch girl," Hud said, his voice sounding crackly. "Just wanted to remind you about taking Boo to see Santa."

Shoot, I'd totally forgotten again. "Yeah, I know. It's on my schedule for . . . today." I crossed my fingers behind my back.

"I'm sorry to be a pest, but Maisie's just frantic about it."

"Boo will have his picture taken with Santa, Hud. I promise."

After he hung up, I turned my phone off. I just couldn't afford to hear from one more person asking me

213

to do something. Somehow today I'd have to find the time to have Boo's picture taken with Santa.

First, find a Santa, I thought, as I unlocked the front door of the folk art museum. Then, bribe him to have his photo taken with a dog.

The minute I got to my office I realized that I'd forgotten the most important thing I was supposed to do today: pick up Abe Adam Finch's painting at the police station. I dialed Gabe's direct number. Maggie put me right through.

"What can I do for you?" he asked.

"I forgot to pick up the painting. Can you—?"

He didn't even let me finish. "I'll send a patrolman over with it right now. Anything else?"

"What service. An extra orange in your stocking this Christmas, Chief Ortiz."

He laughed, sounding more buoyant than I'd heard him in a long time. "Anything else I can do to make you happy?"

"Sure, but that'll have to wait until later on tonight."

"I'll hold you to that," he replied. "Mom and I shouldn't be too late. I'm taking her to Ghost Fish, that new restaurant in Morro Bay. I heard they have great Maine lobster. Mom loves lobster."

"I'm sure she'd enjoy a walk on the Embarcadero too."

"You and Ray have a good time."

"We will. You know there's always something going on at Liddie's."

Thirty minutes later, my favorite police officer, Miguel, came walking in carrying Abe Adam Finch's painting. He was one of Elvia's younger brothers and at twenty-five had been a San Celina police officer for four years now. I still got a kick out of seeing this man in uniform, because I could remember reading all the Dr. Seuss books to him.

"Hey, Benni," he said, setting the wrapped painting down in the middle of the museum's main hall. "Where do you want this?"

"Just prop it up over there," I said, pointing to the spot we'd prepared for it. "D-Daddy will hang it right away."

"So, this is the fancy-pants painting that's going to put your museum on the map?"

I punched him lightly on his muscled shoulder. "Hey, I know it's not as important as a signed poster of Shaquille O'Neal, but it's a pretty big deal in the outsider art world."

"Whatever," he said, obviously not interested. "I'm just the delivery guy." He stretched and scratched his close-cropped black hair. "How's my *hermana grande* doing? Emory said she had a meltdown."

"After a bit of a clothing crisis, she is back on track. I think she spent almost six hundred dollars on maternity clothes yesterday."

"Huh," he snorted. "Not even close to what Mama is spending for the baby. The whole house looks like a baby store. You'd think it was her first grandkid."

Elvia had six brothers, four of whom were married and had children. Elvia's baby would be Mrs. Aragon's seventh grandchild.

"It's probably because it's her only daughter's first baby. Maybe she's reliving some of the experiences she had carrying all of you."

After Miguel left, I sent one of the docents to find D-Daddy so we could hang the painting as soon as possible. I stood next to it, unwilling to even walk out of the room until we had it hung and attached to the security device D-Daddy and the alarm people had devised. It would go off the minute someone lifted the picture away from the wall. Granted, an experienced art thief might be able to disarm it, but it wasn't the fancy art thieves we were worried about; they'd probably not bother with a small museum like ours. I was more worried about amateurs who were looking to make a quick buck.

When D-Daddy came in and readied the spot for the official hanging, I slowly unwrapped the painting. I still couldn't get over our museum's good fortune that, at Nola Maxwell Finch's suggestion, her uncle had agreed to donate a painting to our permanent collection. When Constance brought Nola for a personal tour, I had no idea Nola would fall in love with our little museum, admire its simplicity and champion our statement of purpose, to celebrate the artist in all people, regardless of background.

"It's amazing," one of the docents said. A group of them had gathered to watch D-Daddy hang the painting.

It really was more vibrant and arresting in person than in the eight-by-ten photos we'd been sent. The tree with leaves that seemed to be half oak, half pine, was rich with subtle details, faces painted in the trunk, animals and birds peeking out of the foliage. There was so much going on in the painting that you could stare at it for an hour and not get bored.

"That's perfect," I said to D-Daddy, who gave the plain

black frame that surrounded the painting one last nudge. "I'm so glad this is finally done."

"You say it, *ange,*" D-Daddy said, stepping back and letting the small crowd move closer to the painting. He said out of the side of his mouth, "Now maybe Miss Constance will stop hanging around so much." D-Daddy was patient with Constance and always went to great lengths to appease her, but like me, dealing with her took up time he'd rather spend working on the museum.

"We still have the opening on Wednesday night," I answered back in a low tone, "so we'll probably have her hanging around until then. But once that's over, she'll move on to something else."

He slipped his hammer back in his tool belt. "I'll be in back working on the bathroom sink. Someone, they pour paint down it again."

"I'll post another note on the bulletin board," I said.

We had an industrial-size sink in the back of the woodworking shop, but often people didn't want to walk that far and used the tiny bathroom sink instead. It was often clogged up, trying D-Daddy's patience. Things like that were as much, if not more, a part of my workday as unwrapping and hanging famous paintings.

I was giving my speech one more edit when the phone rang. I almost let the answering machine pick it up, then decided since I'd turned off my cell phone, that probably wasn't a good idea. It actually might be something important.

"Benni, is that you?" It was Constance.

I took a deep breath. I shouldn't have answered. "Yes, ma'am."

"We have a lunch date with Nola Finch and Dot St. James at The Brambles restaurant in Cambria."

"Is that the royal we?" I asked deliberately being facetious. She wouldn't have a clue what I was implying.

"What are you talking about?" Her voice was impatient, sharp. "I have a reservation for eleven thirty. Dress nice."

I was tempted to say "as compared to my normal manure-caked clothing?" Except sometimes my boots did reek of, as Daddy would say, "the smell of money."

"Okay," I said, glancing up at the clock in my office. It was ten thirty now. That meant I'd have to make a quick trip home, because I'd thrown on faded Wranglers and an old Cal Poly sweatshirt, thinking that I'd spend most of the day either in my office or giving the museum one last spit shine. "What's the purpose of this lunch?" I foolishly asked.

"What?"

Did I use any words that weren't in her vocabulary? "Why are we having lunch with Nola and Dot?"

"Because they want to," she said, as if my question were the oddest thing in the world.

"See you later," I said wearily, wondering what part of this job was fun anymore. Of course there was no real reason to have lunch. These women didn't actually have jobs or chores or to-do lists. They paid other people, *like me,* to do that.

The house was empty when I stopped by to change into black wool slacks, a simple white shirt and a black sweater. I looked at myself in the mirror and realized I looked like I was ready to serve dinner in an upscale restaurant, so I added a turquoise and black bolo tie in a six-pointed star design. That touch, along with my good Lucchese cowboy boots, made me look a little less like the person serving lunch and more like one of the ladies eating lunch.

I left a note for Kathryn and Ray telling them I'd be home by six o'clock. I added, "Hope you've had a fun day! See you later. Love, Benni." I felt a little funny putting *love*, but I couldn't think of what else to sign.

As I drove the twenty or so miles out to Cambria for the second time in as many days, I decided that after lunch I'd make good use of my time and also go by Pinky's house. Though I hadn't a clue what to look for, at least I could tell Constance I'd done as she asked. If she weren't the person who paid a good deal of the running costs of the museum, I would tell her to take a flying leap into the Pacific Ocean that churned to the left of me for most of my drive to Cambria.

Normally, it was a beautiful trip, one that I enjoyed despite having to stay aware of the crazy drivers weaving across the yellow strip dividing the two-lane highway. Today, all I could think about was getting through this lunch, making a cursory walk through Pinky's house, and possibly getting back to San Celina in time to find a Santa Claus who'd consent to having his photo taken with a certain little corgi puppy.

"Maybe I should move that to tomorrow," I said out loud. I could always lie to Hud when he called . . . and he *would* call again. No, he could always tell when I was out-and-out fibbing. Maybe after Ray and I had dinner we could swing by the house, pick up Boo and find us a

Santa Claus somewhere. Surely the mall had one? It had been a long time since this had been a problem for me. I think the last kid I took to see Santa Claus was Miguel when he was three or four, right before his brother Ramon was born.

At least the Santa Claus dilemma kept my mind off what was really worrying me: Gabe and Kathryn's dinner tonight. Would she tell him at the restaurant or when they were walking along the Embarcadero? Personally, I thought a conversation like that was better off inside the privacy of our home, but no one was consulting me on the matter.

The Brambles was one of the oldest restaurants in Cambria and deserved its long tenure as one of the town's favorite eating establishments. I could remember coming here as a child for Dove's birthday every year, the one time Daddy consented to dress up and "do the town," which meant dinner at The Brambles, then back to San Celina for a movie at the Art Deco Fremont Theater. Dove and I wore dresses, and she made Daddy wear a tie and his best western-style sports coat. She always ordered the split pea soup, prime rib, garlic mashed potatoes and crème brûlée for dessert. As a child, I loved their tiny loaves of molasses bread served in a big basket, a loaf for every diner. Dividing my loaf into as many doll-size slices as my knife would allow kept me occupied during the wait for our food.

Constance, Dot and Nola had already been seated when I arrived five minutes late. I knew I'd catch heck from Constance, but I'd gotten behind a slow RV and didn't dare try to pass on the busy highway.

"Finally," Constance said when I walked up.

"Sorry I'm late," I said, sitting down in the one empty ladder-back chair. We were in the best spot in the room, next to the stone fireplace. The room's dark burnished paneling glowed in the light from the silk-shaded wall lamps. From the shades dangled sparkling jewels that had fascinated me as a child.

"No matter, we've just ordered drinks," Dot said, waving away Constance's admonition. "What'll you have, Benni?" Her voice was as bright as a chirping bird. She wore a black and white diamond-patterned dress that I was willing to bet cost more than my first car.

"Mineral water with lime," I said.

"Oh, live it up," Dot said. "Try one of their marvelous dirty martinis."

"No, thanks, Dot. I have to drive back to San Celina after this, and one drink puts me in the over-the-limit class."

"I suppose," she said, waving down our waiter and giving him my drink order. "With a husband who's chief of police, I suppose you can't be too careful. But you won't tattle on me, will you?" She giggled and toasted me.

"Is it hard?" Nola Maxwell Finch asked, sipping at what appeared to be a cosmopolitan. "Being the wife of the chief of police, I mean."

"Sometimes," I said. "We've been married over four years. I'm almost used to it."

"He's quite handsome," Nola said, setting her drink down carefully.

"Gorgeous, actually," Dot piped up. "He could slip his shoes under my four-poster bed any old time he likes."

"Dot!" Constance's face flushed with embarrassment.

I tried not to burst out laughing at Dot's unexpected remark. I couldn't imagine it coming from a less likely person. I guessed this wasn't the first martini she'd had today. She also wasn't the first woman who'd been attracted to my husband and wasn't shy about admitting it. My mineral water arrived just in time.

"I'm parched," I said, busying myself squeezing my lime and stirring my drink.

"I would love," Dot said, catching our waiter's eye and pointing at her drink, "to hear more about our chief of police's nocturnal habits."

"So," I said, picking up my menu. "Are there any specials?"

Luckily, Dot was sloshed enough that it was easy to distract her. "The lamb is delicious. They have the most divine mint sauce, though I have to admit, the thought of eating baby lambs can often bring me to tears." She gave a loud sniff and fumbled for the bread basket.

I looked over at Nola, whose face was thoughtful. I imagine Dot wasn't the first tipsy society lady she'd lunched with.

"My gramma always gets the prime rib here," I said. "I really like their roasted chicken pie."

"Chicken pie sounds wonderful," Nola said, setting her menu down. "What about you, Constance?"

"I'll have the duck," she said.

"Me too," Dot said, giving a soft hiccup.

The sound startled me, and I had to keep myself from laughing. I thought drunks only hiccuped on television comedies.

After our waiter brought Dot another drink, then took our orders, I asked Nola, "Do you like Cambria?"

"Yes," she said. "I absolutely fell in love with it the first time I drove through town. I have a little house over by Moonstone Beach."

"Beautiful little cottage," Constance said. "Gorgeous view."

"It's a little small, though," Nola said. "I'm trying to find something a little bigger. Perhaps with a studio."

Constance straightened in her seat, looking like she wanted to crow. I could guess why. Maybe Abe Adam Finch was thinking about moving to Cambria. What a coup that would be for Constance. Maybe Nola telling me about her uncle's fragile health was a precursor to this development.

Nola shook her head. "I'm afraid I'm driving my realtor a little crazy. I can't seem to find a suitable house. Privacy is a real issue."

"Well, there's one really nice house going on the market soon," Dot said, finishing her martini. "If you don't mind living someplace where someone died. Then again, I guess most of the houses in Cambria fit that description. We're an aging bunch here."

It took me a few seconds to realize that Dot meant Pinky Edmondson's house. I glanced over at Constance to see what she thought about Dot's outrageous comment.

"That's a wonderful idea, Dot," Constance said. "I think Pinky would be honored to have Nola live in her house."

"What type of house is it?" Nola asked, her expression curious.

During the rest of our meal, Constance told Nola every detail about Pinky's house. Dot, the martinis finally catching up with her, seemed to have lost steam and picked at her duck. While we waited for our crème brûlées to arrive, Constance and Nola excused themselves to use the restroom.

"Nola seems nice," I said.

Dot shrugged, obviously not as enamored of Nola Finch as Constance. "She's just another of Constance's fancies. She'll pal around with her for a while, then move on to someone new."

"Well," I said noncommittally and took another small sip of water.

I knew Dot and Constance were old friends and so had a tendency to freely gossip and snipe about the other one, but I also knew they had a sense of class loyalty that precluded me actually giving my opinion about Constance and her infatuation with Nola. I suspected Dot was right. But Constance's relationship with Nola, whether real or fake, had benefited the museum, so I wasn't about to complain.

"I suppose," Dot said, "it's better that she focus on Nola Finch than continuing on with her ridiculous obsession with Pinky being murdered by me or one of the other aspiring 49ers." She glanced into her martini glass, which had nothing left in it but a green olive. She picked the olive up and gave it a quick lick before popping it in her mouth.

"You know about that?" I stammered. Had she known about it when I conducted that fake interview a few days ago?

"Of course I do. How dim does Constance think I am? Someone should probably warn her that her housekeeper loves to dish about her to anyone who'll listen, including my housekeeper." She gave a wicked smile. "But it's not going to be me, because I like knowing the inside scoop."

Then she frowned, her eyes bleary from the alcohol. "Honestly, I think she's gone round the bend this time. There are plenty of reasons people would want Pinky dead, but getting into the 49 Club is not one of them."

"There are?" I said, hoping that Dot was drunk enough to elaborate.

I was in luck.

She gave a crooked half smile, then pulled at the collar of her expensive dress. "It is common knowledge that Pinky was, shall we say, a bit crazy." Her expression turned dark. "Actually, if she had been murdered, which I don't think for a moment she was, I would be the perfect suspect."

I sat there, stunned, not moving a muscle.

She looked down at her uneaten duck. "Did Constance tell you that Pinky and my husband had an affair?"

I shook my head no, still not speaking.

"Right under my nose when we first moved here twenty-eight years ago. I was pregnant with my daughter." She touched a trembling hand to her perfect curls. "When I confronted her, you know what she did? She laughed. Told me not to worry, that she wouldn't tie him up for very long, that he was a *foot* doctor, for heaven's sakes, not someone she'd ever consider having a real relationship with. Of course I slapped her. That was for me, not him."

It took me two seconds to guess who blackballed Dot both times there was a membership opening.

"I know she was the one who blackballed me," she said, verifying my guess. "As much as I enjoyed it, that slap cost me plenty." She pulled her napkin from her lap and threw it across her plate. "She broke up with my husband the next day. Everyone knew about it, and guess who was shunned? It took my husband and me years to get asked to any of the important parties. You just didn't do something like that to Pinky Edmondson."

Why in the world, I wanted to ask, *would you even want to be friends with any of these people?*

Dot looked liked she would start sobbing any minute. I remembered from her information that her daughter had a jewelry boutique here in Cambria. I wondered if Dot would allow me to call her. She looked like she could use some help getting home.

"She could always get away with the craziest behavior and still be accepted," Dot said in a hoarse voice. "That's what I can't figure out. How do people like her do it? If I'd done half the things she did, Constance Sinclair and the rest of them would not even give me the time of day." Her thin-lashed brown eyes filled with tears. "I follow all the rules, all of them, and still I'm not really accepted. How fair is that?"

I shook my head, not knowing what to say. Fair? What was fair about life at all?

She abruptly stood up, just the slightest bit shaky on her feet, and picked up her black leather clutch. "There's my daughter." She waved over a young woman dressed in a long, gauzy dress standing in the lobby. "This was lovely, but I have an appointment. Tell the restaurant to put my lunch on my tab."

I watched her walk toward her daughter in that careful way that someone who has drunk too much does, like a tightrope walker without a balance stick. Her daughter's face looked resigned when she took her mother's arm, as if this was not the first time she'd done this.

I was staring at the cracked surface of my crème brûlée when Constance and Nola returned.

"Where's Dot?" Constance asked.

"She went home," I said, looking up at my employer's sharp, enquiring face. "She didn't feel well."

Constance rolled her eyes.

For the first time since I took this job, I seriously considered quitting. I didn't need it now. I had a husband who had a good job and a life that didn't need the folk art museum. Why was I still working for this insane woman who had never had any respect or feelings for me and, it appeared, anyone else?

Constance, being Constance, didn't even notice that I was upset. "Dot needs to see someone about that drinking problem," she said, sitting down. "I certainly hope she doesn't expect us to pick up her check. She had four martinis or my name isn't Constance Sinclair."

"She said to tell the waiter to put it on her tab." I stuck my spoon into my crème brûlée, breaking the crusty top with a snap. Normally, I loved this dessert, but I no longer had an appetite.

Nola, obviously more sensitive than Constance, said, "Benni, are you all right?"

I looked up. Her clear blue eyes, the lashes tinged a soft black from mascara, looked genuinely concerned.

"I'm fine," I said, putting down my spoon. "I just . . . I have some errands to run. It was wonderful seeing you again, Nola. I hope you'll enjoy what I have to say about your uncle on Wednesday."

"I'm sure I will," she said, her voice warm.

"Where are you going?" Constance demanded.

I folded my cloth napkin carefully and placed it next to my plate. "Like I said, I have errands to run. And a dinner date at six p.m."

"You can run your errands after work hours," Constance said. "Because I just came up with a marvelous idea when Nola and I were in the ladies' room. I think Pinky's house is just what Nola is looking for. You can take her over there and see if the house interests her."

"I don't know, Constance," I said, wondering if somehow we weren't breaking some kind of probate law by going inside the house.

"It will be fine," Constance said. "Who will know? And if Nola likes it, she can be the first to make an offer. Pinky would approve." Constance sat back in her chair, a smug and satisfied look on her face.

"I don't know," Nola said, appearing uncomfortable with this turn of events. "If it's not even on the market yet . . ."

"It will be soon," Constance said. "I know you only met Pinky a few times, but she found you delightful. She was one of my very best friends, and her cousins back East couldn't care less about her or her things. They'll want to unload everything as quickly as they can."

Constance's eyes started blinking rapidly, and she opened her purse, fumbling for a tissue. Was she going to start crying again? Despite how much she drove me crazy, I realized at that moment that she really did miss Pinky. Though after hearing what Dot had to say about Pinky, I wondered just what kind of a person she was, but it was apparent that Constance really cared about her. Constance had no close family, much like Pinky. It made me feel a little ashamed when I thought about how many people I had who cared about me. Maybe Pinky, with all her faults, was the only person Constance truly felt cared about her. The sister or even the daughter she never had.

Nola looked over at me, her expression a little uneasy. "If you're in a hurry . . . I wouldn't want to impose."

"You're not imposing," Constance answered for me, sitting up straight, her face a mask again. "Benni's going there anyway."

"May I ask why?" Nola said.

Constance's eyes darted from Nola's face to mine. "I have some things that I left at Pinky's before she died. Benni is picking them up for me." She flashed me a triumphant, aren't-I-clever look.

I wanted to smack her. What a big fat lie! I was certain some kind of law would be broken if I removed anything from the house. But if I gave it to Constance and she put it back or gave it to May, wouldn't that cancel out any law I broke? Right now I wanted to strangle Constance, but I also wouldn't mind the feel of my own husband's neck in my hands. He was the one who got me into this crazy situation.

I looked down at my watch. "If we're going out to Pinky's house, we'll need to leave. It's two o'clock already, and I have—"

"Yes, yes, we heard," Constance said. "Dinner plans. Just don't rush Nola. Pinky's house is gorgeous. She spent a lot of time and money making it a showplace. And it's about as private as a house can be. In all the years she owned it, she only allowed it to be used for a charity event once. And believe me, *everyone* made a point to come to that benefit."

"I can't wait to see it," Nola murmured.

After we paid for our lunches, we walked out to the parking lot.

"You can follow me," I told Nola. "I'm easy to spot." I pointed at my purple Ford Ranger pickup.

She gave a delighted laugh. "I bet you never have trouble finding your car in any parking lot."

"That's the whole idea." Then I turned to Constance. "Let me walk you to your car."

"Don't bother," she said, waving me away.

I grabbed her upper arm in a firm grip. "No, Constance, I insist. Let me help you."

She tried to shake off my grip, but I wasn't letting go. "Benni, what is going on . . ."

Once we got out of Nola's earshot, I snapped. "Constance, what in the world were you thinking in there! I'm going in the house to get some things of yours? Nola Finch will be watching to see what I pick up now!"

"So?" she said, pulling her arm away from me. "Just pick up a few things and say they are mine. Heaven knows I bought Pinky enough gifts. Probably half the silver and crystal she has I've given her."

"Constance, some people would call that *stealing*! Including my own husband. You remember him. *The police chief!*"

"Calm down. Anything you pick up you just give to me, and I'll give it back to May. Simple as that. Do I always have to figure out everything?"

I walked away from her, too furious to reply. I didn't understand why she was so insistent on Nola Finch seeing Pinky's house right *now*.

Just get it over with, I said to myself as I started toward my truck. *The sooner you show Nola the house, the sooner you can wipe your hands of this whole ridiculous situation.* After the opening on Wednesday, I would call Constance and tell her to stop this silly pseudo-investigation. I'd tell her that all her society friends, including the three women up for Pinky's position in the 49 Club, know about her suspicions, even though I didn't know if Francie suspected anything. I would tell her that she was a laughingstock. It would anger her beyond belief. It might even cost me my job, but at this point, I didn't care. Frankly, the museum might be better off with fresh blood, maybe with someone who didn't let Constance get away with murder.

Great choice of words, I thought. I pulled off onto the highway that Elvia and I drove only yesterday. Nola stayed close behind me in her gray Volvo. Her face seemed stressed and intent, hunched slightly forward over the steering wheel in that way a person often does when they are not sure where they are going.

231

We pulled up in front of Pinky's Victorian house. The sun had already dipped behind the hill in back of the house, and the yard was full of yellow and orange mums and neatly trimmed emerald shrubs, even though it was December. I really looked at the exterior this time, realizing what a beautiful house it was and how much care had been lavished upon it. It had undeniable flair. The flowers, shrubs, even the natural walk leading up to the front porch, seemed all of a piece, like great thought had been put into where each stone was placed, the shape of each shrub. It had balance and was gently pleasing to the eye, yet you had the feeling there were surprises to be found among the warm-colored flowers.

I realized in that moment how little I knew about Pinky Edmondson. She was definitely a woman who marched to her own drummer. Most society women like her lived closer to town, didn't feel comfortable in such a rural environment. But Pinky had been a widow for a long time. Maybe this house, as isolated as it was, was the last connection she had with her husband. I remember how difficult it had been when I lost Jack and then not too long after that, his mother, brother and I lost the Harper ranch. At the same time I ached for my young husband, I also missed the house we'd lived in, the rooms we'd decorated and the flowers we'd planted in the window boxes. Where we live with those we love is so tied up with our memories of them. I could understand why she'd stay here long after her husband was gone.

A little white Toyota was parked in front of the quaint little guesthouse. I assumed it was May Heinz's vehicle. I dialed her number on my cell phone and told her not to worry, that I had Constance's permission to show the house to Nola. May came to the front window and waved at us. Next to her I could see a large German shepherd dog, ears stiff and alert.

"Remember to shut off the alarm," she said. "The code is 5219."

"Okay," I said.

"What a lovely place," Nola exclaimed, climbing out of her car.

"Yes, it is," I agreed, slipping my phone into my pants pocket. "This is not the first time I've seen it, but I just now noticed how together everything seems, how peaceful, really."

"Yes," Nola said, gazing up at the house. "It really does give off a feeling of peace, not isolation. It just might be perfect for . . . me."

I punched the numbers into the pad next to the front door, disarming the alarm system. Then I opened the front door with the key Constance had given me and stood aside, gesturing for Nola to go ahead of me. She stepped inside the foyer without hesitation, with a promising familiarity. Maybe she'd buy Pinky's house, eventually move her uncle here and make it their home. I imagined briefly the artists at the co-op coming here to pay homage to Mr. Finch, him giving talks about his art, perhaps revealing one of his newest works, our museum and co-op becoming his home away from home.

"May I look around?" Nola asked, interrupting my fantasy.

"Oh, sure," I said, flipping on the foyer light. It bathed

the entryway in a soft, yellow glow. "That's the whole idea. Who knows, this might be your dream house."

She touched one of the textured walls, almost caressing it. "Who knows indeed?"

She started for the large living room to our left, so I decided I'd go upstairs. I remembered when Gabe and I were looking for a house I was always happy when we were left alone to poke around on our own, trying to imagine a life in that particular house, even though it was filled with someone else's possessions.

At the bottom of the stairs, I encountered the cat May was holding the last time I was here. What had she said his name was? Leonardo? No, Lionel. That was it. Like the model trains.

"Hello, Mr. Lionel," I said, bending down to stroke him as he wound around my legs. "I take it you're in charge of mouse patrol."

I briefly wondered who would take this cat when the house was sold. May Heinz? I assumed she was feeding him. Maybe the new owner would inherit him with the house. Did Nola like cats?

The interior of the house was bigger than it appeared outside, something I found to be the opposite in many Victorian houses. I wandered through the rooms, half-embarrassed and half-excited to be looking through someone's personal things. Most history buffs and even academic historians, though they'd hate to admit it, are basically your nosiest neighbor times one hundred. History is, first and foremost, about people, so any chance a history lover has to peek inside someone else's life, it is like being given a precious gift. And, when you thought about it, the minute a person passes away, they pass out of the present into history. Looking through Pinky's possessions felt like studying a piece of history.

As I casually touched her things, the silver hairbrush laid just so on her carved mahogany vanity, or ran my fingers across the fringe of her bedside lampshade, making it dance in the yellow light, I was poignantly aware of Constance's grief and her insistence that Pinky was murdered. There was nothing in the rooms I walked through, her bedroom and three other beautifully decorated guest rooms, that supported that. I truly had to convince Constance to let her friend go, that it was more important to start planning Pinky's memorial service. Maybe it was a good idea for Nola Finch to buy this house. Maybe it would help Constance move on.

In the large upstairs sunroom, I found most of Pinky's impressive collection of folk art displayed across one large, eggshell white wall. She seemed to prefer paintings, though there were a few sculptures and one bright red and yellow Tumbling Blocks quilt draped over a wooden quilt rack. I also recognized a small original Howard Finster painting and another painting that was unsigned depicting a baptism in a bright green and blue river with shocking pink caps on the small waves. The white-robed believers' faces held expressions of rapturous joy.

She owned an original Abe Adam Finch, something that would please Nola, I was sure. It showed an oak tree blooming with the faces of children. Each child's face, though of a different shade of complexion ranging from pale pink to light goldenrod to burnished copper, shared one characteristic, eyes made up of blue, green, brown and black hues, all exactly alike, as if the artist was saying, *Though we possess different skin tones, we all see the world through the same eyes.* It was one of his smaller paintings, about eight-by-ten. I studied his signature, trying to see if there was any difference between it and the one on the painting he gave the folk art museum. Looked the same to me. Then again, I had no idea when Pinky purchased this painting.

The collection in this room alone had to be worth close to a hundred thousand dollars. It worried me that these paintings were out here unprotected except for May Heinz, her German shepherd and Lionel the cat.

I walked over to the large picture window that looked out over the garden. It didn't fit with the Victorian style of the house. It slid open to reveal an unobstructed view of her property, the edge of her garden, the tiled roof of the guesthouse and in the distance tall pine and oak trees etched against the darkening sky. Without screens, the view was spectacular. It mimicked a painting, really, though more realistic than most of the artists whose work Pinky owned. I stood at the window for a moment, admiring the view, especially of the massive old pine tree directly in back of the guesthouse. Its tall, strong presence against the lavender and blue sky reminded me of my mother-in-law's imposing six-foot frame. I thought of her height, how intimidating I found it the first time we met. I couldn't help wondering what the MS would do to her frame. Oneeta was hunched over in her wheelchair, had been round-shouldered and frail from the first time I met her.

I hoped that Kathryn would tell Gabe tonight about her condition. It weighed on me knowing this intimate information about his mother and not being able to talk to him about it.

I heard Nola call my name as she came up the stairs.

"In the sunroom," I called back, picking up a china dog and a crystal box as my "reason" for coming here. This whole charade was ludicrous.

"What wonderful light," Nola exclaimed, coming into the airy room. "An artist's dream!"

She was right. The light in here would be perfect for an artist. "Look at the view." I pointed to the wide-open window, the towering grandfather pine that seemed to be framed like a painting.

She walked over and gazed out across the meadow and trees. I heard a very distinct sigh. "This is the perfect place to paint."

I smiled at her. "Think your uncle would like it?"

She blinked rapidly, touching a hand to her chest. "I guess I was thinking more of myself."

"You paint?" I flinched inwardly, embarrassed by the surprise in my tone. "I mean, I think that's great." That had probably happened to her before whenever she told someone that she painted. Would there be anything more difficult than a relative who was both critically and commercially successful at something you aspired to do?

A flash of consternation told me that she was sorry she brought it up. "There's no reason you or anyone else would know that I've studied art myself. Just a few art retreats, some private lessons, a semester of college classes. I'm mostly self-taught."

"Why did you stop?"

She shrugged, turned back to the view. A sharp, close breeze rattled the open window and caused the top of the pine tree to dip and sway. A bird of some kind sat on one of the top branches, swaying with the wind. "You know, taking care of my uncle's business. All the marketing, finances, making sure he has what he needs. It's a full-time job."

"I can believe it, but it's a shame you have to put your own dreams on hold."

She turned away from the window to look at me. The wind whipped up her red-blonde hair, causing it to fly around her head. She laughed, tried to hold it down with both hands.

"Let me get that window," I said, rushing over to slide it closed. "The one thing about living here on the Central Coast: you better be able to tolerate wind. I imagine you've already discovered we get quite a bit of it."

"I don't mind wind." She wandered around the room, touching her fingers to the pale walls. "Who knows, I might try painting again. This room . . ." She swept her hand to take it all in. "Perfect light, as I said before."

I glanced at my watch. "I hate to rush you, but I need to head back to San Celina. I hope you saw enough of the house to get a feel for it."

"Thank you so much for letting me tag along. Did you find what you came for?"

I nodded, holding up the china dog and the crystal box. Though I hadn't gone through every room like a real search, I reminded myself that this *wasn't* a real search.

We were at the front door when I couldn't remember whether I locked the window in the sunroom. "The alarm will probably not work if it's not locked," I said to Nola. "I'd better go check."

"I'll wait outside."

Sure enough, the window was closed but not locked. I locked it up and ran back down the stairs. On the bottom step, Pinky's striped cat sat with its tail wrapped elegantly around its body. It looked like a statue. I reached down and stroked its head. "Good night, Mr. Lionel. Guard the house."

He merely lifted his single eyebrow and yawned in reply.

CHAPTER 11

IT WAS FIVE MINUTES AFTER SIX AND DARK BY THE time I picked up Boo and drove home. Ray sat on the porch swing waiting for me, his hand resting on Scout's head. Scout bounded down the steps to greet me and Boo. Ray stood up and waved.

"Sorry I'm late," I said, setting Boo down and giving my own dog a hearty belly rub. "It's been a crazy day. Have Gabe and Kathryn left already?"

He nodded. "About a half hour ago."

I pressed my lips together, trying not to worry.

"They seemed fine. This'll all turn out okay, Benni. Your husband and his mother will work this out."

"I hope you're right." I wished I was as certain of that as he was. "At any rate, I can't do anything about it. But I

240

can feed these canines and then take you out for some of the best vittles in the city."

He laughed and scooped up Boo, who was dancing around his feet. "Sounds wonderful. Why don't you let me feed the pups? I've seen how you do it. Then you can go do whatever it is women do to freshen up."

I smiled gratefully at him. "Do I look wilted?"

"Nah," he said, laughing. "Just a little soft around the edges."

"Like I said, it's been a nutty day."

"I've been told I'm a good listener."

While he fed the dogs, I washed my face and quickly braided my hair. I pulled a green wool sweater on over my shirt, changed my dressy wool slacks for jeans and was ready to go.

I slipped my arm through his and told him about Liddie's Café on our walk there. "One of the best things about this house is that Liddie's is within walking distance."

Most of our walk, we strolled down Lopez Street in a companionable silence. Though it was a cool evening, it was busy downtown because of the holidays. With the tiny twinkling lights in the trees that canopied most of Lopez Street and the sounds of Christmas music filtering out from different stores and cafés, it truly was beginning to look a lot like Christmas.

Liddie's Café, about two blocks from the civic center and the police station, was packed with its usual assortment of ranchers coming to town for supper and shopping, chattering students who elected to stay in town over the holidays, police officers on break, retirees who liked

Liddie's inexpensive diner food and everyone else who just flat-out loved big portions of home-style cooking. The sign above the café read Open 25 Hours! Indeed, the owner of Liddie's didn't even close on Christmas, even though he was a good Catholic boy, but, instead, gave a free meal to any homeless people who came in and provided a place where lonely people could partake of a holiday meal.

"Liddie's has been here as long as I can remember," I told Ray when we slid into one of the red vinyl booths in back.

"There aren't too many places like this anymore. Not even in Kansas," he said, looking around at the brown and red fifties decor.

Lucky for us Nadine, Liddie's head waitress and the heart of the restaurant, was working tonight. I couldn't wait to introduce Ray to San Celina's most famous waitress, a woman who'd served me pancakes and chicken-fried steak through all of my most troubled moments as a child, teenager, dates, breakups, squabbles with Elvia and two marriages. Nadine knew everything about everyone in this town. If she didn't know something, it truly wasn't worth knowing.

"Benni Harper Ortiz, I haven't seen you in a coon's age," she said, pulling a pencil out of her pinkish-gray beehive hairdo. Her upswept hairstyle and pink plastic cat-eye glasses hadn't changed style, I'd been told, since Eisenhower was in office. Like the mashed potatoes and the golden French toast made with double-thick slices of sourdough bread, why change what worked?

"My life has been crazy," I said, opening a plastic

menu even though I'd memorized everything on it years ago. "Nadine, this is Ray Austin. He's—"

"Gabe's new stepdaddy," Nadine interrupted. "Good for his mama and, I'll venture, good for you. Congratulations, and nice to meet you."

I stared at her, struck dumb for a moment.

"Close your mouth, Benni," she said, giving a screechy cackle. "I knew about Ray and Kathryn ten minutes before they hit town."

I looked at an amused Ray and shook my head. "For years I've said the CIA should look into Nadine's information gathering methods."

She gave a sharp nod, taking my comment seriously. "I could clean this country up in no time. First thing I'd do is make it a law that everyone eat a hearty breakfast and get at least eight hours' sleep."

"Hear, hear," Ray said, lifting up his water glass. "You've got my vote."

She narrowed one tobacco-brown eye at me. "I like this man. But I hear Gabe doesn't."

"Nadine!" I felt my neck turn warm.

She shrugged and pulled her order pad out of her apron pocket. "I'm only repeating what I've heard."

Ray reached across the table and patted my hand. "I understand small towns, Benni. And I keep telling you, Gabe will come around."

"He's right," Nadine said. "Gabe will eventually accept his new stepdaddy. He's just still all in pieces about his cousin and whatnot. Mark my words, this will all turn out for the better."

I looked up at her, wanting desperately to believe that.

"I guess we'll have to wait and see. Gabe and Kathryn are having dinner tonight in Morro Bay . . ."

Nadine checked her large Timex wristwatch. "They finished their shrimp cocktails about ten minutes ago and have just started on their main course of mahimahi."

I could feel my eyes widen.

Nadine gave another loud cackle. "I was just putting you on. I have no idea what they are doing."

Ray laughed, and so did I. Coming here had been the perfect thing. She took our orders; hamburger for me, grilled cheese with beefsteak tomatoes for Ray. In no time, Nadine delivered our food, including a strawberry malt for me.

"I didn't order this," I said, accepting it gladly. So what if my jeans were already pinching my waist?

"You look like you need it," she said, glancing at me over her pink glasses. "Not your thickening waist, mind you. But psychologically."

"Thank you, I think."

"Constance has you running around with this Pinky Edmondson silliness like you were her personal slave."

This time I didn't act surprised that Nadine knew about what Constance had me doing. I took a long drink from my malt. "So, what do you think?"

"I think Constance Sinclair is completely bonkers, you know that," Nadine said. "But this time . . ." She clamped her thin lips together. "Pinky Edmondson did her share of stepping on people's toes. The things I hear would put hair on a seal."

"Like what?" I said.

She narrowed her eyes. "You know I don't gossip, Benni."

"Of course not," I said, not looking at Ray for fear I'd laugh out loud. "But I do want to know what you know about Pinky's affair with Dot St. James's husband."

She looked at me over her glasses again. "Wasn't very long, and Dot knew about it from the first time they do-si-doed."

"I knew she knew. But she didn't say when she found out." I glanced over at Ray, who was calmly chewing his grilled cheese sandwich. He'd certainly have a lot to tell his cronies about San Celina when he went back to Kansas.

"Yes, and despite her moaning and groaning, she really didn't care."

I cocked my head. "Oh, c'mon. She didn't care that her husband was having an affair with one of her friends? I know everyone's trying to be all modern and stuff, but people still care about adultery. I watch *Dateline NBC*."

She gave a triumphant smile. "Not if a person is busy do-si-doing themselves."

"Dot St. James was having her own affair? She didn't tell me that!"

"You're surprised? Those 49 Club women are like a bunch of rabbits from what I hear. Lucky for us they are all too old to procreate."

"Who was she seeing?" I picked up a French fry and took a small bite.

Nadine's white eyebrows scrunched together in frustration. "I don't know."

"What?" I said. "The great Nadine Brooks Johnson does not know a significant piece of San Celina society gossip? Call the newspaper."

She bonked me over the head with her order pad, causing Ray to chuckle. "You watch your mouth, missy. I told you, I do not gossip."

"Okay, important social commentary," I said, not wanting to annoy the woman who brought me a significant portion of my meals. "So, who do you *think* it might be?"

She bent closer and said sotto voce, "No one knows. But whoever it was, it was happening at the exact same time as Pinky was seeing Mr. St. James."

After she left, I mulled over this new piece of information as I ate my hamburger and fries.

"What do you think?" Ray asked after his second cup of coffee.

"I don't really know what to think," I said. "You know, somehow I have the feeling all of this is connected, but I don't know how."

"Do you really think this woman, Pinky, was murdered?"

I pondered his question while stirring the last of my strawberry malt. "I don't know, but there is something fishy going on, and I'm nosy enough to want to know what it is."

He leaned back in the booth. "I wish I could offer you some wise insight, but it all looks as clear as pea soup to me."

"On that we agree, Ray." I drank the last swallow of strawberry malt and looked up at the Elvis clock hanging above the kitchen pass-through. "Want to head back home? Maybe Gabe and Kathryn are back, and everything is hunky-dory."

He raised his gray, bristly eyebrows. "One can hope."

Gabe's car was in the driveway when we got back home, and the porch light was on. I said a quick prayer that everything had been settled between him and his mother. When Ray and I walked into the empty living room, I didn't get a good feeling.

"It's too quiet," I whispered to Ray.

"Yes," he agreed. "I'll go check on Kathryn."

"I'll lock up and go upstairs. Maybe they're just having an early night."

When I opened our bedroom door, both dogs jumped up to greet me. Gabe was lying in bed reading. Though I tried to immediately get a vibe from him, all I felt was . . . nothing.

"Do the dogs need to go out?" I asked.

He looked up at me over his wire-rimmed glasses. "Yes."

That one word said it all. The evening did not go well.

I took the dogs downstairs, let them out in the backyard and contemplated how I would handle this. Like many times when I was faced with an emotional dilemma that confused me, I tried to channel my gramma Dove and consider what she'd likely advise. It was past nine p.m., and though I could call her and get real live advice, I was trying to learn to figure things out on my own. I would be thirty-nine years old in March, it was time for me to stop running to my gramma every time I had a problem.

While the dogs sniffed around and had their last constitutional, I thought about what I would say to Gabe when I went back upstairs. When the dogs had their bedtime treat and we went back upstairs, I heard Dove's voice in my head: *"Sometimes, honeybun, the best thing you can do for a man is absolutely nothing. Just let him be."*

So that's what I did. I took my shower, settled Boo in his crate and climbed in bed. Gabe was still reading, so I turned on my bedside lamp and picked up the book I'd been reading on outsider art.

"Ray and I went to Liddie's," I said, settling down under the covers.

He nodded but didn't smile. I resisted the urge to ask how his night had gone. I scooted across our wide bed and laid my head on his shoulder.

"What's on the agenda for tomorrow?" His answer would tell me in a roundabout way what happened.

He set his papers down on the floor next to him. "I'm going to work. I couldn't tell you what my mother is doing. She might go home."

I bit my bottom lip, holding back my cry of surprise. It was worse than I thought. I decided to override Dove's advice—or rather the advice I thought she'd give—and just spit out what I was thinking. Who was I kidding? I'd never be as wise as Dove. "What happened?"

He stared straight ahead. "She has multiple sclerosis. She's known about it for six months."

When I didn't exclaim in surprise, his head jerked over to look at me. The truth was written all over my face.

"You knew?" Anger darkened his high cheekbones.

My words tumbled over themselves like water over river rocks. "Not for very long. Ray told me last night when I commented that she didn't seem herself. He asked me not to tell you. He felt so bad, but your mom wanted to tell you herself. It was—"

He held up his hand for me to stop. "I suppose you all had a great time discussing this behind my back."

I sat up, shocked at his remark. "Gabe, that's a horrible thing to say. No one was talking behind your back. I found out accidentally."

"No, my mother's husband *told* you."

He had me there. I knew it looked bad. I knew that he was hurt deeply, just as I would have been in his position. But I didn't know what to say, how or why I should defend my position or Ray's or his mother's.

"My sisters knew." His voice was bitter. "She told them before she came out here."

And Kathryn told them not to tell him. I understood why his mother wanted to be the one to tell her son, but this whole situation had gotten completely out of control simply because she just didn't pick up a phone the day before she flew out here. *Oh, Kathryn,* I thought. *What was it you were trying to accomplish with this trip? To see how many ways you could hurt your son?*

I waited to see what he would do. There was nothing I could say to defend what I'd done. Maybe I had been wrong not to tell him the minute Ray told me. But I knew my husband. If I'd told him, he'd have gone straight to his mother and demanded to know why she hadn't come to him. So, we'd have been in the same spot as we were now. Well, I thought, not exactly the same spot. He wouldn't be angry at *me*. Still, a small part of me was glad I wasn't the one who told him about his mother's illness. I guess in this situation there was no winning position.

"I'm sorry, Gabe," I said. "I was in a no-win position. I wanted to honor your mother's request—"

"Why?" he said, his voice harsh. "She's never been anything except hostile to you. Why would you care what she thinks of you?"

"I . . . I don't know," I stammered. "Because she's your mother."

"I'm your *husband*. You should care more what I think of you."

"I know that." I blinked my eyes, trying to hold back the tears. "I know I blew this. I should have told you, but I just . . . it was just . . ."

"Forget it." He threw back the covers and grabbed a pair of jeans and a sweatshirt. "I'm going out for a while."

I started to ask where, then bit back the words.

He pulled on his topsiders and grabbed his keys.

"Be careful," I called after him.

He didn't answer. I could hear his footsteps go down the stairs.

"I love you," I whispered to the empty doorway.

THE NEXT THING I REMEMBER WAS THE ALARM GOING OFF at two a.m. I stumbled out of bed and pulled on my sweatpants. I glanced over at Gabe's side. At some point he'd come home, though I'd obviously slept through his return. He'd been able to do that to me before, despite me being a pretty light sleeper. He'd learned a stealthiness as a soldier in Vietnam that had never completely left him. It was kind of creepy sometimes, I'd told him. He'd just laugh and say, "One of the many fascinating yet charming aspects of my complex personality."

Boo murmured a doggie protest about being woken up. I stuck my nose in the warm, downy ruff of his neck and made comforting sounds as I carried him downstairs, thinking about my sleeping husband.

Though he joked about it, he was, indeed, one of the most complex people I'd ever known. I couldn't even imagine what it must have been like for his mother raising him. Was she a little afraid of him? I had to admit, sometimes I was. Not physically, of course. Gabe would cut off his own arm before he'd harm a woman, a child or anyone weaker than him. It was his unpredictability that was disconcerting. But it was also part of what made him so interesting. Predictable people were wonderful, but so were the less predictable ones. I mean, in some ways my own gramma was about the most unpredictable person I knew besides Gabe, and I wouldn't want one thing changed about her. Daddy was as predictable as a sunset, and I wouldn't want him any different, either.

Where was I in all that? Predictably unpredictable is what Gabe called me one time. I suppose it all came down to accepting ourselves for who we were. You needed predictability in dentists and train engineers and unpredictability in artists and inventors. The rest of us fell somewhere in between.

CHAPTER 12

GABE WAS UP AND GONE BEFORE I WOKE UP AT SEVEN a.m. A note waited for me on the kitchen counter next to the coffeepot.

"I'll try to make the exhibit opening tonight. It will depend on my workday. Love, Gabe."

I stared at the note a moment, trying to discern his mood from the few dashed-off words. Of course, I couldn't. I didn't have a clue what was really going on inside him.

I checked my calendar and for the first time in weeks, my day was relatively free. Maybe I'd have time to take a nap this afternoon, so I'd be rested for the opening tonight. The phone rang when I was standing in front of the refrigerator trying to decide what to make for Kathryn and Ray's breakfast. It was Constance.

"There's an emergency," she said, her voice harsh and panicked.

My thoughts flew immediately to the Finch painting. Had someone broken into the folk art museum and taken it? Had something happened to the museum itself? Was anyone hurt?

Her voice broke through my racing thoughts. "Our speaker for the 49 Club Christmas luncheon canceled on us. You'll have to take her place."

"What?" My panic turned to annoyance in a millisecond.

"Which part don't you understand?" she asked, her voice impatient. "The luncheon is at noon at the Forum downtown. You'll be speaking at one thirty. Wear nice clothes."

"I thought Nola Finch was speaking today."

"Fifteen minutes is all we need from you. Nola Finch was only half the program. The other half was . . . well, never mind, doesn't matter, she canceled. Don't be late." Then she hung up.

I stared at the phone, whose buzzing dial tone was eerily reminiscent of Constance's voice. This was all I needed. What would I speak about? The only thing I could think of was tweaking the speech I was going to give tonight. I knew Constance would complain after the fact that I used the same speech twice, but what could I do? I had less than five hours before I had to give a talk to forty-eight snooty society women plus three wannabes. So much for my nap.

Twenty minutes later, Ray and Kathryn came into the kitchen just as I was pulling a pan of muffins out of the oven.

"Good morning," I said, my voice unnaturally cheery. "Banana muffins coming right up."

"Sounds wonderful," Kathryn said, her cheeks looking a little drawn. I hurt for her; I hurt for my husband. What if they couldn't resolve this before she left?

"What are your plans today?" I poured Ray a cup of coffee and started the electric teakettle for Kathryn's morning tea.

"Your neighbors, Beebs and Millee, kindly offered to give us the grand tour of San Celina County," Kathryn said, sitting down at the table.

"Apparently we have quite a full agenda with wineries, old cemeteries, and a tour of the San Miguel mission," Ray elaborated. "If I heard Beebs correctly, we're eating lunch in a cave?"

I set the platter of hot muffins on the table. "That's one of the wineries in north county. Gabe and I attended a fund-raiser there. It is literally a cave." I gave Kathryn a worried look. "You'll take time to rest, won't you?" Then I realized it might not be my place to make that comment. Fortunately, Kathryn took it with grace.

"Don't worry, Benni," she said, her voice warm. "Ray watches me like a hawk. We'll take it easy. I don't want to be sick on Christmas Day."

I gave an inward sigh of relief. Gabe was wrong. She was planning to stay through Christmas. That meant there was still a chance that they would patch things up. "I have a full day myself. I'm a last-minute speaker at the 49

Club Christmas luncheon today, and then there's the outsider artist exhibit opening tonight at seven o'clock. I'd love for you to come if you're not too tired."

"We'll see," Ray said.

"We'll *be there*," Kathryn said. "We wouldn't miss it for the world. Gabe's told me how hard you've worked on this. Isn't it quite an honor to have such a valuable painting donated to your museum's collection?"

I nodded, setting out plates, napkins and silverware for three. "Yes, there's a newspaper reporter coming from Los Angeles. The outsider art movement is just exploding, and our little museum is starting to carve a small place on the map for itself." I opened the refrigerator and took out a pitcher of grapefruit juice.

"Because of your hard work and expertise, no doubt," Kathryn said, smiling.

Her praise, so unexpected, caused me to blush with pleasure. "A lot of people's hard work and help. Even as annoying as our patroness, Constance Sinclair, can be, she's worked tirelessly to promote the museum." I set the pitcher on the table.

"Will Scout be all right being alone all day?" Kathryn asked.

"Ordinarily, but I think I'll drop him off at All Paws with Boo," I said. "It will be his first time in day care, but I think he'll like it."

By nine o'clock I had the kitchen cleaned, was dressed in brown tweedy slacks, a pale green shirt and golden brown cowboy boots. I dropped the dogs off at All Paws and was reminded by Suann that Boo still needed his picture taken with Santa.

"Yes, yes," I said. "I know. Did Hud call you?"

She nodded. "I don't mean to bug you about it, but he mentioned it when he was calling to see how Boo was doing."

"Don't worry, I'll call and reassure him."

Out in my truck, I dialed the number he'd given me and got the housekeeper.

"Mr. Hudson and his family are off on a ride," she said. "May I take a message?"

"Yes, tell him Mrs. Ortiz called and said not to worry. Boudin and Santa, it's going to happen."

"Yes, ma'am," the woman said, her voice not missing a beat. She'd probably taken more than her share of weird messages for Hud. I then dialed the ranch and got the answering machine. I sure wished Sam had convinced Gabe to buy him a cell phone.

"Never mind," I told Dove's recorded voice. "I'm looking for Sam."

I dialed the bookstore and hit pay dirt. Sam himself answered.

"What's up, *madrastra*?"

"Want to earn forty bucks?"

"Sure. I still have to buy Dad and Grandma a Christmas present. Who do I have to kill?"

"No death involved. I need someone to take Boo to see Santa."

His laugh almost rattled the cell phone in my hand. "You're kidding? No *problema*. Easy money."

"You'll have to find a Santa and convince him to have his photo taken with a dog." I had a feeling it wouldn't be as easy as he thought.

"Just a minute." He went away from the phone for a few minutes. I could hear people talking in the background. Elvia must be opening the store at nine a.m. instead of ten during the holiday season. "I'm back," Sam said. "I have a lunch break at noon. Where can I find the little guy?"

"All Paws on Board Doggie Daycare. It's in back of the folk art museum."

"Okay, cool. I'll do it during my lunch hour."

"I'll leave his car seat with Suann. Make sure to buckle him in. And thanks. You're the bomb."

"I know," he replied.

I got out of the truck again and took Boo's car seat inside All Paws, informing Suann that Sam would be by to pick up Boo for his photo op.

"Check that off my list," I said to myself on my way back to the museum. I spent the next hour at my desk at the folk art museum editing my speech for the exhibit opening. With a few modifications, I could use the same one for the luncheon. True, some of the people hearing it would overlap both events, but many more wouldn't. I called the catering company and made sure they had the time and menu right for the opening.

"White and rosé wines," I read off my list. "Sparkling water and ginger ale, cheese platters, crackers, tiny cream puffs, vegetable plates, mini–chicken tacos and those little cherry tomato thingies with the mushrooms." Constance was footing the bill for the opening tonight. There'd be, if everyone we invited attended, about one hundred people. Tonight would be the unveiling and official presentation of the painting to the museum with Nola Maxwell Finch standing in for her reclusive uncle. We'd pulled every string we had to obtain as much media coverage as possible. This was the big time for the Josiah Sinclair Folk Art Museum.

After verifying everything with the caterers, I took a deep breath and sat back in my high-backed office chair. Was there something I was forgetting? D-Daddy was supervising the cleaning of the museum. The artists from the co-op were straightening up the studios and deciding what of their creations should be displayed, hoping to score a little attention for themselves from the visiting Los Angeles journalist. Everything was on schedule.

I contemplated calling Gabe, just to see how he was doing, then squelched the urge. I might be tempted into discussing his mother, and I swore to myself I was staying out of that. Instead, I called Dove to tell her about Kathryn's condition.

"Hey, Gramma."

"Hey, granddaughter. How's things in town?"

I sighed, not knowing where to start. "No murders in the Ortiz household yet, though we've come close a few times." I updated her on the most recent development between Gabe and Kathryn, including her MS.

"What a shame. How's Gabe taking it?"

"I don't really know how he's taking her condition because he's so wrapped up in being upset about being the last to find out."

Dove's voice was sympathetic. "Can you blame him?"

"I suppose not. But it was a sticky call for me. I didn't want to be the one to tell him about his mom's condition, but I hated holding out on him."

"That's just one of those places where you just can't win, honeybun. Don't worry too much about it. He'll come around. You said he seemed more settled this morning?"

"His note didn't sound angry."

"Then if I were you, I'd get on to whatever business you have today and let things work themselves out."

"No wise homily about mother and son relationships?" I lightly mocked.

"Mind your own beeswax? That wise enough for you?"

I couldn't help laughing. "Okay, guess I can't misunderstand that." I sat up in my chair and brushed some crumbs off my desk pad. "I do have plenty of other things to worry about today. Want to hear something absolutely maddening? Constance roped me into speaking at the 49 Club Christmas luncheon today."

"Didn't they already have a speaker?"

"I guess whoever it was canceled at the last minute. So I have to warm up the audience for Nola Finch, who people are really coming to see."

"You'll do fine. You ready for your opening tonight?"

"Thank goodness for D-Daddy and the docents. They have everything under control. You are coming, aren't you?"

"Me and Isaac will be there in our fanciest threads. Anything you need me to do for you?"

"A little prayer might help. Not for me, so much, but for Gabe and his mama."

"Already got that covered. Now, I have to go feed my geese before they storm the kitchen."

On my way out through the museum, I stopped by Abe Adam Finch's painting one more time. D-Daddy had done an excellent job hanging it. Light reflected off the old hacienda's pale adobe walls, illuminating the details of the animal faces painted among the small odd-shaped leaves. What was he trying to say in this painting? Like a lot of outsider art, his message appeared to be private until he chose to reveal it.

It was now eleven o'clock, still plenty of time to get to the luncheon. The Forum, a large, Greek-style building used for a variety of San Celina's society gatherings, was, fortunately for me, only ten minutes away in downtown San Celina.

I sat in my office for a few more minutes with my eyes closed, trying to calm my nervous stomach. No matter how many times I spoke in front of groups, I always had stage fright. There were many things I loved about my job, but this was not one of them. And I wouldn't even feel relief after the luncheon, because I had another speech tonight. I took a deep breath and exhaled slowly. By tomorrow this would all be over.

The Forum was one of San Celina's newer buildings, where many clubs and private citizens held their special functions, wedding receptions or charity auctions. It had a large kitchen built to accommodate the specific needs of catering companies and had a huge, airy ballroom-size hall that I'd seen decorated in every way imaginable from a colorful, pinata-themed Cinco de Mayo dance to a wedding whose theme was gnomes and fairies to Western hoedowns with fiddle music and tri-tip barbecue to fancy ladies' luncheons that featured models wearing Chanel suits and music by the Santa Celine Mission orchestra.

I arrived a half hour early to orient myself and scope out what type of microphone and podium were being used. I parked in the back next to two pink vans with EmmyLou's Creative Catering painted on the side, and entered through the kitchen where Constance, not to my surprise, was giving the catering company detailed instructions on how to do their job. With Constance's back to me, I gave the woman she was chattering at a sympathetic smile. Her face looked familiar, and I realized I'd seen her photo in the *San Celina Tribune* a few weeks ago. Her name was Prudence, and her catering company was new and was named for her rescued greyhound, Emelia Louella. Being the new kid on the block was probably the reason she was catering this function for Constance. All the established catering companies had, no doubt, been conveniently booked this day. Constance had a tendency to leave chewed-to-the-marrow bones in her wake.

After Prudence assured Constance that everything would be fine, Constance turned to face me.

"It's about time you got here," she said, her thin nose quivering like an anxious rabbit. Her back was to Prudence, so this time I was on the receiving end of a sympathetic smile from the beleaguered caterer. "Are you all ready?"

"Yes, ma'am," I said, not elaborating.

"What are you going to talk about?" she demanded.

I forced a smile and said, "I'm going to talk about Abe Adam Finch and his painting."

"You can't do that!"

"Why not?"

"What will Nola talk about? You can't talk about the same thing."

"I'm sure we'll cover different aspects," I assured her. "I'll talk about acquiring the painting, what it means to our museum and a little about outsider art—"

"No, no, no!" Constance interrupted. "You cannot do that. You must talk about something else."

I have to admit, I was flummoxed. It was less than an hour before the luncheon, and she was telling me I had to come up with a completely different subject? So much for the notes I'd so neatly printed on three-by-five index cards. I lifted my hands in frustration and found my voice. "Constance, I can't believe—"

"Oh, fine," she said, throwing up her own hands. "Just talk about the museum. Try to make it interesting. This *is* our special holiday luncheon."

She turned and stomped out of the kitchen, leaving me to gape at her departing back. The clatter of pans and chatter of the catering staff continued on as if nothing significant had happened. They'd probably seen meltdowns like this a thousand times.

"This is it," I said to no one in particular. "I am quitting this job and going to work at Target."

"I could use a server," Prudence said.

"She's impossible, but she is also the museum's biggest donor."

"Want a cream puff?" Prudence asked.

I declined her offer and went out to my truck to think. What could I say about the museum that these women hadn't already heard? I felt my stomach twist into a knot. This time, I seriously was considering turning in my resignation. What would life be like if I didn't have the museum and, even more important, Constance Sinclair, to worry about? I could spend more time at the ranch working the cattle with Daddy—he wasn't getting any younger—or do some more decorating on our house or even sit on my porch and relax for ten minutes.

I was thinking about what a wonderful lady of leisure I could be when someone tapped on my truck's window. It was Nola Finch.

"Oh, hi," I said, opening the truck door. I glanced at my watch. How long had I been woolgathering? "Is it time for me to go on?"

"No, no," she said, laughing lightly. "I just talked to Constance and wanted to touch base with you." She was dressed in a simple hunter green wool suit with a silk ivory T-shirt. Her apricot hair was pulled up in a neat chignon, and she was wearing an obviously handmade necklace of amber and some kind of dark green stones. She had an elegant, creative flair to the way she put her clothes together. I wondered if she ever regretted giving up her own artistic career to oversee her uncle's.

She smiled at me. "Constance told me that she told you that you couldn't talk about my uncle and his painting."

"Yes, but it's okay. I'll just ramble on about the museum, what we do there, the other artists who work at the co-op. Nothing that these women haven't heard before, but it'll be so boring that they'll love it when you take the stage." Then, realizing how that might sound, I backtracked. "I mean, not that they're not thrilled to hear what you . . . about your uncle, I mean . . ."

She touched my arm. "Benni, it's okay. I told Constance that I actually preferred you be the one to talk about my uncle's painting. I came out here so we could coordinate what we were going to say. I assured Constance, there's plenty to say about my uncle, enough for both of us." She lowered her voice in a conspiratorial tone. "Between you and me, I've done more than my share of these ladies' luncheons, as I'm sure you have. I'm positive half of them will be nodding off and the other half will be fidgeting and wanting us to hurry so they can have dessert."

I laughed, liking this woman more and more. "You are so right. How about I talk about outsider art in general, what it is and why it is so popular now, and end my talk with how important it is to the folk art museum to acquire your uncle's painting. Then you can move right into his life story and what he is doing now."

"That sounds perfect. It'll be over before you know it."

"From your lips to God's ears."

We walked into the decorated ballroom together and looked for our respective place settings. She was seated with Constance and two of the board members of the 49 Club. Their four-person table was front and center of the podium. I found my name at the table that hosted the three nominees. It was set off to the right side, closest to the swinging kitchen doors. Its placement was very telling.

"Welcome to the cheap seats, Benni," Bobbie said. Francie and Dot both shot her aggravated looks. They obviously didn't have Bobbie's sense of humor about our not-so-prestigious table.

"At least we'll get served first," I said.

"Or last," Francie said in a grumpy voice.

"Oh, cool your spurs, Francie," Bobbie said, patting her on the back. "Before you know it, you'll be president of this snobby group of overbred racehorses."

Dot gave Bobbie a horrified look.

"Oh, Dot, you'll get in too," Bobbie said. "I can't imagine why you would want to, but you will."

"Bobbie," Francie said, her voice tight and angry. "Why are you even here if you don't want to be a member?" She leaned over her gold-rimmed china plate, painfully obvious in her desire to be a part of this group. What was sad was, knowing the way women like Constance worked, Bobbie would be the one asked, simply because she didn't want it, and that impressed snobby people more than anything.

"Promised my mama I'd try, so here I am." She leaned back in her chair, her brown and white western-style suit looking as out of place at this affair as a clown costume. The women of the 49 Club definitely preferred to dress in a more Brooks Brothers or Chanel style.

Echoing my own thoughts, Dot said, "No doubt, just because you don't really want it, you'll be the one they vote in." Her tone was bitter.

Bobbie just shrugged and sipped the three-olive martini in front of her.

Please, I thought, *let this be over soon.*

After our lunch of a chicken breast covered with a surprisingly tasty cheese sauce, real mashed potatoes, fresh green beans and hot sourdough rolls, I suffered through the business portion of the meeting. There would be a short break when we were encouraged to look over the silent auction items lining the back of the hall, reminded by Constance that the money would go for books and personal items for needy children. They would be part of the Christmas baskets being passed out by San Celina Social Services in conjunction with local churches, scouting and FFA groups.

"Dig deep, ladies," Constance said into the microphone. She looked pointedly at our table, her message clear.

"For cryin' in a bucket," Bobbie said, standing up. "We're supposed to buy votes now?"

I headed over to the long tables of donations hoping I'd find something appropriate for Kathryn for Christmas. Elvia had solved my gift dilemma for Ray yesterday. She'd found an antique orange crate label: San Celina Express Navel Oranges. It depicted an old steam train barreling through a grove of orange trees. I'd immediately dropped it off at the framer's and would pick it up in a few days. I meandered down the long line of donated items, passing up the impractical gifts like days at a local spa or a weekend at a luxury hotel in San Francisco.

At the end of the table, there was a necklace made by a local jewelry artist who wasn't a member of our co-op. It was an interesting mixture of stones: amber and turquoise separated by carved sterling silver beads. It was the sort of necklace that any woman could wear with either a fancy blouse or a man's T-shirt. There were four bids with the last one being seventy-five dollars. Knowing Christmas was getting close, I rashly put down one hundred fifty dollars. If I won it, I'd tell Kathryn that the money went to books for kids. She'd like that, I was sure. During this time the three nominees mingled with the rest of the club members, obviously trying for that one last impression to secure votes. From what I understood, the voting would take place as they left, with them dropping their ballots in a locked box at the door for Constance and the other two board members to count later.

Both my speech and Nola's went off without a hitch and actually sounded like we'd coordinated them. She didn't reveal anything new about her uncle but gave the same publicity spiel I'd read in countless art magazines: his desire for solitude, his little house in northern Nevada (she pointedly didn't name the town, something I'd noticed before), his love for his art. There was a short question-and-answer period after her talk, and someone asked, "Do you think your uncle will ever come out to San Celina and immortalize our county? We have some beautiful places to paint here."

Nola smiled and shook her head, a practiced sadness to her expression. "I doubt it. Though I don't speak of it much, Uncle Abe's health is not as good as it once was. Travel is not only hard for him psychologically but physically."

"Has he ever been to the West Coast?" the same woman asked.

"He loves his little place in Nevada," she said, not exactly answering the question.

After a few more questions, dessert was served, a layered chocolate-strawberry mousse. By that time the tension at our table was so high that it was starting to give me an upset stomach. Once Constance said her last few words and brought the gavel down to close the December meeting, I quickly said good-bye and hightailed it out of there. On my way out, I went by the auction table to see if I'd "won" the necklace. Luck was with me. I wrote out a check, thrilled I'd solved the mother-in-law Christmas present problem, and picked up the necklace, which was already wrapped in lovely silver paper with bright red ribbon. One less thing for me to worry about.

It was four p.m. when I dropped by the folk art museum for a last check on things. D-Daddy had everything under control.

"I'll be back up here by five thirty at the latest," I told him. "I have to pick up the dogs, feed them and then change clothes. The caterers should be here by then."

"I'll stay until you get back, *ange*," he said.

I didn't ask if he was coming to the opening, because I knew that though he loved readying the museum for exhibit openings, he didn't like attending them. It had become a sort of tradition that I give him a gift certificate for two to a local restaurant so he could enjoy a peaceful dinner with one of his many female companions while I pandered to the rich and influential of San Celina.

"Here," I said, handing him an envelope. I ruined the surprise by saying, "It's to that new restaurant by the creek, Creole Catin." I knew that *catin* meant "doll" in Cajun.

D-Daddy grinned and nodded his head in approval. "Been wanting to try their crawfish."

"I've heard it's great. You'll be eating better than me tonight, for sure."

"I'll bring you the doggie bag."

After picking up a very tired Boo and Scout, I headed home. The house was empty, telling me the twins and Kathyrn and Ray had not returned from their San Celina tour. I briefly worried again that the day would be too much for Kathryn. I hoped I made it clear this morning that it really wouldn't hurt my feelings if she was too tired to attend tonight.

After the dogs were settled, I called Gabe at work. His assistant, Maggie, answered.

"You just caught him," she said. In a few seconds, he came on the line.

"Hey, Chief," I said. "How's your day going?"

"Don't ask. What's up?" I could hear him trying to keep the impatience out of his voice.

"Sounds like you're busy. Are you going to be able to come to the opening tonight?"

A loud sigh came over the phone. "*Querida,* I'm sorry, I won't be able to make it. Things are just piled up here. I've got reports that are already late and a meeting with FEMA first thing tomorrow morning. There's things on the city's new disaster preparedness plan that I—"

"It's okay," I interrupted. "It's really not that big of a deal. I just think your mother will be disappointed."

"She'll get over it," he said, his voice clipped. "Anything else you need?"

Though I probably should have been irritated at him for deliberately avoiding his mother and this important moment in my career, I was only sad. I knew this man better than anyone, and I knew that he was in so much pain that the only emotion he'd allow himself to feel was anger.

"Nothing else. Just don't forget to eat dinner, okay?"

"I'm having dinner with Father Mark," he said. "He's got some ideas about mentors for kids aging out of the foster system. He thought some of my officers might be interested."

"Sounds like a good idea," I answered, sending the Lord a quick prayer of thanks. Father Mark was just the person Gabe needed to see. "Tell him hey for me."

"See you tonight. Hope your opening goes well."

"It will. D-Daddy has everything under control."

I decided to shock everyone and wear a skirt. I paired my swishy black calf-length skirt with a bright red silk shirt and black boots. With the platinum and diamond horseshoe necklace Gabe bought me a few years ago and diamond studs from Emory, it was as classy as I was going to get. I petted the dogs one last time, made sure they had fresh water and, hoping for the best, cracked the back door since Boo wasn't big enough to get through the doggie door yet. The worst that could happen was an accident on our wooden floors, something entirely fixable. I rolled my black skirt one more time with the lint lifter and was off.

The catering truck had already arrived and was unloading their silver trays filled with hors d'oeuvres. I passed D-Daddy leaving and wished him a good dinner. I would have given anything to be going with him. Evenings like this had never been the part of my job I was particularly fond of, but with everything that was going on with Gabe and his mother, I was even less enthralled with chatting up San Celina's elite in hopes they would support the museum.

Still, I was proud to be the recipient of Abe Adam Finch's generosity, and the least we could do was make this night as special as possible for his niece. Did she go back and tell him what these evenings were like? Did it even matter to him? Again, I couldn't help wondering if he was perhaps one of those artistic savants, incapable of relating to people yet able to create art that moved people's hearts.

After a final inspection of the refreshments set up in the artist's co-op studios, I went back into the museum to check the painting one more time.

"It's spectacular," a low, familiar voice said behind me.

I turned around to see my stepgrandpa, Isaac Lyons. "Oh, Isaac, thanks so much for coming. That'll really impress the journalist from L.A." I gave him an enthusiastic hug. "Where's Dove?"

"Already nattering away at someone she knows. I swear we can't walk five feet in this town without stopping to hear someone's life story." He said the words with a huge grin on his perpetually suntanned face, telling me he actually didn't mind having his walks interrupted. He'd just recently cut his waist-length white braid, and his hair was thick and wavy around his face, giving him a leonine appearance to match his name.

Living in San Celina had been a huge change for Isaac, an internationally famous photographer who left his home in Chicago to marry my gramma Dove. But we'd welcomed him into our family as wholeheartedly as he'd wanted to join. His celebrity had been hard on Dove at first, but she'd grown used to it. And at times like this, when his celebrity could help someone she loved, well, she'd stand on a chair and announce his presence herself.

"Hey, honeybun," Dove said, coming over to us. She stopped in front of Abe Adam Finch's *Tree of Life* painting. "My stars, this is magnificent."

"I know," I said. "I'm still pinching myself at our good luck. Mr. Finch could have given it to any art museum in the country, but we were the lucky ones."

"I can't think of any museum who deserves it more," Isaac said.

"Thanks, Gramps," I said. "But you may be prejudiced."

At that moment, Dove's name was called out, and she headed toward a group of ladies I recognized from the Farm Bureau. "Don't forget to try the little cream puffs," I called after her.

Isaac and I turned back to the painting. We were discussing the detail of the colorful animal faces painted on the tree when a man with shaggy brown hair and Ben Franklin eyeglasses joined us. He was wearing black jeans, a bluish tweed jacket a shade too large in the shoulders and black leather Adidas athletic shoes.

"You know," he said, studying the painting. "You can't help but wonder how much of this guy's popularity has to do with the fact that no one has ever actually seen him."

Isaac and I turned to stare at the man.

"You can't deny this is an incredible painting," I said to the man, then glanced up at Isaac, whose eyebrows had shot up in curiosity.

"I suppose it's nice enough if you're into the primitive thing. But you have to agree with me that there is an argument in the art world about the artistic legitimacy of so-called outsider art and how much of its appeal has to do with the artist's odd background or personality quirks as with the art itself."

He had a point, but it was the snarky way he was saying it that annoyed me. It was as if he believed the whole folk art world was trying to pull something over on "real" artists.

"Do you think that's a question that can ever be really answered?" I asked, my voice tart. "It's not so different in the mainstream art world. I mean, would many of the world's contemporary fine artists be just as popular without their weird lifestyles and foibles? Jackson Pollock, for instance?"

The man smiled at me and shook his head. "Ah, we could argue about this all day. The truth is, art, whether anyone wants to admit it or not, is partly in the eye of the beholder and partly politics."

"So you believe there's no objective way to judge art? What about van Gogh? Da Vinci?"

"Van Gogh never sold a painting in his lifetime. That tells you something, though I'm not sure what." He held out a hand. "James Leonard Bradford. *L.A. Times.*"

Great, I thought. *I should have found out who he was before I spouted off. Oh, well, I didn't actually say anything that I regretted, though I would have liked to have known I was talking to a journalist.*

"Is that what your article is going to be about?" I asked lightly.

He glanced up at Isaac, ignoring my question. "You're Isaac Lyons."

Isaac's raisin-dark eyes sparkled. "Yes, sir."

"Love your work. What're you doing here?"

His emphasis on the word *here* said what he thought about San Celina. I could see Isaac considering whether he should put this guy in his place or not. Though a big part of me was hoping he'd verbally cut this guy up like a Benihana chef, another part of me knew that our museum needed the good publicity this annoying guy could give us. Fortunately for the museum, Isaac was more mature than I was.

"I live *here* with my wife," he replied. He shifted his eyes over to me. "Her grandmother."

James Leonard Bradford glanced over at me, his eyes suddenly interested. He turned back to Isaac. "That right? So, would you consider doing an interview with me? Are you planning a new photo series?"

Isaac smiled at him. "It's possible, but I don't believe I'm familiar with your work. Let's see how this article about my granddaughter's museum goes first. You can contact me through Benni."

I wanted to throw my arms around Isaac right there. He virtually assured us a positive article.

"Uh, yeah, sure," the reporter said. He turned back to me, pulling a small notebook out of his jacket. "So, what do you know about Abe Adam Finch?"

Isaac excused himself and left me to talk to Mr. Bradford. I told the reporter the little I knew about Abe Adam Finch and pointed out Nola Finch to him. "She's pretty protective of her uncle, so I wouldn't push her."

He shrugged and grinned at me. "Pushing is what I do. But don't worry, never killed anyone yet."

At seven o'clock, Constance went to the small podium

we'd placed next to the painting and rang a small bell, getting everyone's attention. After a few words about how thankful we are to Abe Adam Finch, how this will put the Josiah Sinclair Folk Art Museum on the map, she then turned the podium over to me.

After the requisite fawning and recognition of the museum's financial supporters, especially Constance Sinclair, I gave my talk, ending with the unsubtle plea about why it was important for a community to support its artists. Then I asked Nola Finch to officially present the painting to the museum. I thanked everyone for coming and told them to enjoy the refreshments.

After the requisite photographs, I was pouring myself a glass of ginger ale when my mother-in-law came up, her face pale and tired-looking. Ray hovered protectively at her side.

"That was a wonderful speech, Benni," she said. "I'm sorry my son wasn't here to hear it."

I could hear the disappointment in her voice.

"I understand. You know how demanding his job is. He can't always control his time."

Her voice was tight, controlled, reminding me of Gabe's. "He's the boss. I can't imagine that, short of a hostage situation, he couldn't break away for an hour." Then her face turned pink, realizing what she'd just said. "Oh, Benni, I'm sorry. I didn't mean to make light—"

I touched her forearm with my fingertips. "It's okay, Kathryn. And, really, I don't expect Gabe to come to every museum opening."

"But this one is special," she insisted.

I couldn't deny that, but I also didn't want to feed the antagonism between my mother-in-law and my husband. Besides, I was sure that this had as much to do with unresolved issues between them as her annoyance at Gabe appearing to not support my career. I glanced over at Ray, who was watching us both with sad, sympathetic eyes.

"I'm sure he would have been here if he could," I said, my voice light. "He's been to tons of these openings. He's very supportive of what I do."

Her face was skeptical, but she didn't comment. I hoped that my words would help put this to rest. I was suddenly very tired and was just looking forward to the day we could stand in the train station and wave good-bye to Kathryn and Ray.

"I'd better mingle," I said. "I'll see you both back at home."

"Of course," Kathryn said, touching her chest. "You must see to your guests. I think we'll go home. I'm a little weary."

After they left, I wandered through the crowd answering questions and greeting people. I saw Nola across the room a few times and waved to her. She was never without a crowd of people surrounding her: art lovers, collectors and folks just flat-out curious about her uncle. I wondered if she ever grew weary of being the sole spokesperson for her famous relative.

A lull came in the groups of people studying the *Tree of Life* painting, so I went back over to it, fascinated again by its rich detail and arresting, otherworldly colors. It was like an intricate quilt with an almost 3-D effect, as if the fantastical tree rose up out of the canvas, and the leaves were real enough to touch. I looked closely at each animal's face, mesmerized by the details. There was a regular Noah's ark of animals, and I wondered if that was the source of his inspiration. He seemed especially fond of cats. There were numerous feline faces in the painting, some smiling, some wide-eyed, but one in particular looked familiar. I peered closer, gazing at its peculiar markings. It was blue and green striped and had one odd marking over its left eye. I swallowed the exclamation in my throat. If the cat were black and tan, it could have been a dead ringer for Pinky Edmondson's cat, Lionel.

CHAPTER 13

𝓗AD ABE ADAM FINCH AND PINKY EDMONDSON known each other?

Had he been to her house in Cambria, seen Lionel who, I remember May Heinz saying, was only three years old? How else would he have put this cat with the unusual markings in this painting? Granted, the connection between these two people seemed unlikely. And surely Nola would have mentioned it when she was looking through Pinky's house.

Unless she didn't know.

I glanced over at Nola, talking to a group of artists from the co-op. She looked at me just as I did, a questioning expression on her face. I smiled at her, trying to appear nonchalant.

Could her uncle have a secret life that he was keeping from her? One that included Pinky Edmondson? The thought seemed fantastic. Where would they have met? What kind of relationship was it? And, to be honest, what difference did it make?

I moved closer to the painting and studied the whimsical cat. The spot over the right eye, making it appear to have one eyebrow, sure reminded me of Pinky's cat.

I thought about it the rest of the evening, trying to be subtle, but drawn again and again back to the painting to look at the cat, wondering if I was seeing something that wasn't there. When the last patron had left and some of the artists helped me straighten up the museum in preparation for its public opening tomorrow, I came to the conclusion it wasn't all that important. I suspected my real problem was I was looking for something to fret about rather than the real problem waiting for me at home, a mother and son who seemed so far apart emotionally and were both so unwilling to give an inch, that their relationship would always be a source of pain rather than comfort.

I found the file in my office that had the photo of the painting as well as all the articles I'd found about Abe Adam Finch. I stuck the folder in my truck. If I had time tomorrow, I'd run out to Pinky's house and see if I was imagining things about this cat. Even if it was the same cat, maybe she'd sent him a picture of it. Maybe it was just a huge coincidence. At any rate, it didn't matter. It would neither add nor take away from the painting to know that Abe Adam Finch and Pinky Edmondson had a relationship. And if Nola didn't know about it, well, maybe that was better, although it would be beyond ironic if she ended up buying Pinky's house. I couldn't help wondering what her uncle would think about that, if he indeed had a relationship with Pinky and never told his niece.

At home, Kathryn and Ray were waiting for me in the kitchen with a fresh pot of herbal tea. Scout lay on his side in front of the sink, and Boo was scampering around chasing a toy that Ray trailed across the floor. I didn't have the heart to tell my mother-in-law I didn't like chamomile tea and so accepted a cup and sat down at the kitchen table.

"Did you enjoy the exhibit?" I asked, picking up Boo, who pawed at my leg. I ran my fingers through his soft puppy fur. Though I hated admitting it, I was getting attached to him. Darn that Hud.

"Oh, yes," Kathryn said. "The painting was beautiful, and the rest of the exhibit was fascinating." She smiled and circled her teacup with her long fingers. "Your speech was delightful."

"Thank you. I'm just glad my speeches are over now. I can actually start thinking about the holidays." I moved my chair back and placed an already-sleeping Boo in my lap. His little face lay cupped in my hand, a comforting pillow of warm flesh. The expression of contentment on his face made me smile. If only I could sleep so peacefully.

We were still discussing the exhibit when Gabe walked into the kitchen dressed in running shorts and a sweatshirt. He'd obviously gone for a late run. A good thing, I thought. He needed something to work off his tension. It certainly beat going to a bar.

"Hey," he said, walking over to the refrigerator and pulling out a carton of orange juice. His tone seemed a tad adolescent, reminding me of Sam.

"Good evening, son," Kathryn said, her tone even but with a touch of steel, much like I'd heard in Gabe's voice on more than one occasion.

I honestly wasn't annoyed that he hadn't attended the exhibit. I'd grown used to the demands of his job, and I didn't feel neglected or ignored because he couldn't make this one. But it was obvious that it bugged his mother.

"Did you have a nice run?" she asked.

I watched, fascinated by all that *wasn't* being said but was absolutely being communicated. Her tone was saying, *So, you had time for a run but no time to come to your wife's event?* I brought Boo up to my chest, cuddling him. He shifted and didn't wake up.

"Yes, I did," he said, not looking at her and drinking right from the orange juice carton. My mouth dropped open in surprise. I'd never, ever seen him do that. My husband had meticulous personal habits and would never have done something so . . . so . . . juvenile. He drained the carton and threw it in the sink.

"The exhibit was beautiful," she said. "Benni did an excellent job."

"She always does," he said. "My wife is very competent."

They stared at each other a moment. The air seemed to crackle in our small kitchen. I almost said something, thinking that maybe Dove's advice wasn't right just at this moment, that perhaps these two did need intervention. I caught Ray's eye, and he shook his head slightly from side to side. Though I hadn't known him long, he'd impressed me as being a wise and thoughtful man, so I heeded his warning.

"Why couldn't you be there?" Kathyrn asked.

"I had to work." He looked over at me. "Didn't you tell her I had to work?"

I nodded my head, not daring to say anything.

"Surely you could have taken an hour out of your busy schedule for your wife's event. Honestly, Gabe, this was a big night in Benni's life, and I would think you'd want to be a part of it."

"I had to work," he repeated, enunciating each word with great care. "*Surely* you know what that's like, not being there for your family because duty calls."

His bitter words took her by surprise, as they did me. But she recovered more quickly. Her voice was cold. "I was trying to make a living for my family."

"So am I," he replied, matching her icy tone.

He left the room without another word. The three of us sat there in stunned and embarrassed silence. Thankfully, Boo chose that time to wake up and start squirming in my hands.

"Whoops," I said, standing up. "I think someone needs to go outside and water the grass."

It was a perfect out for me. The moment was about as awkward as I'd ever experienced. I'd been married to my first husband, Jack, for fifteen years, and had lived within shouting distance of his mother. Nothing close to this kind of thing had ever happened. But Jack and his mother had both been extremely easygoing people. Jack had been her youngest son, the one who had inherited her relaxed and cheerful personality. His older brother, Wade, had been the volatile one, the one more like his father. Gabe and his mother were behaving like Wade and my late father-in-law: two strong-willed people butting heads, both determined to prove the other was at fault.

Though I felt sympathy for Kathryn, I also knew that she'd asked for it a little by springing her new husband on Gabe and keeping him out of the loop about her MS.

And there was all that history when Rogelio died—Kathryn, a traumatized widow with the frightening task of making a living, raising her ten-year-old daughters and coping with Gabe, a traumatized, out-of-control sixteen-year-old boy with raging hormones and a grief he couldn't express. If any family had needed grief counseling, it was probably them, but people weren't as open and accepting about going to therapy back in the sixties.

When I came back into the kitchen, only Ray was there. He was rinsing out our teacups and putting them in the dishwasher.

"Kathryn went to bed," he said. "She asked me to wish you good night."

I set Boo down on the floor and reached into the dog treat jar to give him and Scout their before-bed biscuits. I couldn't help smiling when Boo took his biscuit, threw it in the air and attacked it like it was actually a moving animal. I was beginning to remember why people got puppies. Their spontaneous antics made you forget for a moment the dreariness of everyday life. I turned my eyes back to Ray. "What are we going to do?"

He closed the dishwasher door and turned to look at me. "Benni, this is old, old business that happened way before you or I came into the picture. I don't think we can do anything except wait around to pick up the pieces."

I sighed, reached down and scratched behind Scout's ears. He looked up at me, his golden-brown eyes worried. He was more nervous than usual, obviously picking up on the tension in the house. Like most animals, he hated it when his routine, either physically or emotionally, was interrupted. "You're right. It's basically the same advice Dove gave me, but I can't help but want to hurry things along. It would be a tragedy for Kathryn to go home without the two of them resolving this."

His face looked tired. "I know."

Upstairs, Gabe was in bed with his bedside light already turned out. I put Boo in his crate and took a shower. By the time I crawled under the covers, I'd decided that if Gabe was awake, I would talk to him about this.

"Friday?" I whispered.

"I'm awake." His voice was flat, unemotional, telling me that he did not want to talk about this.

I scooted closer to him, placing my hand on his warm back. The snarling marine bulldog tattooed on his back eyed me with its never-changing anger. "Friday, this can't go on."

"I don't want to talk about this, Benni." He didn't move an inch.

I leaned over and placed my lips right over the bulldog's mean-looking face. "Did you see Father Mark tonight?"

I felt his back stiffen, then he turned over to look at me. "If you're asking whether Mark said anything about my mother, no, he didn't, because I didn't tell him she was visiting."

"Oh," was all I could say. Then, in a moment of frustration, I sat up and decided to ignore all the advice I'd been given and tell my husband what I thought. "Well, I think you're acting like a jerk and that you ought to just forgive your mom for whatever it is that is upsetting you and get on with your life. This is ridiculous."

He didn't move a muscle but lay on his back, his head propped up by his pillows, and just looked at me. The look said it all. "I think," he said, saying each word slowly. "That you should mind your own business and—"

I held up my hand for him to stop. "This is my business—"

He sat up and lowered his voice in anger. "No, it is not. You don't know what it felt like to be left at sixteen with an uncle I barely knew, starting over in a new school, not seeing my mom and my sisters for almost a year. I was the man of the family . . . My dad would have . . ." His voice faltered.

"I'm sorry," I said, moving closer to him. "I know it must have been hard, but, Gabe, that was so long ago."

"She didn't call me for two months," he said, his voice harsh. "My dad had been dead less than three months, and she didn't even call."

"Have you told her this? I mean, did you two ever talk about it?"

He gave a low, bitter laugh. "Right. That would be so easy, talking to my mom. What do you think?"

I moved closer to him, touched his face. "Maybe that's why she came out here. Maybe it's time you talked. Maybe it's time you . . ." I swallowed, then tried again. "Time you forgave her."

"She's never asked for forgiveness. She's never said she was sorry."

I didn't know what to answer. He was right; it would be easier if she brought it up, if she said she was sorry, asked for his forgiveness. "I know that would be the ideal, Friday. But sometimes we have to forgive even when the person doesn't ask us to."

He narrowed his eyes at me, not willing yet to give up his anger. "Easy for you to say."

I looked over at him, thinking of Jack, the night not many years ago when he left Trigger's, a bar down by the bus station, angry and drunk, with a friend. The question of whether he was driving or not remained unanswered. It would never be answered, and did it matter anyway? Months after he died I was so angry at him for being stupid and selfish, for risking so much because of an inconsequential fight with his brother, Wade. I thought I'd never forgive him, never forgive Wade. But I did forgive his brother. And if I could see Jack one more time, I'd hug him hard and say, "It's okay. We all mess up. I forgive you. I'll always love you."

But I'd never be able to hug or talk to him again. But I could forgive. That was the one thing I could do. And when I did, I was able to go on with my life. It was when I was able to feel real love again.

"No," I said, touching his shoulder. "It's not easy for me to say."

He pulled away and turned back over. "Let me handle this." Those were the last words he said to me. I lay in the dark for a long time afterward, listening to his even breathing as he slept.

The next morning, his side of the bed was empty when I woke up. There was a note lying on his pillow. "I turned off your alarm and took Scout and the puppy out at about five a.m." I glanced over at the clock. It was seven a.m. Through the closed bedroom door, I heard the distant clatter of pots and pans.

Downstairs, I discovered Ray stirring oatmeal. Scout and Boo were playing with a crumpled paper sack on the kitchen floor. I glanced out the kitchen window. Gabe's car was gone.

"Gabe went to work early," he said. "I'm making enough for two."

"Thanks." I didn't have the heart to tell him I'd rather have a Pop-Tart.

"Coffee's fresh. And strong."

"The stronger the better." I poured a cup, took a sip of it black, a huge change for me, but I needed the quick jolt this morning. "How's Kathryn?"

"Not awake yet. I'm letting her sleep. Nights are sometimes hard, so she has to sleep when she can."

"Of course." I wanted to ask more about how she felt, find out more about what to expect with this disease, but now wasn't the time. What Ray and I needed to do right now was eat a quiet, relaxing breakfast. "I'll call Gabe later on today. Find out what's up for dinner."

He nodded and kept stirring.

The oatmeal started to softly bubble. I contemplated

apologizing for Gabe's behavior last night, then decided that it wasn't my place to do that.

"What are your plans for today?" Ray asked.

I opened the cupboard and took out two deep bowls. "I'll probably drop by the museum to make sure the tours are going okay, then I'll try to finish up my Christmas shopping. What are you and Kathryn going to do?"

"I think we'll stay around the house today. Yesterday was pretty tiring for her. If you'd like to leave the dogs, we'd be happy to watch them." He smiled and spooned some oatmeal in the bowls.

"That would be great," I said, then reconsidered. "Actually, I'll take Scout with me. He's been a bit neglected since Boo arrived. But if you'd watch the little guy, I'd sure appreciate it. Doggie day care is wonderful, but I think he needs a quiet day. Don't want to give an overly exhausted puppy back to my friend."

"Don't worry a bit," Ray said, sitting down in front of his cereal. "Feel free to stay out as long as you need."

This worked into my plans very well. I wasn't lying when I said I needed to finish up my shopping. I would do that. But I also wanted to go out to Pinky's house and look for that cat, see if he actually looked like the one in Abe Adam's painting. What I thought that would prove, I had no idea. But it beat worrying about my husband and his mother.

I threw on faded Wranglers, my oldest boots and a pale green San Celina Cattlewomen's Association sweatshirt. I also wanted to explore the land around Pinky's house, the land that Bobbie and Pete wanted to include in their easement. I wondered if Nola bought the place if she'd consider such an arrangement. I didn't have a clue about her feelings about the environment.

Thinking about hiking around Pinky's property lightened my mood. I needed to get outside, get my boots dirty, and smell the pine and oak trees. Scout would have a ball, and we'd both come back more relaxed and able to cope with life.

It was a cold, misty day with storm clouds roiling around San Celina's hills like soldiers getting ready for battle. I drove Highway 1 out to Cambria, the Pacific Ocean to my left, gray and flat, almost the same color as the steely sky.

When I got to Santa Rosa Creek Road, I rolled the truck's passenger window down a crack, just enough for Scout to smell things but not enough for him to stick his head out. I'd read enough about dogs' eye injuries from flying debris to do that any longer. But he loved stretching his nose up to smell the passing scent of rabbits, squirrels, skunks and other varmints. Coming out here reminded me that I hadn't been to the ranch and worked cattle with Daddy for over a month. Not that he needed my help anymore. There were any number of young men who needed the part-time work, and Sam was always willing to help him, but I missed it. I rolled down my own window so I could enjoy the scent of damp earth and fresh pine.

Pinky's house was as gorgeous as I remembered, but it definitely looked empty and, if it was possible, a little sad. I wondered who would eventually buy this house and live here. Though Nola was considering buying it, a part of me hoped a young family would move in. This house needed children. Though with the real estate prices being the way they were in Cambria and throughout San Celina County, that wasn't likely. If not Nola Finch, it was more apt to be some idealistic retired couple from Los Angeles or the Bay Area who had visions of living the country life. When they realized how inconvenient rural life was, it would be sold again. And maybe again. If it was lucky, it would end up being a bed-and-breakfast. If it wasn't, if the joint easement with Pete and Bobbie didn't work out, the house might be moved or even torn down and the land eventually sold for an upscale housing tract.

I pulled into the circular driveway and parked. I opened the door and let Scout jump out. While he sniffed around the area close to the truck, I flipped through the folder with the photo of the painting and the articles I'd found on Abe Adam. I glanced over them again, looking for something, though I wasn't sure what. There was something that had been bugging me for a while, something that pecked at my subconscious, persistent as one of Dove's chickens. A piece of the puzzle, the puzzle that was Abe Adam Finch.

Scout gave a joyful bark, chasing after a black and yellow butterfly. He was thrilled to be outside, unencumbered by the small charge he'd taken so seriously. I stepped out of the truck and watched him frolic like a puppy on the emerald grass in front of Pinky's house. It made me forget everything for a moment and just laugh at his obvious joy. He caught scent of a rabbit and turned to look at me, his thick body shuddering with excitement, his shiny eyes begging.

"Go," I said, laughing. "You've earned it." He

bounded through the brush, his tail high, going after a rabbit he and I both knew he'd never catch, but thrilled for the chase, for the chance to just be a dog. He needed to get out to the ranch as much as I did. I looked up at the darkening sky and called after him. "Don't be gone too long. It looks like it's going to rain buckets."

I glanced over at May's cottage. Her car wasn't parked in front, and it appeared as if no one was home. When she returned, she probably wouldn't be alarmed. She knew my purple truck and would think I was here at Constance's request.

I went up to the porch, slippery from the damp air, and set the file down on a small wicker table.

"Here, kitty, kitty," I called out. "Here, Lionel." What an odd name for a cat. Was it because the cat sort of looked like a lion? No, that's not right. He looked more like a tiger. Did Pinky know someone named Lionel?

Then it hit me.

Lionel.

I remembered what I just reread in Abe Adam's biography.

Lionel Bachman was the collector who discovered Abe Adam ten years ago. It was too much of a coincidence that a cat that Pinky owned, one that was apparently painted into one of Abe Adam Finch's paintings, also had the somewhat uncommon name of the man who discovered Abe Adam Finch ten years ago. Either something connected Pinky, Lionel Bachman and Abe Adam Finch, or I was so eager to find something other than Gabe and his mother to think about that I was connecting dots that didn't exist.

I opened the file on the table and scanned it. I was right.

I was sitting on the top porch step, staring at the photo of the painting, when I heard my name called.

I looked up in surprise and saw Bobbie Everette strolling toward me, wearing old jeans and a mustard-brown Carhartt barn jacket, a shotgun strapped casually on her back.

I closed the file. "What're you doing here?" I called.

She licked her lips and smiled tentatively. "Maybe I could ask you the same thing."

I glanced behind her, wondering if she was alone. "I'm just checking on things for Constance."

"Did she lose her cat?" Her eyes pierced mine.

"Why do you ask?"

"Heard you calling one. Your voice carries."

"Pinky has . . . had a cat. I was worried about it being alone out here."

"Isn't the housekeeper, Mary, taking care of things?"

"Her name is May. Yes, but she's allergic to cats and had to leave it outside." That was a complete lie, but I wasn't going to tell Bobbie why I was really here.

"What have you got there?" She pointed at the file under my hand.

"Nothing."

She eyed me suspiciously. "Have you heard anything about who is interested in this property?"

I shook my head no. "Constance might know more about that than me. I don't even know Pinky's family."

Bobbie studied me, her face expressionless. A breeze picked up, blowing a tornado of leaves around her legs.

"I have to go find my dog," I said, standing up. I

picked up the file, held it close to my chest. "You know I'm on your side in preserving what is left of San Celina County's open space. I hope whoever buys this property goes in with you and Pete on the easement."

She gave me a curt nod. "Me too." She turned and walked into the tangle of pine and oak trees. I watched her until she was out of sight. Lionel picked that moment to dart from his hiding place under a hedge and head around the side of the house.

I set the file down on the top step and ran around the side of the house in time to see the cat disappear through a kitty door at the kitchen entrance. I tried the door. Unlocked. That wasn't good. I'd have to remind May that there was some very valuable artwork in this house, and she'd have to be more careful about locking up. I went inside, hopefully to find Lionel and assuage my curiosity about him. Then I'd lock up, whistle for Scout and get back to town. I'd wasted enough of my day on the wild kitty chase.

Lionel was inside the kitchen standing by his empty bowl. May must let him stay inside the house here, rather than with her. Should I feed him or let her? I decided not to interfere. She would feed him when she got home. Home sounded good right now. Who cared if Pinky, Abe Adam and Lionel had a relationship? It had nothing to do with me or the folk art museum.

I left through the kitchen door, locking it behind me, and walked around the house, calling Scout's name.

"Well," a voice said as I rounded the corner. "I guess you're smarter than I thought."

CHAPTER 14

$\mathcal{N}$OLA FINCH STOOD ON THE FRONT PORCH, MY FILE with the photo and articles about her uncle open in her hands.

"What are you doing here?" I asked.

"I could ask you the same thing."

In that moment, I knew that she knew about her uncle and Pinky.

She carefully took each porch step until she was eye level with me.

"I saw you studying the painting last night. So, what do you plan on doing now?"

"About what?" What did she think I was going to do, run to the newspaper and tell them that Pinky and her uncle had some sort of relationship? The truth was, no one cared.

"Please, spare me the innocent act. That's the reason you're here, to expose us and make me a laughingstock."

I stared at her, confused. My brain was trying to wrap itself around her words and what they meant. Why would *she* be a laughingstock?

Then, like a jolt from a cattle prod, it hit me.

"It's you," I said, remembering her own frustrated career in art. "You're Abe Adam Finch." I'd read about this, mainstream artists who masquerade as outsider artists when their own work is not spectacular or special enough to make it in the art world.

Her smooth face gave an almost imperceptible flinch, a flash of pain. "Not just me."

Then I finally got it. "You and Pinky Edmondson?" This was getting more and more bizarre. "You both were Abe Adam?"

"It was ridiculously easy."

"I still don't get it," I said, realizing now that perhaps Constance, as crazy as it seemed, might have been right about Pinky's death being a homicide. If that was true, then the person who likely did it was standing right next to me, looking as normal as my next-door neighbor.

My survival instinct told me to keep her talking until I could figure out what was going on and, even more important, how to extricate myself from the situation. "The first Abe Adam Finch painting was discovered ten years ago. You two have been—?"

"Yes," she interrupted. "We've been carrying on the charade for ten years. I have to admit, at first it was something we did just to see if we could get away with it. Then it actually became lucrative. Very lucrative."

I knew from Constance, or at least assumed, that Pinky didn't need the money. "For you."

She shrugged. "Pinky didn't need the money, but she did love the excitement. I guess when you grow up with money like she did, having everything you've ever wanted in life, you have to dig deep for your thrills. But like so many rich people, she bored easily and wanted to stop."

And Nola didn't. That meant there was a very good chance that Constance was right that Pinky was murdered and that Nola killed her. But how? Not that it mattered at this point. If it was true, I had only two possible ways to escape the same fate: talk my way out or overpower her. In hand-to-hand fighting, I thought I'd be able to overcome Nola, but Gabe had told me over and over that you should never underestimate any opponent.

I glanced over her shoulder, trying to figure out if there was a way I could get around her. Still, getting to my truck was only one of my worries. Scout was still out there. I wouldn't leave without him, not when I didn't have any idea what this woman was capable of doing. So I had to keep her talking until I could figure out what to do.

"Lionel," I said. "Was he named after Lionel Bachman?"

She crossed her arms over her chest. "You are pretty sharp. Pinky thought it was funny. I thought it was taking too much of a chance. But I guess that's what appealed to her about the whole thing."

"Was he in on it?"

"Of course. It would have been a lot harder to pull it off without someone of his caliber pretending to like my paintings." Her lips pulled down at the corners. "And he never let me forget that he was pretending. I hated that man. Best day of my life when he died."

"Okay, so you pulled off this huge trick on the snobby art establishment. What now?"

I saw her draw in a deep breath. "That's a problem. But not as much a problem as you are. Frankly, I never counted on having to deal with someone like you."

My stomach churned as I lied like a sideshow barker. "I don't know what you mean."

She gave a contemptuous laugh. "I'm not stupid. I couldn't be stupid and pull this off. You are one of those tediously honest people who would insist on telling everyone the truth about Abe Adam Finch."

Though I should have kept my mouth shut, I couldn't help saying, "What you're doing is fraud. Why not just paint under your own name?" But before she replied, I already knew the answer.

"Because the art world is a closed, narrow world with impossible rules for entry. This was the closest I'll ever come to being one of the players." Her lips turned up into a bitter slash of a smile. "Pinky just couldn't understand that. To her, it was just a lark. Easy for her because she would always be in just by virtue of her money and her name. If Abe Adam Finch's real identity was revealed, her friends would just laugh and say, 'That crazy Pinky Edmondson, you just never know what she's going to do next.' You see it all the time, rich and famous people getting away with . . . everything! Her fancy lawyers would get her a slap on the wrist. Me, on the other hand . . ."

She was right. She had a lot more to lose. No one would ever take her seriously again in the art world, and she might even be prosecuted for fraud. At any rate, with only her alive now, all the blame would fall on her shoulders. I couldn't help feeling sorry for her. She'd obviously started out wanting to make art and ended up being seduced by the part of the creative world that was as judgmental and unbending as a Third World caste system.

Her eyes were shiny with angry, unshed tears. "I was so mad when she said it was time we ended the charade. What did she expect *me* to do? Where was I supposed to go? You know what she did? Laughed. Said I needed to get over myself. That she'd always meant for this thing to be temporary, for the joke to be eventually revealed to her friends."

"What are you going to do?" I asked casually, glancing over her shoulder, frantically searching the woods for Scout.

She drew a small hand pistol out of her pocket and pointed it at me. "I need time to figure it out now that you've ruined things."

I stared at the gun, trying to calm the rapid beating of my heart. I hadn't expected a gun, which proved what Gabe said was true. Never underestimate anyone. I felt my senses spring to alert, knowing that in a split second, depending on this unstable woman's whim, my life could be over.

"Killing me wouldn't accomplish what you want," I said. *Keep calm,* I told myself. Think of her as a green horse or an angry bull. Don't let her smell your fear.

"I don't plan on killing you," she said. "Like I said, I'm not stupid. I just need time to get away. Luckily, I always knew something like this would happen. I should have left right after Pinky died. I have a plan B. I have *always* had a plan B."

It was something about the way she said Pinky died that told me that Constance had, indeed, been right. But I wasn't foolish enough to say it out loud. Right now, I wanted to stay alive myself.

She waved me toward the front door. "I'm going to tie you up and lock you in the basement. By the time anyone notices you're missing and your husband figures out where you are, I'll be—" She stopped, clamping her lips together. "Gone."

She jabbed the pistol in my side. "Now, I mean it, don't try to be a hero. You can't beat a bullet. Trust me, I wouldn't hesitate to shoot you if I had to." She handed me the front door key. "Unlock the door."

"I know," I said, fumbling with the lock, finally opening the heavy wood door. We walked down the hallway toward the door that led to the basement. Would I ever know if Nola murdered Pinky Edmondson? Right now, I didn't care. All I wanted to do was live.

"Open the door," she said.

The metal knob was icy to my touch. The cold, dank scent of the unfinished basement drifted up. Panic rose in my throat, a salty bile that threatened to choke me. I didn't want to go down in this room under the house. It felt too much like a grave. I hesitated a split second. Enough to panic her.

"Go!" she said in a low voice, giving my back a push.

I felt myself start to fall. I grasped at air, my head hitting the wooden railing. My feet tangled, and I tumbled down the stairs, jolts of pain exploding in my head, my arm, my leg. I hit the concrete floor with a thump, my right arm twisted under me, pain ripping through me, pain so intense that I prayed to lose consciousness. The door at the top of the stairs slammed shut, and in the deep, black silence I heard the faint click of a bolt.

Please, I prayed. *Lord, help.* Then nothing.

CHAPTER 15

I WOKE UP SURROUNDED BY THE COLOR BLUE, A SOFT robin's egg blue. I was in bed, a firm, bleach-scented bed. For the first few seconds, I wondered if I was dead. Was heaven a room painted blue that smelled like bleach? Voices murmured in the background.

I opened my mouth, and something that sounded like a croak tumbled out. Blurry bodies rushed to my side. I blinked my eyes a few times, finally able to discern a dark shape. The shape loomed over me. Gabe's familiar ginger scent eased my racing heart.

"Querida." His voice sounded faraway.

"Gabe?" My lips formed the shape of his name, but no sound came out.

A soft hand touched my cheek. It smelled of sweet, toasty almonds. In the background I heard the rumble of voices: Daddy, Emory, Elvia.

"Dove," I said in my soundless speech. Tears burned my eyes. If I was dead, then so was everyone I loved.

"Now, now," she said. "You're fine, honeybun. You're going to be fine. You got a concussion and a broken wrist. Sam says he wants to be the first to sign your cast. You're going to be fine."

"Nola," I said. This time I could hear my own voice, jagged and harsh as a thirty-year smoker. "She tried to . . . Pinky . . . she . . . where's Scout . . ."

"Everything's under control," Gabe said, his wide, warm hand touching my face. "Scout's fine. Go back to sleep. I'll be right here."

Knowing I was safe, I let myself lapse back into sleep. Every so often someone would arouse me, and I'd murmur answers to their questions and go back to sleep. I woke up again hours later with a splitting headache. It was dark outside my window, and Gabe was the only one left in the room sitting in a visitor's chair close enough for me to touch.

"Scout?" I said, remembering what happened.

Gabe bent down to kiss the top of my head. "He's at home with Mom and Ray. He earned his kibble for the rest of his life. His barking brought you help."

"He's a good dog," I said and started to cry. Gabe moved to sit on the edge of my bed and pulled me into his arms. He didn't say anything but just let me cry out my fear and relief.

Once I calmed down, he told me what happened after I

302

was knocked unconscious by my fall down the basement stairs.

"You were lucky," he said. "You could have broken your neck." His face hardened, imagining the possibility. "Constance was probably right about what happened to Mrs. Edmondson. If I'd only listened to her."

I placed my hand on his forearm. "There's no way you could have known, Friday. It didn't look like a murder. Even the medical examiner wasn't suspicious. And, frankly, Constance has always been as loony as a . . ." My head throbbed and I couldn't think. "A loon."

His blue-gray eyes darkened in the pale morning sunlight. "Still, I should have . . . I don't know . . ."

"Been able to predict the future?" I touched my aching temple. "Do you know how Nola killed Pinky?"

He shook his head no. "She's in custody, but she's not talking."

My eyebrows went up, surprised. Then I flinched. Even that little movement hurt. "You caught her already? How?"

He smiled, touched my cheek with his warm palm. "You told us."

"I did?"

He filled in the details of what took place right after my unplanned meeting with Nola Finch. Apparently, Scout had sensed that something was wrong when he came back to the house. It was luck or, I'd rather believe, God's providence that Bobbie was still out hiking around the property. She heard Scout's barking and came upon him scratching at Pinky's front door. She saw my car and naturally assumed I was inside. She knocked and knocked, and when I didn't answer, she took a chance and broke a window. Once she let Scout in, he ran directly to the basement door and barked. Bobbie unbolted the door, ran down and found me. Though I don't remember, apparently I woke up for a few moments when Bobbie checked my pulse. As I lapsed in and out of consciousness, I managed to say Nola Finch's and Pinky Edmondson's names when Bobbie asked me what happened.

"My training as a cop's wife," I said, smiling.

"Thanks to you, she only had a few hours' head start."

He went on to tell me how Bobbie called 911, then immediately called Gabe, whose number she found on the cell phone still in my pocket. She told him what I'd said.

"We caught Ms. Maxwell attempting to cross the border into Tijuana," Gabe said. "She was wearing a wig and carrying a fake ID."

"Wow," I said.

"After our APB, she was recognized by a sharp-eyed border patrol agent who, fortunately for us, happens to be a part-time folk artist himself. He'd just read the story that morning in the *L.A. Times* about your museum's acquisition of the Abe Adam Finch painting. We were lucky enough that one of the newspaper's photos showed Nola Maxwell. Which, by the way, is her real name."

"Where is she being held?" I asked.

"Down in San Diego. I sent two detectives down there."

"You said she's not talking?"

He shook his head no. "Already has a lawyer. Did she say anything to you about killing Pinky Edmondson?"

I almost shook my head, then remembered how much it hurt. "Not really. She confessed to the art fraud, and she seemed very angry that Pinky was going to reveal their secret."

His expression was slightly confused. I realized that he didn't know the details about why she killed Pinky, or at least what it sounded like to me. Slowly, I told him about discovering the picture of Lionel the cat on Abe Adam Finch's painting.

"I really didn't think I was doing anything dangerous by going out there," I said. "Since I thought I hadn't done anything to make anyone suspicious about the painting."

"Obviously, something you did or said worried Nola Maxwell."

I thought for a moment. "I don't know what."

"When did you recognize the cat in the painting?"

"At the opening. I was studying the painting, and that's when a lightbulb went on."

"She was obviously watching you and, as I've told you before, you aren't the best poker player in the world." He softened his comment with a smile. "After that, it is likely she followed you, waiting to see what you'd do with the information."

I inhaled deeply, causing a sharp pain in my side. "I've been stalked enough in my lifetime for ten people. I hope this does it."

"You and me both," Gabe said.

"Maybe it just came down to greed. Or envy. Or both. She really liked the social position being Abe Finch's niece gave her and didn't want Pinky to end it. Do you think she'll ever confess?"

"Doubt it. She was smart enough to hire a lawyer as soon as she could. Because of what she did to you, we can charge her with aggravated assault, assault with a deadly weapon, maybe even kidnapping. The DA's figuring all that out. And anything you've figured out is just speculation. Since we don't have any physical evidence on Mrs. Edmondson, there's not much we can do now."

"She'll get away with murder."

The edges of his lips turned down in a frown. "Not the first person who has and won't be the last. But she'll do the most jail time possible under the law."

"I wonder how she did it."

Gabe shrugged. "I asked the medical examiner, and he said if he had to speculate, he'd guess that she used Mrs. Edmondson's own medicine against her."

"What medicine?"

"Digitalis. Pinky Edmondson had a heart condition. She also, apparently, had trouble sleeping, because she had a prescription for sleeping pills. Our guess is that, somehow, Nola managed to trick Mrs. Edmondson into taking too much of her own heart medication. Maybe gave her some sleeping pills, then convinced her she hadn't taken her heart medicine when she actually had. We've checked with her pharmacist, and Mrs. Edmondson had a prescription filled two weeks before for a month's worth. The detectives found the bottle of sleeping pills but not the digitalis. Nola Maxwell likely got rid of it, since it would have shown more pills missing than was logical."

"So many ifs. I guess we'll never know for sure."

"Not unless Nola confesses, and though I don't underestimate the interrogation experience of my detectives, Ms. Maxwell sounds like she is not one who can be easily tricked."

"Not as easily fooled as the rest of us," I said, meaning me.

"Don't beat yourself up, sweetheart. These kinds of people are walking geniuses when it comes to using people."

"I wonder what will become of the painting? And what it makes the rest of his . . . or rather, their work worth."

"That's not my field of expertise," Gabe said. "For right now, since there isn't a charge of murder against Nola Maxwell, you can keep the painting."

"I suppose I need to make an official announcement. We'll get media coverage, all right. Just not the kind I'd hoped for."

"You know what they say," Gabe said cheerfully. "All publicity is good publicity."

"Who says that?" I said.

He laughed and kissed me. "I don't know. The people who don't get publicity? But if what you wanted was for your museum to become known, that's in the bag now."

"Except we'll be a laughingstock."

"Not as much as the people who paid thousands of dollars for a fake Abe Adam Finch painting."

"You're right," I said, feeling a little better. "At least this didn't cost us anything." Then a feeling of sadness swept over me. "It cost Pinky Edmondson her life."

Gabe's face was more thoughtful than sad. "Yes, that's a tragedy, but one she could have prevented by simply not perpetuating a lie."

"It's still tragic," I said. "To die for something so small." I groaned. "Do you realize what my life will be like once Constance Sinclair finds out she was sort of right about Pinky being murdered?"

"Not as bad as mine."

Within the next hour, the rest of my family had come back: Dove, Isaac, Daddy, Sam, Emory and Elvia. I had an entourage to help me check out. As Dove and Elvia helped me dress, Gabe filled out my paperwork. In the next hour, I was back home sitting in the living room holding Boo in my lap, Scout at my feet.

"You're the best dog in the whole world," I told Scout, bending down to scratch him behind his left cheek, a favorite spot of his. "Extra premium dog treats for the rest of your life."

"He already gets those," Gabe said, bringing me a tray with a grilled cheese sandwich, tomato soup, hot chocolate and homemade butterscotch pudding, compliments of Kathryn.

"Yummy," I said, digging in, thankful it was my left wrist broken rather than my right. I'd taken a pain pill about an hour ago and was feeling hunger for the first time today. "This meal is almost worth what I had to go through."

"I hope not," Kathryn said, walking into the living room. "I'd be happy to make you those things any time you like without you risking your life." She smiled at me, then at Gabe.

Gabe smiled back, which relieved me. They'd obviously come to some kind of truce. Had they talked about the past or just silently agreed to let it go? I looked from

Gabe to his mother and back to Gabe. Nothing on their unexpressive faces told me. Ray came in, and for the next couple of hours we sat around chatting about a lot of nothing. For the first time since my mother-in-law had arrived, it felt like the air between Gabe and his mother wasn't thick with resentment and anger.

In bed that night, after taking an awkward shower with my wrist wrapped with plastic wrap and taped to keep it from getting wet, I asked Gabe about his mother.

"Are you two okay?" I crawled awkwardly under the covers. I watched Gabe pick up Boudin and hold him in his arms, stroking his puppy fur, his face visibly relaxing.

"We're fine," he said.

"Did you talk?"

He bent down and put Boo in his crate, taking his time to settle him in, fixing the soft blanket around the puppy, stroking him again, murmuring assurances before closing and locking the gate.

"Things are fine," Gabe repeated, not actually answering my question.

I almost pursued it, discouraged that they hadn't confronted the issues between them. What had happened with me had obviously eased things between them, but it hadn't solved the deeper problems. Maybe that wasn't possible. My husband carried so much anger inside him, so many questions, so much sadness, but, it seemed, this was not the time that things would be resolved between him and his mom. All things had their season. Perhaps this was not the season for that.

The pain pills brought me wonderful, painless sleep, but they only lasted four or five hours. It was dark when I woke. I sat up, looked over at Boo to see if he was awake and waiting to go outside. He was fast asleep. Scout, sleeping next to my side of the bed, sat up, alert. As always, he was ready to accompany me wherever I needed to go at two a.m.

"I'm fine," I whispered to him. "Down." He obeyed with a grunt of relief. "Go back to sleep." I leaned down from the bed and stroked the warm top of his broad skull.

By this time, I was awake enough to realize I was alone in bed. Where was Gabe? The master bathroom door was open, and in the dim light from the half moon, I could see it was empty.

I struggled out of bed, worried. Gabe rarely wandered the house at night. Though he often had troubled dreams, insomnia never plagued him. I pulled on my robe and slowly made my way downstairs.

I was at the bottom step when I heard it, the sound of two voices talking, the timbre of anger obvious even before I could hear the words. I froze where I was, knowing that me walking into the living room at this point might halt something that had been coming for a long time, something that needed to happen.

"You should have told me about your MS." My husband's voice was low and angry. "Being the last to know was humiliating."

"That wasn't my intention," Kathryn said, her own voice tight, controlled. "You know that."

"I don't know anything apparently. I am your son. I am your oldest child. Even Benni knew before I did."

"Perhaps it's because she pays more attention," his mother said, her voice now just as angry as his.

"How can you say that?"

His mother's voice softened. "Gabe, honey, I'm sorry. Is that what you want from me? I'm sorry. You're right; I should have told you immediately. I just didn't want to ruin our Christmas."

"I don't believe you," he said, his voice sounding adolescent now. "If that were true, you would have called and told me about Ray over the phone. You wouldn't have sprung it on me in public."

She was silent for a moment. "That was cruel, I know. I was just . . . afraid."

"Afraid of me? Mom, I'm your son. I'd never hurt you."

"Not physically," she whispered.

My heart ached for both of them. My husband didn't understand that the intimidating presence that made him such a trusted commander in an emergency was often more than a little scary to those who loved him. And my mother-in-law didn't understand that the distance she kept was like a slap to her son.

"I don't mean to . . ." Gabe's voice cracked.

"I know," she said, her words so low I almost couldn't hear them. "I know that, son. I made an error in judgment. Surely you understand that?"

What he said next completely floored me. Only in retrospect did it occur to me that he'd been wanting to say this for so many years.

"You sent me away." His voice was raspy, agonized.

Kathryn gave a small gasp. "Gabe, I didn't—"

"Yes, you did! Dad was only dead for three months, and you sent me to Uncle Tony."

"You were almost a man," she said, her voice sounding desperate. "I didn't want to, but you were out of control. I didn't know what to do. Your sisters were so young, and I was alone and had to work."

"You never called me."

"That's not true! I called Tony every week to see how you were doing, but I was afraid to speak to you. Don't you remember the horrible things we said to each other? I didn't want that to happen again. We needed time to cool down. I never stopped thinking about you for a minute. I missed you every day. I'm so, so sorry. If I could do it over again, I wouldn't send you away. I wouldn't. Please forgive me."

Before she finished I heard something else, something I never thought I would hear in my lifetime. A sound that flooded me with sadness and relief.

I stood up without thinking, making my way to the living room doorway. My husband sat next to his mother on the sofa, his head bent down to his knees, his back heaving with the tears he should have shed years ago. His mother's arms surrounded him, her cheek against his black, tousled hair.

"*Lo siento, Mamá,*" he said. "I'm sorry, I'm sorry Papa . . . Luis . . ."

"It's okay, son. It wasn't your fault. Luis is in God's hands now."

"You can't die, Mom. You can't."

"Oh, sweetie," she said. "I'm not going to die."

Her words turned into comforting murmurs, the sound that mothers make, soothing nonwords that somehow a child, no matter what age, found comforting.

Before they noticed me, I moved quietly away. There would be many times in our future when I would hold Gabe to comfort him, not the least when the day would come when he would lose the woman who now held him, the first woman he loved. Right now, it was her place to care for him, this woman who'd cradled him for nine months inside her body, who taught him to walk, to talk, to read, who kissed his skinned knees and hemmed his jeans, who'd sent him away in fear and guilt and love when he was sixteen, who, no doubt, prayed for him every day he was in Vietnam and every day afterward, this woman, who, no doubt, if asked, would die for him. Right now, it was her arms he needed.

I went back to bed. Soon it would be morning. I would rise before everyone else and take muffins out of the freezer. Lemon muffins I'd made a week ago. I would serve hot tea and lemon muffins with warm, rich ginger butter. Gabe's favorite. This was what I could do for him, for her, for us. When all the crying was done, I would be ready with hot tea and warm lemon muffins.

CHAPTER 16

THREE DAYS LATER, CHRISTMAS EVE, I WAS FEELING much better, though I was still taking pain pills at night. We were driving to the Aragon house for their annual tamale feed when Hud called my cell phone.

"Hey, ranch girl," Hud said. I could hear "White Christmas" playing in the background. "How are you?"

How was I? That was a good question. Right at that moment, I was grateful that my family was well and safe, grateful that Gabe and his mother were finally at peace with each other. He'd even managed a couple of laughs with Ray. I had a feeling that my husband was actually relieved that his mother had someone who cared for her. Most important, I was grateful to be alive.

"I'm thankful," I said, sparing him the details. We'd have time to talk when he picked up Boo.

"Yeah, I know what you mean. How's Boudin?"

"He's doing great. We're all headed over to Elvia's parents' house for tamales and presents. Sam is bringing both dogs in his car."

"Did you get Boo's photo with Santa?"

I hesitated. The only picture of Boo that Sam had managed to get showed the puppy screaming in terror while attempting to escape from the red and white scary monster he was certain was trying to puppy nap him. Nevertheless, it *was* a photo with Santa.

"Sure did." No use ruining his or Maisie's Christmas.

"Good," he said, his voice relieved. "I have no idea why Maisie was so obsessed with that picture, but with what she went through this year, it seemed a small thing to give her. You have my undying gratitude, *catin*."

"No problem," I said, my stomach sinking into my feet. Somehow, I'd have to figure something out before they returned from Texas. "See you soon."

"We're flying home the day after Christmas. I'll be by to pick up Boo about six p.m. or so, depending on whether the planes are on time."

"No hurry," I said. "I'm actually kinda getting used to the little pumpkin head."

"Yeah, they do have a way of stealing your heart, don't they?"

"Merry Christmas, Clouseau."

"*Joyeux Noel,* ranch girl."

At the Aragon house, Gabe, Kathryn, Ray and I were the last to arrive. Sam had been there for about an hour, and Boo was in puppy heaven as he was passed from arms to arms of cooing girls and women. All of Elvia's family was there and even Uncle Boone, Emory's father, had flown in.

"What a wonderful surprise," Dove exclaimed, hugging her Arkansas cousin.

So many conversations were going on at once, some Spanish, some English and even more a mixture of both. I glanced over at Kathryn and Ray. I was happy to see a flushed expression of joy on Kathryn's face. Was she remembering times with Rogelio and his family? It occurred to me for the first time how much in common she and I had, being widowed at a young age. But we'd both found love again with two extraordinary men.

At that moment, standing there watching all these families become one big family for this evening, a mixture of races, ages, backgrounds, histories, sorrows and joys, I felt the real presence of God flowing through the room, like a cool, refreshing breeze, a reminder of what this holiday was really about.

We ate tamales and chicken verde and Dove's twice-baked potatoes and Christmas butterscotch cookies and Mrs. Aragon's Mexican chocolate cake until we were stuffed. Then we sat in the Aragons' huge family room, squeezed in like sardines, and watched the kids open presents. The rest of us would wait until Christmas Day. This night was always for the children. I watched my best friends open the present I bought for the newest little Aragon-Littleton. It was a stuffed pony, of course. When you turned it upside down, it gave a spirited neigh.

"It also comes with one thousand and one horseback riding lessons," I said, laughing. "My wrist should be healed by the time your little *niña* or *niño* is ready to sit a horse."

Elvia touched her stomach, her face flushed with joy. "Thank you. It's our baby's first present."

Sam came over to me with a wrapped gift. "Here, stepmom. I got you something."

"The adults aren't supposed to open their presents until tomorrow," I said, protesting.

"Well, it's not exactly for you."

I took the shirt box–size package and tried to tear away the wrapping with one hand. When I finally got it open, Sam laughed, making me instantly suspicious.

Nestled inside thick white tissue paper was a framed photo. It was a photo of Boo sitting on Santa's lap. And the dog was smiling.

"Oh, my stars, Sam! Thank you, thank you, thank you. How in the world *did* you get him up there? And smiling?"

Sam grinned. "A gifted animal trainer never gives away trade secrets."

I stared at the photo, amazed. "You're in the wrong profession."

"I agree," Gabe said, winking at his son. "Computer graphics might be a good career avenue to explore."

"This picture is fake?" I exclaimed. I peered closer at the photograph. It was incredible. You really couldn't tell that Boo wasn't actually sitting on Santa's lap. "This'll do just fine. Thank you, stepson. I owe you big time."

"You know it, *madrastra*."

We ended the night gathered around the old upright piano in the corner of the family room. People took turns singing Christmas carols, harmonizing on old Beach Boys songs. Sam and Ramon, Elvia's youngest brother, made us all laugh singing some silly verses they'd written to "Jingle Bells." They'd replaced a one-horse open sleigh with a low-ride Chevrolet.

I looked around the room at all these people I loved, each with their own story, their own beginning, middle and end. I thought about what I'd read somewhere about how each ending was only the beginning of a story we hadn't read yet.

For a moment, I thought of Pinky Edmondson and Nola Maxwell and felt a pang, wishing that things had turned out better for both of them. I wondered where Constance was spending Christmas, knowing she was probably missing her friend. I was sad for them and thankful for where I was right now, at this particular moment in time.

I could not have guessed in a million years when I was a little girl how my life would be at this age, how many twists and turns it would take, how much sorrow I would endure, how much fear I would encounter, how much joy awaited me. It did feel like another beginning. I looked over at my husband, his face relaxed and happy. I sent up a quick prayer thanking God for the time we have had and for whatever time was still ahead. Then I rested my good hand on his knee and turned my attention back to our families, waiting for the next song to begin.

Earlene Fowler was raised in La Puente, California, by a Southern mother and a Western father. She lives in Southern California with her husband, Allen, and a semi-obedient Pembroke Welsh Corgi, Boudin. You can visit her website at www.earlenefowler.com.

THE
SADDLEMAKER'S WIFE

By National Bestselling Author

Earlene Fowler

After the death of her husband, Cole, Ruby McGavin arrives in Cardinal, California, where she has inherited part of a cattle ranch. But she is shocked to discover that Cole's family, despite what he told her, is still very much alive.

Though intent on selling out to the McGavins and starting a new life, she cannot help but be drawn to them—particularly handsome saddlemaker Lucas McGavin. And the more she learns about them, the more she wonders if she ever really knew Cole...

"[A] sweetly told narrative."
—*The New York Times*

"Emotionally powerful."
—*Publishers Weekly* (starred review)

penguin.com

EARLENE FOWLER

Don't miss any of the Agatha Award–winning series featuring Benni Harper, curator of San Celina's folk art museum and amateur sleuth.

Fool's Puzzle
Irish Chain
Kansas Troubles
Goose in the Pond
Dove in the Window
Mariner's Compass
Seven Sisters
Arkansas Traveler
Steps to the Altar
Sunshine and Shadow
Broken Dishes
Delectable Mountains

BERKLEY PRIME CRIME

penguin.com

ISBN 978-0-425-22123-5

0 71831 00799 5

In the new novel in the "breezy [and] humorous" (*Chicago Sun-Times*) series, Benni Harper is carrying a bundle of holiday stress—as she unveils an elite and possibly murderous society...

Photo by Sharon Kay

San Celina's most exclusive society suddenly has an opening. And Benni Harper has been tapped—not to join, but to investigate. The upper crust, female-only 49 Club is restricted to exactly that many members, and one must die before another can join. When the latest socialite de-pledges in her sleep, Benni's boss wants the mystery solved—and naturally, it's landed on Benni's to-do list. But with a famousl... ...nni's quilting museum or... ...aw soon to arrive—Benni's holiday is already hectic. Nevertheless, she'll need to crack this privileged circle of suspects before another gourmet goose gets cooked...

"Benni delves into the secrets of the town's elite with her usual flair, unraveling a plot that is as dangerous as the bulls on her father's ranch and as cozy as the quilts she reveres."—*Publishers Weekly*

www.penguin.com

ISBN 978-0-425-22123-5